D1553278

The Lake

From the same author

The Sister

The Lake

Paola Kaufmann

Translated by Miranda France

ALMA BOOKS

ALMA BOOKS LTD
London House
243–253 Lower Mortlake Road
Richmond
Surrey TW9 2LL
United Kingdom
www.almabooks.com

The Lake first published as *El lago* by Planeta Publishing in 2005
This edition first published by Alma Books in 2007
Copyright © Paola Kaufmann, 2005
Translation © Miranda France 2007

Paola Kaufmann and Miranda France assert their moral right to be identified
as the author and the translator of this work in accordance with the Copyright,
Designs and Patents Act 1988

This is a work of fiction. Names, characters, places and incidents either
are the product of the author's imagination or are used fictitiously, and any
resemblance to actual persons, living or dead, business establishments, events
or locales is entirely coincidental.

Printed in Great Britain by Cox & Wyman Ltd

isbn-13: 978-1-84688-010-0
isbn-10: 1-84688-010-6

All rights reserved. No part of this publication may be reproduced, stored in or
introduced into a retrieval system, or transmitted, in any form or by any means
(electronic, mechanical, photocopying, recording or otherwise), without the
prior written permission of the publisher.

This book is sold subject to the condition that it shall not be resold, lent, hired
out or otherwise circulated without the express prior consent of the publisher.

The Lake

1

Víktor

Lago del Hoyo, Chubut 1922

Sitting on a tree trunk that looked as disheartened as he felt, with his shirtsleeves rolled above his elbows in spite of the cold, and with his face half-hidden by a felt cap, the Engineer watched the surface of the lake.

At some point during the journey he had lost his sense of humour, his famously easy disposition – but when, and where?

He did not want the dejection to be too obvious in his face; all the same, he was sure that his stooped shoulders gave him away. He had been weary and uncommunicative over the last few hours, and had surely revealed his true feelings about the expedition, even while hiding his face under the brim of his hat.

"Damn it all," he said, without thinking that he was speaking to no one.

He let the words slip out, he who never raised his voice, or tolerated shouting, who never lost his temper or got irritated, nor let others do so either – at least not in front of him.

Fortunately at that moment there was no one close enough to hear him. A few metres away, among the trees, some members of the expedition were struggling to erect the tent where they would all be spending the next few days – although the Engineer felt increasingly certain that, with any luck, it would be not a matter of days, but one day only. The rest of the group, chipper as boy scouts on their first ever outing, were busy arranging the equipment around the lake, putting in place devices to measure salinity and temperature, colanders for algae samples, ropes, rifles, a small telescope, maps, wet-suits and some waders tough as sealskin that a relative of Andueza's had found in a flea market. They looked more like something you would find in a medieval torture chamber.

What was he going to say to Andueza? The mission is pointless if what we are seeking is *really* what we have been sent to look for? Did these people have any idea, even a vague idea what they were doing in Patagonia, other than meeting the demands of government propaganda?

The Engineer had been entrusted with a list of secret instructions, penned by Onelli himself. He was, perhaps, the only one who *did* know what they had come to do and – even if it was not his habit to keep his men in the dark about the general purpose of a mission – in this case he had the feeling that it did not matter much whether they knew or not. Either way the objective was the same: to hunt down a creature as yet unknown to zoologists or otherwise regarded as extinct. Whether it was the ridiculous swan Sheffield claimed to have seen, the beast that regularly popped up in Mapuche folklore, the creature spotted by geographers on the Última Esperanza Sound, or by sailors on the coast of Santa Cruz, or by English prospectors in the nineteenth century – what did it matter? As far as the press and the world were concerned, it was simply "the monster".

Each one of them had different reasons for being there. He had no doubt that José had been lured there by the thrill of the chase, just as he had once been lured to Africa, and might one day be lured to the moon if physicists ever proved there was some unusual creature there deformed by the absence of gravity. José Cinaghi would be there, ready for action, his ruddy face and the tumorous patch on his neck the irrefutable

4

badges of his personal battle, his bulky frame affecting a great lethargy. Cinaghi was actually surprisingly agile: he could move quickly, dodging behind trunks, or climbing impossibly tall trees like an animal – and all this without ever dislodging his hat.

Before arriving at El Hoyo he had caught a huemul, a young female still with reddish fur, weighing some fifty kilos. They were rare in that region, but perhaps the early winter that year had driven the huemuls down from the mountains sooner than usual. Anyway, that is what they had all eaten, saving the tinned food for the camp. Cinaghi bled and butchered the animal in no time, armed with a pair of knives and an iron hook, while Andueza prepared a fire in the shelter provided by the wagon. Andueza, who had been recruited for the precision of his marksmanship, had fun watching Cinaghi's clumsy manoeuvres. Finally they had roasted the huemul still in its hide, the long pieces of loin and rump threaded onto some stripped branches of eucalyptus – as if there were no utensils appropriate to such a basic task among their equipment. No – they wanted to eat in the wild, and Engineer Frey had laughed and drunk with them, had told them the regulation horror stories and cautionary tales, in the hope of securing good luck for his own group.

None of those present was too sophisticated to think himself above this ritual of all expeditions, except perhaps Merkel, the taxidermist in the group.

At that moment, though, on the banks of the lake, the Engineer would have paid good money for a bar of chocolate or some strawberry jam. But it did not befit him, or any group leader who prided himself as such, to give in to such a weakness, so he made do with a few bitter herbs, torn out of the ground by the trunk where he was sitting, and sucked on them without enthusiasm.

The men had just finished putting up the tent.

"What do you think this time, sir?" asked the journalist from the Associated Press with his usual irrepressible cheer.

Lopsided, like before, thought the Engineer, but he did not say so. He made a gesture of approval, and returned his gaze to the dark, dirty and poorly oxygenated water of the famous Hoyo Lagoon.

In El Bolsón, further north, supposedly, was the place where Sheffield lived, and on the other side, close to the lake, was a hut that was more like a shack made of sticks and hides, used by the gringo as his hunting base. Up until then, or rather until the day when Onelli showed him the letter, the Engineer had never heard of the gringo, and that was strange, because everyone in the South knew who he was: Martin Sheffield, like Andueza, was reputed to be an exceptional shot, and also a cheat, a rogue, a practical joker, an opportunist and a hero. God only knew under which of those aliases the gringo had taken it upon himself to write his blessed letter to Onelli, but inevitably the text of it had ended up in the press before a decision could be made to send a scientific committee to look into the matter. The Engineer still had the cutting from *La Nación* in his rucksack, although he had read it so many times that he knew it by heart.

Esquel
19th January 1922

Dr Onelli
Director of the Zoological Gardens, Buenos Aires

My dear sir,
Knowing the dedication with which you have always worked to advance the institution under your worthy direction, I wish to draw your attention to the following phenomenon and feel sure it will be of great interest to you,

since it concerns the possible addition to your zoo of an
animal hitherto unknown in the world.

Let me explain:

For several nights now I have been able to make out tracks
in the grass close to the lake where I have a hunting lodge. The
tracks resemble marks left by a very heavy paw; the grass is
flattened down and remains so, suggesting that the animal
that dragged itself that way must be of some considerable
weight. I have been able to make out, in the middle of the
lagoon, an enormous animal with a head similar to that of
a gigantic swan and, from the movement of water around
it, I would surmise, the body of a crocodile.

The purpose of this letter is to secure from you the
material support for a fully equipped expedition, that is to
say, a boat, harpoons, etc.; the boat could be built here. In
the event of our not being able to bring the animal back
alive, we should also need embalming materials.

If you are minded to proceed in this matter, please be so
kind as to authorize the outfitters Pérez-Gabito to supply us
with all that we need for the expedition.

I would kindly request a prompt answer to this letter, and
take this opportunity to send you my deepest respects,
Martin Sheffield

The gringo had made only one mistake: he had not taken
into account, when sending his letter, the motives of Onelli
himself. The Engineer remembered them perfectly.

Not only had Onelli not believed a word written by the
gringo – he had roared with laughter as he showed the
Engineer the passage describing "the monster" one sultry
summer's day in Buenos Aires, when they met in the director's
office at the zoo.

"Do you see, my friend, the things people will invent for a
fistful of dollars?"

"So you don't believe him?"

The Engineer was quite taken aback. He had believed the director of the zoo to be naturally curious, and with a tendency to get carried away by his own enthusiasm. In any case, he had not expected such a sceptical reaction, and had been all ready to play the devil's advocate against what he had imagined – wrongly – would be Onelli's overexcited endorsement of the project.

"Believe what exactly? Forgive me – believe that there is an enormous aquatic animal with a swan's neck in some shitty little lake? A prehistoric marine reptile trapped in fresh water, which nobody ever spotted before?"

"The thing is the Hoyo Lagoon—" The Engineer began to say, but Onelli immediately cut him off with a smile that shut down any serious discussion on the subject, or indeed any kind of discussion at all.

"'The Hoyo Lagoon', my esteemed friend, is the least of it. It's the place where that rogue lives, his stamping ground. It's where he sits down in the evening to drink his whisky and contemplate his empty coffers. That man is notorious in Patagonia, don't go worrying that there's any chance of finding this monster…"

Then suddenly he grew serious. Like someone who is about to confide an important secret, Onelli leant towards the Engineer and murmured:

"You know, there *is* an animal, but it's not the one described by Sheffield."

The Engineer looked at him, bewildered.

"What is it, then?"

"Help me to organize a fully fledged expedition. I can't leave Buenos Aires, not now, not even for something like this – and, believe me, I regret that very much, but it can't be helped. I need someone who knows the area, who can get to the lower slopes of the sierra before the cold arrives, and who can manage people and keep within the limits of a tight budget. I need you, Frey. What do you say?"

"You still haven't told me what for. I mean, the mountains, the cold, the people, the budget – all that's fine. But if Sheffield's description isn't credible…"

"The gringo's letter is handy for us, without that no one would cough up even a peso for an expedition at this level. I've already told you: there *is* an animal, but it's not that one. The possibility of their being the same is, let's say, remote."

"So?"

"Look."

Without speaking, Onelli showed him a diagram made in his own hand, then another that someone had made at the bottom of a letter (the Engineer could not see the sender's name, only that the text seemed to be written in a language similar to German), then a picture from an old encyclopedia lying open on his desk.

"The bones of one example were found in a cave in Última Esperanza, as I told you, in a gelatinous state. Fresh, if you know what I mean. If you want my opinion, *this* is the animal that's alive, not some marine reptile. This is the animal I'm looking for, Frey. Of course, if you also happen to find something remotely similar to a plesiosaur swimming in a freshwater mountain lake, that would be splendid. If this gringo really is able to raise the dead, you can even get us a couple of Cretacean dinosaurs, that would be nice…"

"What do you mean 'raise the dead'?"

Onelli shrugged.

"It's what some people say. But don't worry about it – they're just stories people like to tell around campfires when the light's fading, right? Let's get back to my proposal. What do you say?"

And what could he say? The Engineer knew that, since the beginning of the last century, there had been rumours that some creature from prehistory, or at least one unknown to modern zoology, was roaming around the south of Patagonia. On the banks of Lake Blanco, they said that in the light of a full moon you could clearly see a kind of giant reptile that made horrible guttural noises, then vanished, as if it had only emerged to worship the night. Some time afterwards a Norwegian Engineer who worked, like him, in border demarcation, had found the tracks of a supposed plesiosaur on the banks of the River Tamango, and further south, the famous gelatinous remains of that prehistoric quadruped that interested Onelli so much. According to him, this was the only one that would have stood a chance of surviving the isolation of the Andean cordillera, protected in no small part by the very absence of man and his modern, sophisticated ways of wrecking things. From then on until the time of Sheffield's letter, there had been no end to the sightings and descriptions of animals; in various places creatures of different kinds, monstrous or chimerical, kept cropping up in the stories of natives and travellers, so much so that the accounts had reached Europe and North America and there was now some excitement brewing about the possible discovery of a "Patagonian Lake Monster". The Engineer suspected that an expedition would prompt both support and scepticism in the northern hemisphere.

Of course, against his better judgement, he had said "yes", and it was only now that he saw how clearly that had been a mistake. Now as he sat beside the muddy, calm – damnably calm – water.

But on the hot summer's day that he had talked to Onelli, it had even seemed like a good idea. There was money, not for him personally, but certainly enough to pay for equipment and to bring specialists on board – the right people, trained, and with experience in the field. Some of them, like Cinaghi, had even worked on other continents. There was also enough money to pay for transport, for a trip to Lutz and Shultz to buy the best photographic material, and to fund the expedition for a month, if it proved necessary.

The whole thing had been almost completely organized that same afternoon in Onelli's office. They had also ordered from Lutz and Shultz the surgical instruments necessary to perform a partial autopsy, although, even at that stage, they considered including a taxidermist in the group, to embalm the specimen in case it proved impossible to bring it back to Buenos Aires alive. In a provisional budget, they included the cost of a wagoner for the roughest leg of the journey – from El Bolsón – or even before that, allowing for early snowfalls, which could never be ruled out. Andueza and Cinaghi were included in the expedition right from the start. Next they added Merkel, whose reputation as an embalmer was beyond question. Only later did the Engineer learn that most of the money for the trip had come from the coffers of the newspaper *La Nación*, which explained the addition of two more people: Señor Estrella, a cheerful reporter from Associated Press, and Señor Vaccaro, a freelance journalist.

Following the instructions that Onelli had laid down, they left the station in Buenos Aires under separate steam. Meanwhile the press had been informed that all the party would take the train to Patagones, then the boat to San Antonio, in the Gulf of San Matías, and then take the shortest route west, got up, no doubt, in the garb of far-flung explorers and carrying all the paraphernalia that the popular imagination associates with hunting terrifying, gigantic dinosaurs in Esquel. The fact that nobody knew if it really *was* terrifying did not matter very much, just as it did not matter that they were using the word "dinosaur" to describe the prehistoric marine animal which, after thousands of years negotiating glaciers, might now have made its home in the freezing freshwater lakes of the mountains. At any rate, the journalists, opportunists and hangers-on were deliberately put off the scent, so that they would not interfere with the true purpose of the mission.

The "secret list" of instructions Onelli had so carefully drafted, many of them in consultation with the Engineer, included advice on how to behave in the presence of the creature, when to keep watch and when to sleep (this was based on previous sightings at Criptoterio that preoccupied Onelli, rather than on any speculative description of the behaviour of a marine animal that had been extinct for around sixty-five million years). They were also told how and under what circumstances to kill the beast – should such action proved unavoidable – which parts of the specimen to embalm, which to leave behind and which to attempt to transport back to Buenos Aires.

"You should rest during the day and be alert at night," Onelli had told them when he said goodbye. "Always have your weapons at hand, your searchlights and flares, your cameras loaded and ready – you don't want the creature to appear and then have nothing with which to document it."

They had also been entrusted with the special job of finding certain animals that had been named by the Indians, such as the *bullín*, the *lobito de rio*, the *cuyá*, or *pequeño hurón* and also any grasses, fossils, skeletons or skins that were interesting, to add to the collection in the Museum of La Plata.

So it was that they arrived separately at Bariloche, and by 20th April they had reconvened to travel together south by car. On the way, however, they got wind of some accounts that were consistent with the sighting of a creature Mapuche mythology knew as the *cuero* or *calueche* on the banks of the river Correntoso.

12

According to the locals, a bulky creature, red like a swollen bloodsucker, boasting several rows of talons along its extremities, appeared in the area at the end of summer and beginning of autumn, always at the same time. This creature travelled from one inlet of a lake to another, and even from one lake to another, as if it had the capacity to turn amphibian for these crossings, or as if the lakes themselves were linked underneath the mountains like a set of connecting chambers.

So before they took the road south – and given that the Engineer had to return urgently to Buenos Aires for a few days – they had decided to go to Correntoso, to clear up any doubts. They went by land, which was certainly the harder option, but at least it saved on the cost of sailing across a large part of the Nahuel Huapi Lake.

The Engineer had been sorry to interrupt the trip so early on, but he explained that his presence in the capital was unavoidable and placed the lake operation in Cinaghi's hands. The huntsman set off some sticks of gelignite in the deepest part of the lake's bed, but the *cuero* did not appear. In fact nothing appeared, other than some sediment thrown up from the bottom. This was brown and of a slippery consistency, probably plankton moving in the mass of water thanks to gas bubbles produced by some volcanic phenomenon imperceptible to the human eye.

But they did find something just before they left Correntoso, and that was an old friend of the Engineer, if "friend" was the right word for Víktor Mullin. He was a man of unkempt appearance, more corpulent even than Cinaghi, and he spoke a mixture of German and Spanish and some words of a language the expeditionaries recognized much later as Mapuche, the Indian tongue. He was of European origin, but had been in Patagonia for so long that he considered himself Argentine – or perhaps stateless, a wanderer. These insignificant details were all that they managed to coax out of him, and over the next few days they scarcely learnt any more: Víktor Mullin became the group's new member, incorporated by tacit consent on the pretext that he would act as guide, showing them the best routes. He never explained how he knew the Engineer, nor did the latter ever shed much light on the circumstances of their friendship.

Cinaghi was the only one to mention Víktor's enigmatic presence on the 1922 expedition, years later, in an interview with *La Razón* newspaper. From what he said, the Engineer seemed both to respect and fear the German, though perhaps it was not so much fear as a wariness that comes of knowing someone really well. He had not hesitated in accepting the help when it came from such an experienced source.

However, everyone in the group noticed a certain uneasiness in the Engineer's expression; or perhaps it was a more ambiguous sentiment: a mixture of admiration and contempt that gave his smile a bitter twist, as if he were unable to enjoy fully the thing he knew best how to do – explore the great unknown. And they also felt that Víktor's arrival had shut them out of something, but they did not dare question him about it. All in all the presence of the German signified only a minor contretemps in the Engineer's otherwise buoyant mood.

Even as they left Correntoso empty-handed, the members of the group were still brimming with excitement. So with their enthusiasm undinted, they had continued to Epuyen.

Horses and carts were waiting for them at the coal mine to take them on the irregular and winding road that lead to Cholila and Esquel. So far everything had gone too well. The members of the group were in high spirits, and even looking forward to meeting the gigantic beast described by Sheffield in his letter. All of them believed there was "something" out there, even if that something might be very different from a dinosaur or a marine monster. Merkel was the only sceptic in the group.

Before arriving at Hoyo, a little after passing El Bolsón, Cinaghi had allowed himself the satisfaction of killing with one shot the little female huemul, and that night, what with the wine and the impromptu barbecue, they had felt like the first men on earth. They were nature's sole witnesses, its only "rational" witnesses, thought the Engineer, and he remembered what Víktor used to say whenever they arrived at one of those stranded spots you find among the gentle foothills of the cordillera, so beautiful that it hurts your chest to see them: "Nature, my friend, does not need you or me, nor any human being. Everything you see will endure, but not for us. For us it disappears as soon as we close our eyes, just as dreams disappear when we open them."

Once he had suggested to Víktor that art might be a way to hold on to that emotion produced by nature in the human soul. Without even looking at him, Víktor replied, "If you find the idea of art or memory comforting, then good for you."

Scarcely had they arrived at the lake's edge when it dawned on the Engineer that, even if Sheffield's monster were alive – even assuming it had managed to overcome all the obstacles of evolution, the vagaries of climate, geography and the presence of man – they were not going to find it here.

The Hoyo Lagoon – home, supposedly, to a prehistoric and elusive creature the size of a whale – was at that moment about three hundred metres in diameter and, judging from the measurements they had made that morning, no more than five metres deep.

In other words, as Onelli had so witheringly put it, it was "a shitty little lake".

What sort of animal could they expect to find in that stagnant mud, that dominion of horseflies? What exactly were they hoping to snare with all the metres of steel cable they had lugged down here?

They had taken on some manual labourers in Bolsón. Now the Engineer ordered them to "go and look for Sheffield. If the directions in his letter are to be believed, his hunting lodge is that hut you can see on the other bank, just past that clump of rushes."

Of course the gringo was not there. But much later, when the men had made a start on their work as instructed, a boy turned up claiming to be Sheffield's son. He said his dad was very ill and that he had not been able to leave the house in Los Repollos, but that, if they wanted, he himself could take them to see the dinosaur's tracks.

The Engineer raised his eyebrows, bemused to hear the word.

"Is that how they know it here? As a 'dinosaur'?"

The boy shrugged. "Only the outsiders call it a dinosaur. So do you want to see its footprints?"

After circling the lake from the west, they had arrived at a place where the bank seemed to continue between high rushes towards a gentle rise in the land. Just beyond the slope, there was a patch of broken rushes and dried mud leading towards the water. There was no sign of the print of a paw or a fin. In fact there was nothing more than a muddy oval, two metres wide at its greatest point, with a small trail that suggested a continuation into the lake.

"It's much smaller now than it was before," insisted Sheffield's son, looking with disappointment at the shapeless patch of mud that was clearly not going to get anyone excited.

The Engineer tried to hide his rising impatience. "Could we get to Los Repollos before nightfall?"

"I don't think it's wise – not with the storm that's brewing over there," said one of the labourers.

"It's further on than Los Repollos, you would need to go nearly as far as Foyel," said the boy.

"Are you on your own here?" asked Cinaghi.

"No, I'm staying with Don Salazar until my brothers arrive."

"And where does this Salazar live?"

"Three kilometres from here, on the way to the ranch."

The patch of flattened rushes and that detail about Salazar had been the only fruitful outcome of the first morning. They could not count on Sheffield leaving his sickbed and appearing at their camp to stand by his claims or to offer to lead an expedition in the area. They could not count on José, his son, either, but perhaps they could count on Salazar...

In the end they got to work on the Engineer's orders, measuring up the lake, collecting earth so that they would have something to take, even if it was only a bag of El Hoyo dirt, back to the Museum of La Plata.

Hours had gone by without anything disturbing the surface of the water, apart from the westerly wind which, just as the labourer had predicted, was threatening rain – and perhaps snow, too, judging from the colour of the clouds and the sharp drop in temperature.

Huddled in his woollen poncho, the Engineer watched everything over the others' shoulders, issuing orders while also noting down measurements and making plans of the area under survey: during the first day, as well as putting up tents, they had made all kinds of measurements. Even Vaccarro and Estrella had joined in, in childishly high spirits, intoxicated by the feeling of being in the middle of nowhere. This was a land still inhabited by Indians, by Europeans who had come to Patagonia either with their pockets bulging, to buy up land, or empty-handed, to work like dogs. Criminals and hustlers had been drawn here, gold-diggers and madmen obsessed with legends – like Víktor Mullin – and then priests, the hopeless and the desperate. This was a no-man's-land: *Tierra de nadie*.

Merkel had discovered the skeleton of an animal, either something unknown or too badly disfigured to classify, and he was now concentrating on cleaning it with some chemical products he produced, like a magician, out of a little leather knapsack that went everywhere with him. Meanwhile Cinaghi and Andueza were zealously exploring the area, shotguns at their shoulders, ready to fire. As night fell, they ate a light stew, then prepared to mount a guard. In his instructions, Onelli had been very precise about the times at which the creature might appear, since all the sightings to date had occurred at dusk or shortly afterwards. The natural trepidation the watchers felt was heightened by the confusion of shadows, strange animal cries, the creaking of branches and grinding of teeth.

Three of them stayed up all night beside the fire, feeding each other's fear with stories of ghosts and apparitions. As dawn was breaking, they had been startled in the half-light by a llama, a scrawny orphan, wandering as though lost, near the lake.

Since that moment – 4.15 on a freezing cold morning of relentless sleet – the Engineer had not been able to get back to sleep. Perhaps that was why he was now in such a bad mood, he thought, and his feelings were exacerbated by the lack of sleep, the lack of a monster or the simple lack of anything, even a measly ferret, to see up close. No – the obvious conclusion was that Sheffield's letter had been a well-planned joke – he had probably been looking for a handout for some fictitious project. The mark in the mud was a sly recreation made with a flat-bottomed implement and a bit of guile. Onelli's animal was no more likely to appear than Sheffield's, and the journey from Buenos Aires – two journeys in his case – had been a monumental folly.

In spite of the unremitting cold, the Engineer stayed on by the lake, still in shirtsleeves, though with his poncho wound around his neck – because the last thing he needed was to get ill.

At midday the famous Salazar had appeared, a local expert who much admired the gringo, which meant that the Engineer could not even let off any steam in front of him. At least Salazar came across as an honest man who had always lived in the region and claimed never to have seen anything, though of course he had heard stories about the *cuero*. This was precisely what concerned the Engineer: he had the feeling that the myth of a lake creature – more credible in some versions than others – held sway throughout the cordillera, from Neuquén, through Chalten and on to Santa Cruz, judging from the two recent sightings there. But then the story of the werewolf was also a myth that people kept alive, even though it flew in the face of scientific evidence. And weren't there people who believed in the Lost City of the Caesars, in the treasures buried by Foyel, that great Indian cacique who haunted the dreams of anyone that dared to approach his tomb? So where was the line between reality – as defined by logic, evolutionary theories, physical limitations – and the most atavistic desires of men?

That was what kept him watching the surface of the lagoon, that great volume of unaltered water: the tiny possibility, a chink of belief that he wanted to guard against his better instincts, because it was human nature to believe in these things, even if it turned out that the monster could not be a part of the natural world he knew.

And as if all that were not enough – the waiting, the watching, the anxiety, the disappointment, the speculation, the tiredness, the storm and the cold – they had gone and run into Víktor. That German did nothing but maraud around the encampment like a caged animal, his brow furrowed, consumed by frustration, then occasionally possessed by a fanatical enthusiasm that sent him rushing into the woods – among the fallen tree trunks that were half rotten from humidity and piled upon each other, like a mossy green trellis – as if he were suddenly not a man but an animal, a wood sprite or sorcerer.

"Don't bother going there – there's nothing," Víktor had warned before even greeting him, when the Engineer had joined the rest of the party close to Gutiérrez after returning from his impromptu trip to Buenos Aires. And all the way from Gutiérrez to Epuyén, for at least two hours, the Engineer had listened to his observations, both acerbic and persuasive (in so far as persuasion was possible for Víktor Mullin) about the futility of their expedition, at least in the area around Epuyén.

"Why did you come here with us, then?" the Engineer had finally asked, exasperated by his woeful litany and the demoralizing effect it was likely to have on the rest of the group.

"To save you from wasting time," Víktor had answered. "There are unexplored areas in the north, in the Rincón Sound and right here, in Hess there were sightings recently. Why make a mockery of all your organization and equipment?"

And so it went on, but the Engineer could not disavow Víktor. He could not ask him to go his own way, to leave them in peace – he owed him too much.

Silently he cursed the exact moment that the other members of the team had met Víktor. He cursed the German's incurable obsession and his own bad luck in having to abandon the party so soon after they had arrived at Bariloche, leaving the others in the hands of God. But better God's hands than Víktor's – because the Engineer suspected that Víktor had trailed them, and was trying to use them in his own search for a monster. Now he also cursed his decision to follow up the eyewitness accounts of the *cuero* all the way to Correntoso. That was where they had found Víktor, or so they told him afterwards – but the Engineer found it hard to believe in coincidences, especially in such vast areas. It was obvious that Víktor Mullin had been living in the mountains since the accident in the Futaleufu, that he had continued to search for something that eluded everyone else: a shadow, some imperfection in the landscape, a warm gust to fill the bloody vacuum in his own life and his bloody determination not to belong any-bloody-where.

But how could he have found out about this? The German had been living like the Indian nomads who no longer even existed, here and there, always alone, like an anchorite, in the mountains and valleys of the Andes. Now he had appeared again, like someone back from the dead, from nothingness: the mad foreigner, the adventurer, the hunter, the hermit living a rough and almost animal existence in the mountains, and the travelling companion on that trip organized by Perito Moreno that the Engineer would much rather have forgotten, because the death of three men would weigh on him all his life, all his waking and sleeping hours.

At that time, under Perito's orders, they had been investigating the tenuous edges of a world that was completely unknown to them, a mixture of paradise and stony purgatory, condemning them to perpetual discovery. They had to work like Sisyphus against the instant forgetfulness of geography, because borders never remember themselves, even when you mark them down in black pencil on a piece of paper. That journey had been a nightmare, but not at the beginning, and not because of Víktor's presence. In fact the opposite was true: it was thanks to the German's knowledge of every tree and every twist of the River Futaleufu that they had been saved.

Not everyone, though: only the ones who had been able to save themselves. The rapids of Futaleufu had already swallowed up dozens of men, but the Engineer had paid no heed to its dangerous reputation, and ordered the boats to be got ready anyway, overladen as they were. Their boats were tossed about like toys in the arms of the river, which had looked so clear and was really so full of trickery. Soon after they had passed the confluence, the wind had changed direction; first the wind was blowing in the same direction as the torrent, then came the whirlpools, springing up everywhere, as if the river bed were full of holes connecting to the other side of the world, or harbouring terrible gods all glugging down the water at once. And then on the bank a great grey rampart had appeared, a vertical and pitiless wall: they had entered the gorge that the Indians called Chel-Curá, or "stone ghost". It was a short, enclosed stretch of water, impossible to reach by land and almost impossible to leave, unless you followed the river downstream. Stones from the river bed protruded at the surface, giving the impression that the river itself had hardened. Now they found themselves in a stony wind tunnel. The heaviest of the boats had suddenly been trapped in the tangent of a whirlpool that was so powerful you could see the edges of its funnel, perfectly circular and dark. The boat spun around with the light elegance you would expect of a dry leaf, then it disappeared, together with two of its men. In the other boat, Víktor was on his back in the flooded hull, desperately trying to manoeuvre himself into a position to use a lasso, while the Engineer had one man by his jacket who was half submerged and being dragged along by the current, flapping against the side of the boat, and all the while he was trying to use his body as a counterweight to stop the boat striking the rocky banks.

You should never fight the current, the Engineer thought, not for the first time in his life. There in the Futaleufu, the only other option was to let yourself drift with it to wherever it wanted to take you. You had to let your boat be overturned or broken up if the river ordained it, but you should never try to fight. It was useless: straight away your muscles got cramps and next came paralysis of body and mind, because freezing water quickly undermines even the sharpest survival instinct. And that was something Víktor knew full well, having experienced it himself several times. For that reason, no sooner had the first boat been swallowed by the whirlpool than he ordered the others to be still, to hold on as tightly as they could and to succumb to the current – to let themselves go.

The Engineer understood that they would have to face death in order to get out at all; his stiffened hands were now barely able to grip the jacket of the man outside the boat. When he retrieved him from the water not long afterwards, he found that this man was dead, like the other two.

After some time, a little more than fifteen minutes – though it seemed an eternity to the Engineer – the wall of the gorge began to taper off and was rounded out with patches of earth, until a sudden veer in the river's course brought them into a stretch that seemed less wild, at least by comparison with what they had been through. Even so, it was a miracle that the boat stayed upright as it followed the capricious design of the torrent, because it was beyond the power of any of them to control its navigation.

It was a willow tree – one of those anomalies in the landscape that so intrigued Víktor – that finally saved them. In fact Víktor himself had remembered the position of that old tree on the bank, as it began to level out just beyond the gorge, and he managed to throw a rope around the strongest part of the trunk, and pull the boat onto dry land.

The expedition on the Futaleufu cost three men their lives, and from that moment onwards the Engineer had not crossed paths with the German again, nor had he wanted to return to the area, and certainly not to the Futaleufu.

He had only received one letter from Víktor since the accident, and that was several years later, when his physical wounds were completely healed, though not his spiritual ones. In the letter Víktor described his latest peregrination, an exhaustive trail through western Patagonia, from south of Futalaufquen to Lake Espejo. He wrote:

...in Cuyín Manzano, further north and to the west, there are traces of human settlements dating to 8000 BC. You know as well as I do the ideas of Wegener. Even though everyone insists on finding him mad, there is proof that the continents have been moving since the very beginning of the world! What is Patagonia today was once part of Africa, joined to Europe and North America in one single and perfect form. According to our mutual friend, Herr Dr Windhausen (I've translated this directly from his notes in German), "since the middle Cretaceous period, there is clear evidence of the existence of an open sea between Antarctica and Patagonia: it is the upper Cretacean marine fauna found in the Tierra de Graham by the Swedish expedition to the South Pole in 1901. This fauna indicates the existence of a biological centre in which marine fauna evolved with their own characteristics and in considerable abundance, so giving rise to other faunas that were dispersed northwards, as the great cleft of the Atlantic Ocean opened up". If we add to this Doctor Guzmán's hypothesis regarding the glacial straits which have led human beings to America from the Old Continent three times since history began – what may they also have brought here from the sea?

As he sat observing the almost marshy stillness of the lake, the Engineer knew that the answer was plain to see: they had brought nothing. Neither Wegener nor Windhausen was mad, nor even Guzmán who had often been written off as a "loony" – and with some justification, given the high-pitched tenor of his campaigns. Víktor was the only mad one among them.

And perhaps there was nothing to find simply because nothing was left. Of sabre-toothed tigers all that remained was the puma, which attacked cattle, plundered stables and was useless either to breed or to eat. Of the famously tall Tehuelche people, with their high cheekbones and artisan's hands, only a few fugitive Indians survived, spectres who wandered the land as though in search of their old horses. It was Spanish horses that began the destruction of these peripatetic tribes. Their patient work as hunter-gatherers, their rigorous crafting in wood and stone of bows and arrows had given way to lances, bolas, the greedy pursuit of wild horses, which could be traded for alcohol or money, or leather hides that were easily incorporated into the restless wandering that had made them lose touch with the earth and, worse still, surrender ownership of the land that had been theirs since their race began.

Generals Rosas, Alsina and Roca had all done their best to defeat the Indians. For the Mapuches, Namuncurá put up a resistance; Calfucurá was defeated. Many more came to take their place, and there were more soldiers, and more Indians swelling the ranks of prisoners, war-wounded, the sick and disabled – all of them died sooner or later. Their ghosts also wandered like shadows across the plains, like coirón trees with no roots. Nothing remained of the Mapuche who, as legend had it, were transfigured into fish, nor of the haughty Tehuelches. If they had remained, no doubt they would have been wiped out by evolution, or by the many expeditions to Patagonia.

No, there was nothing. In addition to his physical exhaustion, the Engineer felt an overwhelming desire to go home and have done with this farce. During the three days of their observation, not even that bastard Sheffield had appeared to give some account of what he had written. Onelli had come up with a system of code words for them to transmit their discoveries to Buenos Aires, in which key places were replaced with alternative names, such as Vertiente (Lake Kruger), Esquel (Lake Menéndez), Colorado (Cholila) and more complicated phrases denoting certain actions. The famous system had not been much use since, according to Estrella, the newspaper *La Razón* had begun publishing a satirical daily column recording the exploits of the "magic team" as it called them. Worst of all, it had the facts more or less right. Who was leaking the information?

The Engineer preferred to think that the problem was in Buenos Aires, and they should sort it out there, but it was still quite funny to think of the absurd care Onelli had gone to, all for nothing.

What would there be to say now, or rather when they reached the first telegraph post? He had even been ordered to pay Sheffield one thousand pesos if their mission was successful, and five pesos a day should it fail, for "time wasted", when it was quite clear that he and his team were the ones wasting their time here.

Weary of thinking about it for so long, cold to the marrow, the Engineer decided to put paid to the question once and for all: if there was something in the depths of the lake, he was going to make it jump. He saw that Cinaghi was still on the lake, on board the ridiculous raft made of cypress wood that he had brought especially to sail on the "monster lake" – when the only really monstrous thing here was that raft itself, so out of keeping was it with the landscape.

"Andueza!" he shouted suddenly, and too loud – so that everyone looked round, startled.

Víktor, who perfectly understood the Engineer's tone of voice, came bounding up, as though walking on springs.

"Are you giving up already?" he asked.

"Not yet. Andueza! How much gelignite is left?"

"Are you going to dynamite the lake?"

"Andueza, hurry up for Christ's sake. How much is left?"

"Six cartridges."

"Save them for something worthwhile," remonstrated Víktor. "What do you think you're going to find here, in something that's less than five metres deep?"

"Use them all, Andueza."

"You're making a mistake, Engineer," said Víktor. But the Engineer was so furious that he did not notice that the German, for the first time ever, had just addressed him by the informal "tu".

"Whatever you say, sir," said Andueza, and he went to look for the explosives.

"Has anyone found the gringo?" the Engineer asked, even though no one apart from Víktor was close enough to offer an answer.

"With any luck, that bastard will be the one thing you do find," said the German, frowning, his arms obstinately folded across his chest.

Those were the last words the Engineer heard from him in Epuyén before the nerve-jangling din of the explosion left them literally deaf for a few moments.

They were also the last words from the expedition to stay with the Engineer – along with the image of the miserable fishes thrashing about in the muddy water by the bank, their mouths gasping with shock.

They returned to Bariloche during the storm, the snow already several centimetres deep, their party complete but for the German.

No sooner had they arrived than they were surprised by a crowd of people swarming the civic centre; the shouting and uproar were incomprehensible to the Engineer, who observed the kerfuffle with bewilderment, as did the others, all of them wrecked by exhaustion and a sense of failure. When their group was spotted in the middle of the hubbub, some sign was communicated, like a murmur going around everyone present, and then, from a corner of the room, slow and creaking, appeared a monster made from strips of pine attached to a float pulled by two horses. Its gigantic frame, covered with brown sackcloth, was in the shape of a swan, with crocodile's teeth painted in its enormous mouth and humorous, sardonic yellow eyes. The Engineer regarded the construction in amazement. Andueza began to laugh, but was cut dead by a look from Cinaghi.

"What's the meaning of this stunt?" the Engineer asked quietly, while the excited crowd made the wooden beast turn around, before the astonished eyes of the expeditionaries, to reveal one of its flanks, on which was written in large white letters:

I AM THE PLESIOSAUR YOU HAVE BEEN LOOKING FOR

Primo Carpario, the Mayor of Bariloche, well-known in the city for his practical jokes, stepped forwards, struggling to keep a straight face.

"So, Don Frey – what do you make of the creature we've managed to find you?"

"It's good. Very good," said the Engineer, and he forced his lips into a wan smile. "Now, if you'll forgive me, I must send a telegraph to Buenos Aires."

The cheerful mass of people thronged around the monster, men with children, with wives on their arms, everyone enjoying the impromptu carnival. Some applauded, others whistled.

It was a long, long time since they had laughed so much.

From a dusty back room in the post office, the Engineer telegraphed to Buenos Aires a single sentence, one of those ridiculous, cryptic formulations prepared for the occasion and which Frey, up until now, had never imagined he would need to use – at least not so soon. It read:

ALL HOPE LOST STOP VOLCANO EXTINCT STOP

Even in there he could hear the sound of laughter, muted now by the wind. He was the new town idiot and soon, once Vaccaro had splashed the story of their frustrated expedition on the pages of *La Nación*, he would be a national laughing stock.

On the journey to Bariloche, he had asked his men to do one thing only, and now he was glad he had asked it then, before they had been subjected to the townspeople's spectacle – otherwise it might have seemed like an act of cowardice: that was not to mention the German's presence on their expedition. To anyone. The men – thank God – had agreed, gravely, without asking any questions. But could he rest easy now?

His expression sombre, locked in a room that smelt of glue and damp, the Engineer thought for a moment about the man they had left behind at El Manso, alone with his rifle and his thoughts. He had feverish eyes, a look of being lost, and it was probably true that he was in some way unhinged. But if anyone, one day, was *really* going to find the monster, it was without any doubt Víktor Mullin – or some other wretched soul pursued by his ghost.

2

Ana

"And so ended the only ever formal expedition to hunt the lake creature," said Lanz, with a long sigh of satisfaction, "according to what was published in the newspapers, and what Víktor said. That is, when Víktor said anything, because it was hard for Víktor to talk, very hard..."

And then, after watching me for a few seconds with a slightly annoyed expression, he added:

"But who is this girl, Mutti?"

And from her rocking chair, she answered as though his question were as natural as her own answer:

"Ana, Víktor's daughter. You've known Ana since she was little – remember?"

"Do I know her? Of course I know Víktor's daughter – poor little thing."

The old man, absorbed as he was in his memories, was also at the whim of a cruel dementia. He could remember me for periods of time that went from a few hours to, on occasion, a few days, but whenever he told this story he always ended up referring to me as a "poor little thing", as if my own life were genetically condemned by the imbecility and obstination characteristic of that Captain Ahab type he had reckoned my father to be.

Ilse – only Lanz and Klára called her "Mutti" – stroked his head or kissed his brow while shooting me apologetic glances, and I smiled to reassure her, just as I smiled at Lanz, putting on my best "poor little Ana" face.

Exchanges such as this are what I remember most clearly from those months. Our conversations became soothing in their frequent repetition. For just as Lanz must have told me about the famous expedition to Epuyén hundreds of times, his forgetfulness regarding the present, the care Ilse took to reassure and calm him and the invariable "poor little thing" in the story were repeated like a mantra or an incantation during that whole summer.

It sounds odd to say "that summer" as if others had passed since then. It's actually only nine months since Christmas, and yet it seems like another time altogether. What is this story really about? Lanz's fears, Ilse's premonition, Nando's denial, my own quest or the mystery surrounding Pedro? Everything started at Christmas 1975 – and now, nine months later, the only thing I can say for sure is that it was about the monster.

In fact there was a different monster for each of us.

When I first came back to the "villa" (we all call it that here, although Lanz says it's pretentious, a way to flatter our illusions of sophistication) fifteen years ago, my father was dying in this very bed, the one that I used to lie on as a child, watching the lake.

The bed was really an old divan that Lanz had restored when he still worked as a wood-turner, and innumerable layers of varnish had given it a reddish hue. It was positioned beneath a window made of thick cypress beams that today looks onto the same dark forest as then, and also onto the lake, onto the two banks of a natural harbour, the deep and lonely inlet that my father used to call Melancolía Sound. I was twenty-three years old when I came back to this wild, godforsaken place, having just gained a diploma from the University of Bahia that I never bothered to collect, and my father was dying, finally succumbing to a slow and stealthy cancer.

My father always knew about the monster, and he was far from being the only one. The expedition Lanz talks about so much was unusual only because the government took such an interest in it, and because of the secret presence of my father. Speculations and theories have abounded in every era among the communities in this area – although those places now seem much less close-knit than once they were. However, for my father, the monster embodied more than mere speculation or theory: it also represented the cancer that had impregnated his blood and which the Buenos Aires doctors had diagnosed, with a certain elegance, as an advanced case of leukaemia.

Leukaemia... When I first heard the doctor utter such a technical word it was all I could do not to laugh. I made an effort to suppress a smile, but it was not enough to satisfy the doctor, whose expression shifted rapidly from serene piety to one of suspicion (Dr Hansman, was it? Dr Hauselbach?).

The two of us were in the corridor of the German hospital, a clean, sombre place, as calm as a mortuary. Hearing our conversation, a pair of nurses in white uniforms had stepped out of the sepulchral dark and ambushed the doctor, like little ambulances waiting for toy victims.

"You're not the daughter, are you?" asked the doctor.

"Not the daughter?" came a sharp echo from the one who seemed to be the Sister, judging by the bonnet that was arranged over a hairstyle that had been lacquered and combed stiffly back.

I looked at them, smiling, but with a forced and unconvincing solemnity.

"Why are you laughing?" asked the other one in the starched uniform.

"Do you understand what I've just said? Perhaps you don't know what leukaemia is?" persisted the doctor.

I saw no reason to discuss what I knew or not with such a strange trio of marionettes, though I certainly regretted that such an ill-disguised gesture should have caused my relationship with the chief doctor to deteriorate so quickly and to such an extent, especially as it then proved much harder to get my father out of that hospital.

I am sure that the people living in this area have been talking about a monster for thousands of years, ever since men used primitive language to tell their children that in Lake Nahuel Huapi there was a black creature with no tail or head, whose shapeless flank appeared as a sudden dark reef every time that a certain wind found its path from west to east, filtering through the massive grey cracks between mountains in the cordillera. Perhaps they described how the surface of the water became choppy, and a reddish, oily layer of strange algae rose like vomit from the guts of the lake to be exposed, brilliant as obsidian in the light of day, then dragged to the shore where it formed a great rotten cadaver, pecked on by birds who would die hours later on that shroud of algae, leaving a rosary of dark carcasses among which one could scarcely distinguish the beaks and the claws.

The sole testimony of those primitive men were some vague and tremulous pictures drawn on cave walls – rough paintings that were underrated in many cases preserved solely by people's ignorance of their existence – together with an oral tradition that had struggled to survive in spite of genocides, expeditions, the march of civilization and the shame of speaking Mapuche, not to mention other misfortunes which weighed on the Indian people.

Very few people know about the drawings, or about the oral tradition. My father, whom I found on my return here dying more out of frustration than of cancer, was one of the few who did know. Lanz was another, but around the time my father began his final decline, the first signs of alcoholic dementia had already appeared in the mind of the old Hungarian, in the shape of a marked and instant forgetfulness of everything relating to the present time – and in Lanz that was a clear sign that something was not right.

During the last two days of his life my father – who rarely used his voice unless it was to issue orders or to imitate animal sounds – sought out opportunities to be alone with Lanz to talk. He spoke then for hours and hours. I think he was looking not for clarification or understanding, but simply a kind of expiation, a confession that could be safely entrusted, not to a priest or a friend, but to the only mind he knew was too fragile to retain the details of his wretched life.

When I finally got up the courage to ask Lanz about those conversations, he had already forgotten almost everything. And if he did remember something, he was not able to tell me it. I suspect that had less to do with forgetfulness than with a compassion for me, for his "poor little thing".

My father and Lanz met near here, when my father was building this stone house on the banks of the river and Lanz was working in the Chileans' sawmill. The two of them shared memories of Europe and a passion for the monster, although my father's passion was more like a morbid obsession, while Lanz's was a metaphysical quest, possibly bound up with his experiences in the war. My father had not only seen the monster: he had drawn it hundreds of times in his clumsy hand on bits of paper and tree trunks, on rocks, with pieces of coal, with his finger in the sand on a beach; he had pursued it, he had tried to hunt it on various occasions, he had frightened it and courted it, and he had studied it in his own way, zealously, with adoration, always watching out for it.

Lanz, on the other hand, was the only one of us to whom the monster would continue to appear, as if it intuited the irony of his hazy memory. I have often thought that the old man, with his gentle and unconscious dementia, represented for the monster what the monster itself was for my father. After a whole life of pursuit there must be a kind of unhealthy bond between the hunter and the hunted, a link that is as necessary as air or water. They end up not being able to live without each other. I'm sure that is what happened to my father: the leukaemia was germinated by the loneliness he felt when the monster disappeared, when there were no longer any tracks or signs, or even the slightest suggestion of its presence. If there had been a sign, I'm sure that my father would have continued living – he would have clung to it in desperation, because that is how a man who is alone and searching for answers gets by. My father lived for these trifling, barely significant signs, without ever allowing his mind to fabricate them. For a man like him cannot deny reality or invent it. All he needed was a sign, however small – but one day the monster disappeared without leaving even that. As Oscar Wilde says in one of the cobweb-covered books in the library of this house, "the true mystery of the world is the visible, not the invisible". My father was scrupulously faithful to the evidence of his eyes. For him it constituted all that was real.

After all these years, during which I myself have become caught up in my father's quest, I no longer know if all humans need monsters, or if that is simply the human characteristic that most interests me.

Why did they look for it? Why did *we* look for it?

I suppose that my father was driven by his obsession, by an irrational need to see himself reflected in an impossible mirror. Lanz was motivated by curiosity, or perhaps by some early manifestation of his mental deterioration.

For me it was dissatisfaction, which is surely one of the most powerful motors that exist. Hatred is another, and in recent months I have begun to see that love can also be an explosive element.

My father once claimed, so Lanz says, that my grandfather had been a great sailor, and that during one of his journeys west to the frozen coast of Maine, he saw "Gloucester's Monster", a kind of greenish-black reptile with terrible yellow eyes, as long as my grandfather's boat and as wide as the trunk of an oak, slithering calm and magnificent through the waves of a tempest. That moment changed his life for ever. Lanz believes that Víktor's father had seen nothing less than the mythical basilisk, the crested king of all serpents, which burned alive all those who approached it and split open rocks with its fiery breath. The only detail that caused Lanz to doubt the story was the water: no one had ever seen the basilisk floating far from its infernal swamp. Several members of the crew died, their bodies found mysteriously charred in the lighter that took them to port, while my grandfather was in the grip of a fever, doubled up in the hold, his boat anchored far from the coast, because of the storm. No one ever knew how the fire started. An article from the local newspaper – one of the few papers that my father conserved among his books and drawings – argued that it was a case of spontaneous combustion. Lanz, of course, attributes the flames to the monster's wrath, and asserts that only the crowing of a young cockerel could have prevented it.

Apparently, it was only when my grandfather managed to return to Europe after his odyssey that he discovered that his wife had killed herself "because of that", drowning herself in a muddy stretch of the Rhine. I was never sure what "that" was, but I suspect that my grandfather had lost his mind as well as the family money, and finally he got my grandmother to kill herself and leave him in peace.

Genetics is an ominously truthful phenomenon: the offspring of a mad sailor and a suicide, my father naturally turned out to be violent and introverted, much more so than people round here tend to acknowledge, because they are still prey to an excessive and sometimes baffling gratitude. Lanz, in his way, admired my father; Mutti felt sorry for him; his various partners, when he had them, put up with him the way one puts up with a case of gonorrhoea – proud in some secret way to carry the evidence of one's exploits in one's flesh. Some of them have even come to believe that Víktor Mullin had dealings with the Devil, such was his rage, his merciless and terribly inconsiderate behaviour towards humanity, not least himself.

My father searched for the monster, but it was in order to find himself, just as Narcissus looked in the mirror of calm water to contemplate his own face. The one good thing he did in his life, Ilse says, was to distance himself from me. That act alone redeems him a little, whatever the motivation was. That, and building this house, La Pedrera, something he also did for selfish reasons – not that it matters now. So he did at least two things well. That's no small feat. Some people never accomplish anything in their lives, and all that justifies their invisible, futile lives, existences unworthy even of an epitaph, is the recourse of death. The ultimate recourse.

One of the few times I saw my father relatively healthy and lucid was in a bar in Buenos Aires, one of those classic saloons on the Calle Esmeralda, smelling of coffee, floor wax and a strange mixture of bleach and damp. This light perfume seemed to rise from beneath the tables, from the tiles, even from the waiters who moved around with an exasperating and slow formality, as if they were more accustomed to serving English people. It was a bar for the chronic tippler, for the quiet alcoholic who pops in at any time of day for a whisky. But it suited my father down to the ground. He did not look so different from the waiters. Nothing in his demeanour was out of place, not his rigid expression, nor the shadows under his eyes, framing his gaze with a greyish tinge, nor the sparse grey hair combed back from his forehead, nor the liver spots that covered the skin on his head and arms. Although it sounds strange, I prefer to remember him like that, in the context of the bar, because by the time I arrived at this house, my father was no more than a clutch of bones that breathed; only by God's grace (or the Devil's) was he still in a condition that could technically be classed as "alive".

But I do not want to speak any more about my father – my intention was to explain more recent events. At the moment, from this window I can see three divers in suits of lustrous neoprene preparing to enter the lake. They have tied a wooden platform to a boat and on top of it they are placing tanks of compressed air and other objects I can't make out – I suppose that they are instruments for seeing and manoeuvring in water.

I've been watching them and thinking that they won't know what's hit them when they reach the bottom of the lake – their gear could only be considered appropriate for the surface of this icy clear water.

Ilse, sitting in the rocking chair across the room, wants to know if another letter from Klára has arrived, and also if anyone is going to take the gas cylinder to be refilled. She asks what I am watching with so much interest. Sometimes I have misgivings about telling her the truth, but Ilse is not a woman who can easily be fobbed off with slippery answers. She's been around too long and, in contrast to Lanz, growing older has not clouded her mind or her memory; nor has it affected her movement, although she says she cannot stand for as long as once she could, preferring to rest in the rocking chair with a blanket over her knees. Sitting in the sun, gently swaying, like a willow tree beside a river, she certainly looks like an old lady, white and languid as a candle, almost ghostly pale – but you only have to see her in action to know that this old lady is no phantom, nor is her body as frail as it appears.

Like Lanz, Ilse has been through the worst of this century: both of them are survivors of the world wars, of flight, exile and new beginnings. So perhaps "strong" is not the right word: Ilse has a hard shell that has helped her to weather life's storms. Sometimes I think that the woman will never die, that she is a kind of phoenix, approaching the end of her five-hundred-year life, and quietly preparing to be reborn among handfuls of cardamom and myrrh. I would love to believe that she is a little immortal, but at other times, when I see her dozing in her chair, the sun shining on her white chignon as if it would like to let it loose, I think that Ilse is very soon going to be seventy-six, that she does not want to hang on much longer, and that one day she will simply slip away, while she is rocking herself, as she is now.

I try to put off answering her, but now she demands to know why I am spending such a long time gazing out of the window at the lake.

"Don't be asking me to get up, Ana. What is there?" she asks. (Although she speaks fluent Spanish, she still constructs sentences with unexpected verb forms, some of them invented, others learnt in old grammar books.)

I can't lie to her. "The people from the prefecture, Mutti. It looks like they're going to drag the lake."

For some minutes Ilse says nothing. One of the divers has entered the water and is still holding on to the platform. The others are putting on their equipment and preparing to follow him.

"They'll die of cold," she says finally, in the same soft, almost tremulous tone that has characterized her voice for these last few years.

No one else, with the possible exception of Lanz, would be able to detect that inflexible vibration, the steely core hidden by her old lady's voice. For her, the word "die" is never casual.

I smile, and silently agree: a death by freezing would be quick and solemn. Almost elegant.

* * *

Ilse, Lanz and Klára are Hungarian, though in Klára's case one cannot be so sure, because her parents died on the boat that was bringing them to South America at the end of the Second World War. She was found dying of dehydration, a baby wrapped in a blanket beside her mother's cold body. Who knows, says Ilse, how long her mother had been too sick to feed or tend to her? In a pouch beside the corpse there was a bottle containing the dregs of some crystalline liquor which the mother must have taken to numb her pain. She had also given it to her daughter, judging by the baby's breath, perhaps to quell her suffering. Fortunately, someone had realized that the baby was still breathing, that her skin's bluish tinge was caused simply by a lack of water. Again, by good fortune, there was drinking water and milk on board the boat, something that could not have been reckoned on, given the conditions in which they had fled.

Ilse says that the war spawned many stories like Klára's, hers and Lanz's. In fact these stories constitute the proper definition of war: people who meet other people while fleeing death; people who escape death; people who die.

I don't really know much more about them than that, which is strange because this old couple is the closest I have to family. They have been at this house ever since I was about four or five. They are the only people to have had a close relationship with my father, and who can explain some aspects of his life – and therefore mine.

To start with they lived, I vaguely recall, in a cabin behind the house. At that time Lanz was working at the sawmill. Some time after I went to boarding school, the business was wound up by its owners, who moved to Chile, frightened off by Perón's new labour laws, rather than (as they claimed) by this country's political instability. With the sawmill cut adrift, Lanz tried to keep on working for a time, while the other employees went one by one, until finally he was the last one there.

That was when his illness began to manifest itself, very subtly at the start, with little mix-ups that struck people as funny, because he was usually so meticulous and precise. Later, as some tiny but vital region of his brain began to disintegrate, faults in his memory cut him off once and for all from the present time – the reality of his life – the break occurring at some point which is impossible to fix exactly, but it seems that, for him, the real "today" is a day from twenty or thirty years ago. In fact the illness was much worse than that even, because in addition to the devastation caused by Korsakov's Syndrome (for that was the name of the disease) there were minor bleeds in other parts of his brain that might pass unnoticed by observers and yet caused insidious damage. These haemorrhages brought an unexpected dimension to his inability to create new memories: slowly they began to annihilate those recollections that *were* still impressed on his memory, starting with the most recent ones, as though someone were sweeping his life away from him within his own mind.

Korsakov's Syndrome has no cure. It does not rearrange memory, or hide it, change it or distort it: it destroys it. It negates the possibility of creating a new "past" in place of the old one, of modifying it, reconstructing it, pardoning it. There is no possible redemption for him: Lanz is trapped in a time that torments and haunts him, and that will be the case for ever, because nothing that he has lived through since can appease that past – nothing that has occurred in the interim really exists in his memory. The present brings him no relief, because it leaves no impression. All that is in his memory, standing in for his "present", are twisted recollections of the war. It is an atrocious plight, but at least he has no awareness of it, and that is the only concession this disease makes him. He does not know that he is being deprived of his life, or worse, gradually being cornered in its worst era.

In retrospect, this strange illness of Lanz's seems to have been a premonition. It was during dinner, last Christmas, that one of his haemorrhages caused the old man to retreat a few years on the game board in his mind, and for the first time we all saw it happen. For Lanz, that jump back in time meant returning for good to face his monster – not the creature that haunted Víktor, but something much more terrible. The episode also bestowed a disquieting aura on that dinner which I feel marked the start of everything: that night we all witnessed the moment in which Lanz lost a part of his past, as though neatly excised by a rigorous surgeon. But it was also the first night in the summer, and the first in many years – more than ten – that we were able to observe a phenomenon that had been spoken about Indians and by my father himself: the algae reappeared on the river.

The day before Christmas Eve, all anyone could talk about, between Ilse's panics in the kitchen of the big house and Lanz's in the cabin behind, was Klára's arrival. Lanz was supervising the last distillation of liquor as though his life depended on it (and later, during dinner, Ilse would assure me that that was the case – that Lanz's life depended on the same substance that was killing him – like some exquisite assassin working so stealthily that his body and mind were incapable of detecting it).

It was Christmas Eve 1975 – and summer, of course, but a mountain summer. Spherical grey clouds threatened to conceal the thin strip of sky framed by the mountains and the lake. Rain was forecast too, but a little after midday the sky had begun to clear sufficiently that at about seven o'clock we were able to put the iron table on the porch with some chairs brought from the living room, the hammock Lanz liked and some candelabra with thick candles, like church ones, that Ilse insisted on arranging on a folding table. That sort of

ornament, however pretty or romantic, is useless here. Never
since I can remember – and certainly not that summer – has
there been one day, or any notable stretch of time, without
wind. Wind is a constant presence, like the massive body of
the mountains, like the twisted cypress trees behind the house,
and like this house itself. But the candelabra are important
to Ilse because they were among the few things she was able
to save from her home before the shelling started, and to
take with her across the Atlantic. Usually we all try to bring
something cherished to this ceremony which, Lanz says, owes
more to Middle Eastern traditions than to Catholic ones.
None of us here is Catholic anyway – certainly not practising
– but Christmas is an atavistic feast, and we celebrate it like
pagans, in our own way.

I tell a lie – actually at least two of us have been christened:
Ilse and Nando, and as for Klára, we know nothing about
her life before the boat. Ilse's father converted to Catholicism
at the height of the Austro-Hungarian empire, the "Double
Monarchy", as Lanz calls it. Her mother came from an old
family of Magyars, aristocrats with refined habits who lived
in a castle with turrets and a rampart at the top of a mountain in the Carpathians, with gardens, statues and all the
trimmings one associates with fairy tales, except that in Ilse's
case it was all very true.

Ilse's father was a secular Jew from Szeged, a city of merchants and intellectuals to the south of Budapest – someone
much more interested in art and business than in religion.
So when the time came to choose, he opted to abandon his
family and the thousands of years of religious tradition, of
which he was largely ignorant, and stoically to convert to
Catholicism, a popular religion in Hungary, but one to which
he was at heart equally indifferent. In any case, none of this
helped to save his children: neither the conversion – though
that was hardly painful – nor the protection of his newly

acquired aristocratic relations, nor even the money he had made in the generous and honourable service of the country he considered to be his home.

Ilse was born years before the break-up of the Empire. After the First World War, the redrawing of political frontiers meant that the family ended up living in Romanian territory. Like so many sudden and unexpected exiles, they had to abandon Hungarian as their daily language and, given the proximity to German settlements over various centuries, they took up not Romanian, but German. In the following years, Ilse was the only one in the family accepted into the gymnasium to continue her studies, but only because she was a woman, and the university quotas for 1920 restricted the number of Jewish boys in any kind of educational establishment. Ilse's two younger brothers would not share her luck – they had been born at the end of the First World War, like so many other babies conceived in the fear of death. By the time they reached an age for university, the Nazi party was governing Germany and leaning on Hungary, too. So thanks to a restored antisemitic law, they were rejected by the University of Debrecen for having Jewish blood, once more falling outside the permitted quota for young men. Later they would both be sent to spend several months carrying out forced public works in one of the few metallurgical factories left in Hungary, and from there on a fast train to Auschwitz.

During the period that separated the wars in eastern Europe, Ilse led a quiet life in the suburbs of Budapest, with a few sporadic trips to the Austrian city of Graz. She doesn't speak much about that time, other than to say that she played the piano and got by teaching art and German to a few lucky Magyars. The German occupation found her in Budapest, perhaps the best place to be in a time of such catastrophe, Ilse says, because in the city the Germans were obliged to moderate the savagery and excess of the deportations that they were carrying out more freely in the provinces. Anyway, she managed to hide for a few months. She does not speak about that time, either: her obstinate silence on the subject is a counterpart to Lanz's illness.

By the time Ilse managed to return to the family home in Romania, she discovered that there was no home any more, that her father had died and that her mother was living under the protection of some distant relatives, hidden in the basement of a restaurant that had closed down. She sold some clothes and a few valuable objects on the black market, and with the proceeds – abandoning her university studies in philosophy – at the age of thirty-eight she fled across the Romanian border to Yugoslavia, and from there, by boat, crossing the Adriatic, she arrived in Italy, post-Mussolini. There, thousands of other exiled European Jews, political refugees and war-wounded wandered the streets of Rome or Genoa seeking everything from false passports and visas from South American countries to safe conducts to Palestine or political asylum in Africa.

Among that mass of impoverished and terrified men and women was Lanz.

That was the way they met each other – then they ran into each other again while trying to buy special visas, first for Brazil. But rumour had it that no Jew could disembark in Brazil, so they ended up buying a second visa for the Argentine Republic, a country they scarcely knew how to find on a map.

Klára's parents died during that Atlantic crossing to Rio de Janeiro, but no one knew where they were from, or anything about the mother beyond the fact that her hair colour, like Klára's, was of a kind of red that signified bad luck in Patagonia. The emaciated body of her father (whom they had also found in the hold, unconscious – he died two days later) had the same thin, long face that his daughter would grow to have, and very white skin that hunger and a lack of water had turned as grey as his wife's. It was an image that Ilse says she will never forget – for, lying against the mother's dead cyanotic skin, on the wet floorboards of the hold, and so bundled up in rags that no one had yet noticed her existence, was Klára, dehydrated and quiet, but with her black eyes wide open.

That is the story Ilse tells, in more or less detail, every time she settles down to polish the pewter candelabra; they look deceptively strong, but are really as delicate as porcelain china. We call them, with a certain solemnity, "the Count's candelabra", because it seems that they belonged to her maternal grandfather, who bore the title "count" – in addition, of course, to an unpronounceable Hungarian name.

That evening we carried out the iron table, in spite of the wind and the cold, and Ilse told the story again, almost as if to herself, checking some of the historic details with Lanz, while she finished cooking her own version of goulash with lamb and potatoes, and the famous fish soup that always opened our dinners, whatever the occasion, seasoned with her no less famous sour cream and paprika. The cream was made with goat's milk provided by some mangy animals, with yellow coats that were forever full of thistles and whole families of leeches. The old folk insisted on keeping them in a paddock beside the wood. The cream was Ilse's speciality, but the pâté was exclusive to Lanz. The whole process is something that Lanz keeps to himself, from catching the wild geese – which are abundant, fortunately – to making the liver pâté, with herbs that are carefully cultivated in a greenhouse behind the big house. His most important investments have been his greenhouse, the goats and a collection of hens, not forgetting the cockerels which serve both the hens and the household as a very noisy alarm system.

Anyway, by the time the old folk had finished cooking, Nando had arrived, and the liquor bottle we had opened a couple of hours previously was already nearly empty.

We always began with a home-made musket-rose liquor. It had a deceptively smooth texture that made everyone less hungry – and more talkative – than they should have been. Nando would bring a couple of good bottles of wine from the city, and these were reserved for the meal. Finally, after desert and a coffee, came the digestif, a mix of different herbs – some macerated and others distilled at home – that the old folk had been preparing all year. Some herbs grew in the secret shelter of the greenhouse, others were wild, and the rest, I suppose, had a superstitious value. Lanz and Ilse claimed never to have altered the recipe. The truth is that the lack of finesse in the distillation – the technique involved no element more sophisticated than a live flame and a few misshapen bowls – resulted in a murky and powerful alcohol, a dark-green liquid, irritating and bitter to start with, that seemed to filter through your tongue straight into your bloodstream. Its smoky flavour was a bit like mescal, although this ritual did not call for worms (and Ilse said that putting a dead creature in the "bosom" of a liquor was bad luck). However they did, at the very last moment, throw in an extract that they called wormwood – this softened the extreme bitterness which would otherwise make the drink almost impossible to swallow: it was a tincture of absinthe, a herb that Lanz grew in the colder reaches of the greenhouse. Instead of putting the drops – which were of a darker green than the colour of the night sky above the cypresses – straight into the liquor, Lanz often used the tincture to moisten a block of hard molasses, which he then set about with the enthralled expression of an opium addict.

"It's the only way to take it," he claimed, without any attempt to justify himself, and Ilse, smiling, went about her own serene ritual, adding the blackened drops to her glass of liquor.

I am sure that in some part of Hungary there are secret caverns, damp tunnels under the floor of certain black forests, caverns where virgins were tortured in antiquity and the power of pagan amulets invoked, where today a different version of this liquor is drunk, laced with the leaves of some endangered tree, the botanic name and origin of which no one knows. Some place like the rancid opium dens of Victorian London, but more impenetrable, much more secret and profane.

That night, at the table in front of everyone, I must have described my theory about the existence of such a place, because Ilse suddenly looked at me with astonishment and Lanz burst out laughing, mocking with his alcoholic mirth the indignation of his wife.

"It must have been a dream," said Nando, also smiling.

I don't know why, but I was sure that it was not a dream.

Some things are like that, like the monster – about which we suspected nothing, certainly not its proximity, until some time later, as though my vision had been some sort of premonition.

But I am getting ahead of myself: it was not yet the night of Christmas Eve.

By this time Nando had arrived, with his bottles of wine; after that we had drunk the musket rose aperitif, we had put the tablecloth and cutlery on the iron table and, while the old folk were toiling in the kitchen at the big house, Nando and I gazed at the lake and the darkening sky, and observed how the mountains around us were turning violet, then grey and finally black.

While that liquor seems to throw a blanket over all outside impressions, at the same time it brings a clarity to one's

vaguest sensations, revealing them directly to the consciousness. Perhaps it was that clarity of mind bestowed by the
alcohol that made me aware, for the first time, of Nando's
uneasiness.

He seemed – as usual – calm enough, comfortably sprawling
in a chair, with his eyes half-closed and his gaze fixed on the
surface of the lake. I remember him knocking his foot against
the table, making a noise that sounded overly rhythmic
against the random movement of the wind – but that was also
typical of Nando: he liked to regulate his own tempo, as if
the mountains of the Andes, with their imperturbable rivers,
lakes and woods, were not enough of an anchor for him, not
already a perfect demonstration of the world's immutability.

No: his body language certainly wasn't giving anything away
– all the same, I sensed a jarring, discordant note in Nando's
apparent composure. What I did not know was that, at the very
moment I had realized that something was wrong with Nando,
Klára's red Fiat was coming up the road from the shore, that
stony path that could be seen behind the belly of the lake,
curving up the hill until it was lost among the cypresses. I did
not know that Nando's gaze was not fixed on the lake, but
beyond it, on the red car that was beetling up the slope.

It was only much later that I realized Nando's trepidation
that night had everything to do with little Klára, my childhood
friend, the adopted daughter of Lanz and Ilse, who every so
often returned to La Pedrera to visit her parents, bringing
European-style goodies: traditional cheeses, paprika that was
more yellow than red, fine preserves.

This time, she would present for our delectation a gigantic
Nussstrudel for desert, a bottle of artisan vinegar, much
coveted by Mutti for her cooking, and a tin of caraway seeds
for Lanz.

Klára parked the car anyhow beside the house, then came
up to the porch with her "swag bag", a large, rough knapsack,

woven in bright sisal and immediately recognizable to all of us because it was one of two mementoes that Lanz and Mutti had kept for her from the boat that had brought them to America. On the other arm she carried another bag, a plastic shopper. As she came towards us, a balancing act weighed down with Christmas presents, her red hair drawn up in a ponytail and wearing a leather jacket that was too big for her, no one would have said she was more than twenty-five years old. Klára has always been beautiful in a classical way, and irritatingly so – at least for me, because I can never look in a mirror with any pleasure. However there were other things we shared: the same age, for example, and the fact of having been born in an indeterminate place on the planet. She had been rescued from the boat, while no one knew who had rescued me, but when Lanz and Mutti arrived at La Pedrera, we two little ones began our time together as sisters.

Neither Klára nor I have the slightest memory of our earliest days. Sometimes we say that the stork brought us both together to save on the celestial air fare, and that he dropped her first in the northern hemisphere, while I was dragged onwards to Patagonia, caught among his pink feathers thanks to my large nose.

We used to laugh about that sort of thing, but I think, in fact, it is good that neither of us remembers anything from that time.

Klára was brought up here in the area, while I was sent far away to board at a convent. Ilse so often protests that my father did the best thing for himself and for me that I suspect she was behind the decision. Anyway, it doesn't matter. Klára and I are nearly the same age (in her case it's hard to know – her exact birth date is a mystery that Ilse, with her ancestral gift for astrology, has tried in vain to pin down at least to a particular month) but Klára is much more beautiful.

I had never been impervious to the fact for sure, but neither, until that night, had it caused me to suffer the way I did in the moment that I watched her coming up the sloping path to the house with those bags and her enormous jacket, diminutive and slender, with skin so pale that she stood out like some vivacious ghost. By the ochre light of the candles, her cheeks flushed from the climb, Klára was, if it was possible, even more beautiful than usual. She looked sad too. I suspect that Nando had observed her, like me, with the same pain that is provoked by beauty in those who do not have it, but I was not watching him, so I did not notice him get up and swiftly leave as she reached the porch – although that could not be counted as unusual behaviour in Nando, who obeys no basic rules of etiquette. In fact, as far as he is concerned, they are the only kind of rules that don't count.

"Sister," said Klára finally, dropping her Father Christmas sacks on the floor as she threw her arms around my neck like a little girl. For a moment I had the impression that she was about to start crying, but this was fleeting, like so many strange and incomprehensible sensations that night. Perhaps if she had made some observation about Nando's bad manners, I would have picked up what was going on between them. But she didn't, and I didn't.

I embraced her. "How come you're so late, skinny-ribs?"

"The Beetle broke down, I swear it packed up and I couldn't get it started until an angel of the road come to my rescue."

"What did this 'angel' do, if I may ask?"

Klára burst out laughing. It was not something she did very often, though it was wonderful to hear her laugh. She was, on the contrary, a serious person, quiet and introverted. And she liked to be enigmatic about her personal life.

"Well, the angel siphoned off some petrol for me. I didn't realize that my tank was nearly empty."

"How are things in Barda Roja?"

Klára looked at me, no longer smiling.

"Why?"

"What do you mean 'why'? It's a perfectly reasonable question."

She fell silent with that sadness in her expression that I had noticed when she first arrived.

"Things are OK. They closed the school," she said, "but don't say anything about it; it's probably temporary – you know how these decisions are."

Forestalling anything I might say, she pushed my hair back with her hands – something she often did – and went quickly to the kitchen, calling out to Mutti and Lanz. She had said nothing about Nando, but I began to wonder where he was, and went to look for him.

I found him in the greenhouse, which occupied a corner of the hen house, as neat and colourful a display of plants as one might find on a European farm. The room was in darkness, there was no electricity, and no one went in there after dusk, at least not without the express consent of Lanz, or accompanied by him. Nando's back was to the door, and he did not see me come in. He was leaning against a tall bundle of alfalfa which Lanz kept tightly banded, providing a sort of shelf for his watering cans and shovels. Rather than leaning, Nando seemed to be trying to get his balance, or catch his breath, as if he had just run a race. It was a long time since I had seen him looking so dejected and lonely. I wanted to leave him in peace, to turn back and tiptoe out, but my entrance had alarmed the hens, and their hullabaloo alerted him to my presence.

"Ana?"

"I was looking for you. You got up so suddenly that I thought... Klára's arrived," I ended up saying, confused. I felt again that something was not right with him, but could not work out what it was, except that Nando seemed overwhelmed and his choice of such a gloomy refuge was ominous.

"I'll be there in a minute. Lanz asked me for some mint, and I came to get it, but I can't see it with so little light."

"Are you all right?"

"Why?"

"No reason. The mint is in the little pot on the left."

I watched him for a second or two longer, without knowing what to say, unable even to move towards him. What purpose would it serve? How would it help him? Nando did not appear to have been looking for herbs, and Lanz was not the kind of man to let someone else loose among his blessed plant pots. However there was nothing in my inklings to which I could give concrete expression. Finally I went, taking care not to let the hens escape from their enclosure.

That was all. I went back to the porch where Klára and Mutti were about to serve the fish soup. In the kitchen Lanz was uncorking the first bottle of wine.

I kept thinking about it during the dinner. Part of me, the part that was already a little drunk, wanted to ask Lanz if he had really sent Nando out to get a handful of mint. But I had a nagging worry that, if my suspicion were confirmed, I would not know what to do next, how far to press Nando or what to ask him.

Dinner went smoothly until, after many hours of unusual calm, the wind suddenly got up, blowing out the candles and sending us scurrying indoors with our plates, glasses and cutlery. Inside, Mutti insisted on lighting the candles again, so that now our faces were dappled with mysterious chiaroscuro, illuminated by the spectral light from the fire as it rebounded off the harsh stone walls. The living room was the largest room in the house, square and very high, and, apart from the cypress beams in the ceiling and floor, the rest was pure stone.

Sitting at Víktor's very long, Franciscan-style table, with our old china and pewter candelabra, we were suddenly converted into five souls lost in time, five shipwrecked survivors from the Middle Ages huddled around our provisions and the flickering warmth of the flames. That evening, even the wind was strange, seeming incapable of deciding from which direction to blow. The curtain in the window that looked onto the lake rippled furiously, at the behest of what felt like a whirlwind or an Indian simoom. Klára got up silently and half-closed the shutters to stop the candles from blowing out again.

The room had acquired a texture that fell between lugubrious and sumptuous; Ilse, with characteristic black humour, began to tell an old Magyar tale about a boy who spent his life looking for his father, following the clues of a totally false surname, since, by law, every child born in Hungary must take his father's name. In this case, as the mother had not been able to reveal the true identity of her lover, she had decided to invent a surname which happened to be one of the most common in Hungary. The only thing was that the child, when he grew up, dedicated all his days to the search for this father who could be everywhere and nowhere at once, like an elusive shadow, until bitterness drove him to suicide and he threw himself in front of a train. Ilse told the story in a mixture of German, Hungarian and Spanish, and Klára watched her with a disheartened expression, her black eyes impenetrable, and her fingers interlaced, as if she were praying to a cruel and sceptical God.

Meanwhile, I was studying Nando and his efforts to appear happy and nonchalant over at his end of the table, far from the rest of us, while he obsessively checked his watch. Lanz was at the head of the table, dozing off listening to Mutti, though every so often he roused himself to correct something or add a shocking detail. One could not imagine a scene that was more pagan and less Christmassy – in the Christian sense of the word – than this.

I collected the empty plates and took them to the sink in the kitchen. Nando got up to help me. In the kitchen, without saying anything, he hugged me, and it was that secret embrace, limp and ambiguous, that determined me to ask Lanz what Nando had been doing earlier in the greenhouse. I thought of taking him aside with some plausible excuse, of creating an opportunity to talk to him alone, before dinner was finished and the older ones started going off to bed.

At least that was my intention, but it turned out not to be possible. Soon after we had started dessert, Lanz suddenly sat very upright in his chair, and began to blink and rub his eyes, looking around himself in bewilderment. Mutti noticed before the rest of us, and moved quickly to pin him to the back of the chair, while the old man's thin body seemed to bow to some supernatural force that made every part of it writhe. When the rest of us went to him, we saw that his eyes were violently bloodshot, so much so that for a moment we thought that his eyeballs had exploded, leaving two blackened sockets. The poor man began to babble Hungarian words in a high, childish voice.

"What's he saying?" asked Nando helplessly.

"It doesn't matter," said Ilse. "He'll never be able to remember it. These are the words and events that his mind is losing. Hold him firmly, hold up his head. This will pass."

Ilse had spoken with extraordinary serenity. Before our very eyes Lanz's brain was being buffeted as surely as our candles were in that frightening mountain wind. A large part of his life would never return to him, and these were the experiences he was murmuring about in broken words, conjugating the verbs of a language that would also soon be lost to him, as if he felt a final and supreme need to speak aloud, to give voice to all the things he was losing.

The episode did not last more than five minutes in all, perhaps less, but from then onwards Lanz was not the same.

In the following months he would suffer two more attacks, both of them silent, but of a shocking subterranean potency. Each one robbed him of whole years of his life, and left him less able to remember what was happening in the present time. Sometimes, when he was feeling well, he could contend with a whole day, but at other times he remembered no more than ten minutes.

Everything that happened on Christmas Eve was extraordinary and strange, full of signs that each one of us might or might not have been able to decipher, depending on the moment in history in which we found ourselves. As for Nando, I was left to make assumptions that I would only much later be able to prove (although the word "prove" in this case comes closer to conjecture than it does in even the case of the monster).

After the attack we carried the old man, half-aware that something had happened to him, to the cabin at the back, to his own bed, so as not to befuddle him any further. It was a blessing that he did not fully realize what had happened to his brain. He would not have been able to bear it. No one could bear it. Mutti went to make a medicinal herbal tea for lowering arterial blood pressure, and I stayed at Lanz's bedside, while he watched me through a thick, transparent haze.

Lanz's cabin room looked onto a communal area between the two living quarters, a "garden" as Mutti liked to call it, which separated their cottage from the big house. From his room the illuminated rectangle of the kitchen window was clearly visible, lit up like a cinema screen. And there, standing beside the table, were Klára and Nando, arguing with gestures that were wild enough to draw anyone's attention – but especially mine. Nando's face was livid with rage, Klára's as white as candlewick. The whole scene, however, was very brief. He struck something hard with his fist, the table top, perhaps, and then he went, leaving her alone in the kitchen. Her expression was one of resignation or sadness, as if she had tried to explain something to Nando, all the while knowing that he could not understand it. When Mutti entered the room, a few seconds later, Klára quickly wiped her cheeks, then helped her to prepare the tea.

I got up from the rocking chair and tugged the curtains closed: I did not want to see any more. It was bad enough that I had lost, perhaps for ever, the chance to air my concern with Lanz. The obvious thing, in fact, would have been to speak to Nando, to ask him what was happening, what was going on with Klára, but that wasn't my style – had never been my style. On the contrary, my way was to try to understand the world by induction, using the same scientific method of observation, trial and error that I applied to the study of sediment and the primitive life harboured within its layers. Rigorous, immune to the mind's tricks, that was the method I applied to an understanding of the world – and, true to that same protocol, I could never speak to Nando. So I drew the curtain, completely covering the window along with my own uncertainty, but I did not have much time to think about the rights and wrongs of the matter, because just then Lanz started to mumble incoherently from his bed, words that were both hurried and disconnected, with such an urgency that I decided to sit beside him for a while, and try to calm him down.

"It was a very little, yellow notebook... a jotter... Darko, the gardener wasn't bad, and I think that he gave him the pencil too... He wrote *költemény*... so tiny on the yellow pages... Miklós only had that one notebook, just one, and he kept it hidden with his pencil in a sock, against his ankle, or tucked inside the waistband of his trousers..."

"What are you talking about Vati? Do you feel well?"

"The guards weren't the ones who came later, not the *Volksdeutsche*. They were worse than the Germans... the man gave him the notebook and he wrote poems... he walked, we all walked and in the train station we boiled up straw from the fields to eat... and also maize."

Exhausted, with his eyes still reddened, the old man covered his face with both hands. He wept silently, as animals weep, without tears.

"Everything will be all right," I said, stroking his head and making him lie down again. "Shhh, everything will be all right."

For a few moments his agitation abated; he lay still with his hands over his face, and I thought that he had gone to sleep. I pulled the blankets over his body, which was still dressed in the evening's attire; none of us had dared to undress him, nor to move him much.

Suddenly transformed, he sat up in the bed.

"They're killing us all. Like dogs," he said.

His eyes had begun to recover their usual limpidity, the watery blue of the iris sharper against the pale pink of the sclerotic.

"Face down, next to the road. They come by and they shoot at the head, shoot to kill, randomly, five, ten, fifteen, one hundred. Half of the cadavers get up to carry on walking, the other half can't any more. He still has the notebook in his hand. He survives this time, both of us survive. But he doesn't care. I still want to live."

Lanz's voice was marked by pain, but also an inhuman clarity; there was no doubt that he was describing something that was happening at that very moment before his eyes, as if he were looking through the same window from which I had just seen Klára and Nando argue with such strange violence.

I didn't know what to do. I tried to get up to call Mutti, but with the same determination, with the same desperate resolve that had moved him before, Lanz gripped my arm.

"Don't go yet, Sashenka."

Sashenka? I was about to correct him, as usual, about to tell him that I was Ana, Víktor's daughter, "poor little Ana", not Sashenka. But I realized that Lanz's gaze was still crystalline, as clear or clearer than before, and that he was not wandering off but looking straight through me, penetrating perhaps that other reality, which was so much more powerful for him than was ours. At that moment, I'm sure Lanz was not at all delirious and that I, in some way, was indeed Sashenka.

Then, as suddenly as he had sat up, he fell back onto the pillows.

Mutti had come silently into the room, carrying a tray, and had remained in the door frame, observing the scene without entering further into the room. She watched Lanz with a kind of resigned pain, and with some surprise. I wondered how long she had been there.

"He called you Sashenka," I said.

"No," replied Ilse. "He wasn't speaking to me."

Without asking her any more, I offered her my place on the bed beside Lanz. She came forwards, holding the tray, and briefly touched my cheek by way of thanks.

I went back to the house, overwhelmed by everything that had happened that night, by worry and doubt.

The howling wind reverberated between the black forest and the scarcely visible silhouette of the mountains, urgent and sharp like a woman in labour. The elements of landscape felt out of place to me, although I knew that the lake was where it should be, the house also, and the old folk's cabin behind it, flanked by the hen house and the yard where a goat was bleating, as though startled, perhaps by a fear as ill-defined as my own. Everything was where it should be, including my father's grave, but it all felt disconnected, like some scene imagined in half-sleep.

Nervous of stumbling across Nando and finding him in a similar state of confusion, I decided to walk down one side of the porch; I always kept an old fisherman's jacket, made from alpaca wool and misshapen from years of use, hanging on a peg there. It was one of the few things I had kept that had belonged to my father. I put on the jacket and set off down to the edge of the lake, the only place in the world that I found calming, taking the lateral path which was rough and barely lit by the flickering orange light thrown through the windows by Ilse's candles.

It seemed a supernatural light, like that of a star that has been dying for thousands of years.

What I call the "lateral path" is an unpaved track of flattened earth with stretches of rubble, testing to walk in the dark and even more so under that evening's overcast sky. Lanz had once baptized it "the Verecke Pass" in honour of the first Magyars to cross the Carpathians by that very narrow mountain track that took them to the other side, to the plain with shining rivers that was Hungary. Verecke, according to Lanz, was the route only victors, conquistadors and madmen would choose, and I knew that if I went that way, no one at the house would see me.

From time to time the clouds parted to reveal an intense, silvered, crescent moon. The cold was finding a way through the woven wool of my jacket, and I could not help shivering.

Why should the landscape suddenly cause me so much apprehension? I was all too familiar with this scenery. Why, then, this feeling of treading foreign soil? I walked as far as the wooden bench on the shore, groping a way through rocks and the atrophied roots of ancient trees, but to my surprise (it seemed that there would be no end to the surprises that night) there was already someone sitting there, his back to me, watching the lake.

It was Nando. I decided to go to him, trying to make no noise – just as I had tried a few hours earlier in Lanz's hen house – and, once again, without luck. Nando knew it was me without even turning round.

"Sit down here with me. If you like," he said quietly.

I did as he said. The night was profoundly dark, so that I could hardly see Nando's sharp, bluish profile as he gazed out at some indefinite point on the lake, or further away, into the mountains that merged with the night.

I lit a cigarette; it was an occasional vice because Mutti hated the smell of smoke and in Lanz it brought on a kind of hypochondriac asthma – a minor problem in the light of episodes such as the one we had just witnessed. For that reason I always carried a packet of cigarettes in the shapeless pocket of my father's old jacket, together with a box of matches that could be renewed whenever I went to the city and sat down in some bar to have a drink. Nando called that stealing, but more often than not he was the one who brought me the little boxes from bars. Klára did too, but only when she found one that appealed because of the coloured heads of the matches. The glowing tip of the cigarette made chinese shadows on my hand.

"How's the old man?" asked Nando.

"He's with Mutti now. What happened was so odd, wasn't it?"

"Odd? Lanz has been putting up with this crap for years now, Ana, and he's seventy now. The brain can only cope with so much."

"But this was worse than the other times. Or maybe it was just that this time it happened in front of us all."

"Was he conscious? Awake?"

"I don't know. Not at the beginning, but later... it was as if his expression cleared, as if the pressure normalized inside his head. He wasn't delirious. He said something about a notebook and how people had 'killed them like dogs'."

"The war."

"I suppose so. But he was very specific about the notebook. He talked about it with such sadness, such pain. Has he ever said anything to you about it?"

"Not that I remember. It could have been a random memory, like the way you suddenly remember your teacher's face…"

"It was a horrific memory, very precise, very clear. And he called me 'Sashenka'. I thought he had said it to Ilse, who was standing in the doorway, but…"

I did not know whether to tell Nando about Ilse's answer. Who was Sashenka? I suspected that not even Lanz could answer that, and that Mutti would not want to compromise her dignity by elaborating on what she had said at the time.

"He must have confused me with someone. It happens more and more often to him – don't you think? He always recognizes Mutti and Klára perfectly well, though. I must admit, it makes me feel rather envious."

"You shouldn't feel envious about it. The day those two disappear in the quagmire of his mind, he's sure to die. He can live without you, but not without them. It's a question of life and death – you shouldn't go taking it personally."

"No? You're very wise all of a sudden. What is this? A New Year's resolution?"

Nando did not answer. He bent down and picked up something from the ground.

"Here – I brought you today's paper."

And he passed me the newspaper, wrapped in a nylon bag.

"And an infrared light so that I can read it here?"

Finally I had made him laugh, and I felt emboldened to ask him the question that had been preying on my mind.

"Why were you arguing with Klára?"

It was as if the question had come out of the blue. For the first time since I had arrived at the lakeside, he turned to face me. The thing about Nando is that he is as transparent as a sheet of ice; even in the dark the lines on his forehead betray him in a way that is almost touching. I am sure that for a second he thought of lying to me, of denying that there had been an argument, but his mind was too quick to fall into such an obvious trap. He must have worked out that from where I was, in the old man's room, I would have been able to see all too clearly what was happening in the kitchen of the big house – and he preferred to own up to the fight. Looking back, I think that if he had denied it, in spite of everything, I would not have confronted him about what I had seen, in fact I probably would have apologized for questioning his words and his actions. As it was, he acknowledged the contretemps.

"Politics," he said simply, and moved away from me, turning his face back to the lake. "We were arguing about politics."

Now he could lie to me, for I no longer had the advantage of being able to study his gestures and those lines around his mouth that were so telling, so revealing to me. His tone was level, a little wearied, as though my question had irritated him.

"You are all living in a country that does not exist. This is not real, Ana, this… peace. Some time it will stop. It will end. Very soon."

"What are you talking about?"

Nando dropped his head between his shoulders. He wore the same jaded expression I had seen through the gloom of Lanz's greenhouse. For a moment I was tempted to believe his story about the argument with Klára.

"Sometimes I wish they had television down here, so that you could see what's going on – and not a million miles away from here."

"We've got the old man's radio, the Grundig, and the newspaper you bring. Isn't that enough?" I said, shaking the bag he had given me.

"No. It's not enough. Shall we go inside?"

"You're staying, then."

"Don't you want me to stay?"

"Yes, I do. Anyway it's late, you're not going back to the city at this time of night, it's nearly one o' clock."

"Anyway it's late," repeated Nando in a monotone. "And Klára?"

It was the first time that night that he had spoken her name, and it startled me, as though he had mentioned someone dead.

"She must be in the cabin. Mutti's been getting her room ready for two or three days, poor thing."

"Why 'poor'?"

"I'd love to have someone like Mutti to adore me the way she adores Klára."

"You're not yourself today. Ever since I arrived you've been strange," said Nando, taking my face in his hands and looking into my eyes. A gust of wind seemed to drag away the clouds that had covered the moon and suddenly we saw each other clearly, standing now beside the lake. Nando leant towards me, his enormous rough hands around my face, holding me firmly but with a strange care, like a doctor who examines a difficult patient to reassure her more than anything else.

Now that we could see each other so clearly, I found it hard to hold his gaze. I knew that what had happened with Klára was not to do with politics – or at least not just that – and that his pretence at normality was false, but I did not want to keep going over the matter, not then, not there.

"I'm just worried about the old man. And a little drunk. Nothing out of the usual – right?"

"No," he said quietly. "Shall we go in?"

That night was also one of the last times that I slept with Nando, one of the last times that we made love with patience, rather than an urgency to establish sovereignty over one another's bodies. Usually we were more like conquistadors than lovers; we were lieutenants charting the boundaries of newly won land.

For years now, ever since I first arrived here and first met Nando, we have had this feudal agreement to copulate, to serve one another's sexual needs. It does us good, for some reason. We know that the skin, orgasms, the viscosity of saliva or semen belong to a foreign body that aspires only to this transaction. And we ask nothing more (of that body) than the same in return: skin, orgasms, the viscosity of saliva or semen. We launch simple, frontal attacks, free of passion. There is no desire between us, it's something else, like an instinct to procreate in a void.

We went up to my room, taking off our clothes as we climbed the stairs, as if that might buy us an extra few minutes in a night that was, at any rate, bound to end at dawn, with Nando secretly and silently leaving the bed before the light of the new day disturbed the shadows on the stone walls – or before I could wake up and ask him, if I were ever brave enough, not to go. The truth was that I was nearly always awake when he left, and he knew that, but we both kept up the pretence.

There are perfect lovers that one meets too early in life – when inexperience, foolishness or misfortune cause those paths that have crossed just once, like the lines on a palm, never to converge again – and perfect lovers that one meets when it is too late to break the threads of the great spider web which life has become, in order to start again with nothing. Both kinds of relationship are impossible. And there are imperfect lovers, met at the right time, with whom one stays. This is the material of which most human relations are made, and society generally, together with the fantasies of those who refuse to accept the status quo, the misgivings of those who gave into it and the various frustrations of those people who find no lover at all. I like to think that Nando and I contribute no more to society than our regrets and neuroses, our sad and empty houses.

I know that Nando does not subscribe to this theory. If I were to expand on my ideas I am sure he would regard them as the pathetic maunderings of a spinsterish naturalist. That is why we can attack one another without mercy or shame on the nights he stays at the house, kissing with a fury, possessing each other with no other feeling than ardour, frustration and loneliness. That is why we can be as daring and deceitful as the gambler who knows exactly which face of the die is loaded. Christmas Eve was no exception. We ended up ridiculously entwined in sheets on the floor at the foot of the bed, and a few centimetres from a remorseless mirror that had reflected all our movements. I think that we slept for a few minutes before Nando carefully extracted himself from the tangle of sheets and limbs, and some or other article of clothing knotted around a heel, and I got up to wash myself.

The freezing cold water in our house comes from the old pump installed by my father. It is water regurgitated from the land, as hard as the soap which coagulates before you can coax a lather from it. The source of our water supply is a mystery. My father used to say that is came from a sub-surface water table, fed by various underground channels connected via the Andes to the Pacific. Nobody has ever been able – nor, I think, have they really tried – to prove the existence of these. You would think that the difference in altitude between the lake and the ocean would make such a network impossible. Topology itself refutes it. But of course Víktor Mullin jumped on any theory that might support the existence of the monster, and this one looked promising to him.

Lanz once said that it was not continuity that was necessary between the ocean bed and the lake, but *contiguity*, and that a phenomenon of filtration could alter the mechanism of communicating vessels, transforming it into something very similar to osmotic movement: thus the salty water of the Pacific would flow upwards to that hidden water table that is connected to the bed of our lake, thanks simply to a difference in concentration. Though highly unlikely, Lanz's hypothesis is not impossible, and it is true that the water flowing from our taps has neither the texture nor the composition, nor even the temperature of the water in the lake, which seems completely to invade the surrounding landscape. After bathing, I returned to bed, where Nando was sleeping face down, snoring peacefully. I sat beside him and stroked him for a long time. I placed the palms of my hands between his shoulder blades, and I may have kissed, gently, the warm curve of his neck, holding my breath like a vampire who fearfully kisses his own child. Later I lay down beside him, my back to him, and with my eyes closed, I waited for the moment when he would get up and leave the bed, as usual, without making a sound.

So it was that many things happened that night, and all of them were signs, subtle indications of what was to come, symbols which now, nine months on, have taken on a historic significance. They were omens that spoke of the power of memory and monsters, of nature, of perfect love, betrayal and honour.

Pedro had still not arrived – that did not happen until January. However, a few days later there was a sign, the first indication of what the Indians, explorers, early travellers in Patagonia and, above all, my own father had considered as tangible proof of the monster's existence (or even of its "coming", because the creature in the lake had always been regarded as a kind of Messiah, especially by the Indians, who used to tie up goats on the shore as an offering to prevent the spirit of the water taking any of them).

Early accounts talk about a "season of the monster", a time during which the Indians regarded Nature as capable of anything: famine, droughts, frost, children dying, puma attacks, inexplicable diseases. They would say that the lake was "rotting". There are descriptions of this phenomenon in the caves where very few humans have ever set foot: The lake is putrid with algae, and the fish give themselves up to death, showing their white bellies to the sky. *The lake is covered in white bellies, like other-worldly lilies, so we must tie goats to the rocks on the shore, close enough that the monster can devour them alive in the air, because that is what he wants: living blood. Dead things do not please him, and he will not eat them because they cannot talk, and the monster is tired of the profound silence of the water. His body has suffered silence for a long time, and when he wakens he needs to feed on life, to consume and suck it dry, so that it can sleep again and then be reborn again, amid the algae that announce it, as clearly and unquestionably as the star of Bethlehem.*

The spare room in the house looks onto a strip of unkempt ground where grass, dichondra, broom and a pair of plum trees are growing wild. That is the room where I keep my father's papers and everything that he owned – apart from the house itself – from the time he arrived here. When Nando is not staying, I sometimes use the room as an office (the divan in here is where he sleeps, after leaving my room in the early mornings). The sole window does not look onto the lake, but onto the garden, and the cabin where the old folk sleep. The forest is so close that it lends a sadness to the sky, colouring it a shadowy verdigris in the day, and an impenetrable green at night. The sky is permanently dark, and the air in that room borrows the dark, vegetal property of the trees.

After a struggle to get it into the room, I had managed to place against the window the walnut desk I bought years ago near Alicurá from an old German who was tired of missing his homeland and had finally decided to return there, leaving behind all the things that he had once brought with him. I found it hard to imagine a German abandoning everything like that, so capriciously; Lanz would say it was behaviour more befitting a Hungarian, or maybe an Austrian, but here was an exception. From some nameless corner of Middle Europe had come a man who so sorely missed his country that he was prepared to sell everything he owned in the world to return. That desk of solid wood and brass hinges had come from his wife's family. It was the only piece of furniture that they had managed to bring in the boat, apart from their trunks, and that was only because the hold had a tendency to flood – thanks to a few holes that would have been impossible to mend without putting the vessel out of circulation – and an object of that size could usefully prevent the rest of the luggage getting damaged during the voyage.

That was how the desk that holds my father's treasures arrived at this house, from a plantation of walnut trees in the Black Forest, via the workroom of one Freiburg's finest carpenters, the flooded hold of a second-class boat and the dusty compartment of a train travelling south from Buenos Aires.

Inside the desk, my father's books and maps are kept in a box among little bits of raw pork that are supposed to ward off moths. And it's from my studies of his notes, as well as soil samples, stones, fragments of bone and fossils, topological maps and the testimony of explorers, that I have come to a conclusion about the algae on the lake: I believe that they are an indication of an important ecological phenomenon, one that occurs cyclically every ten or twelve years and which, curiously, follows the cycles of the sun.

However extraordinary it sounds, Lanz's theory (the one about water flowing upwards through very narrow channels which connect the lake bed with that of the sea on the other side of the Andes) simply adds another mysterious angle to the phenomenon of the algae's appearance; in effect there is a change in the composition of the water, a subtle but detectable change. This has occurred at least twice in the last thirty years, three times if we include this summer's event – and that is a figure that tallies with the natives' accounts.

On Christmas morning I woke up late, very dehydrated after the liquor, and tired, but pleasurably so. Nando had got together his stuff and taken a boat out into the middle of the lake to fish for trout for lunch. Lanz watched on from the shore and, from time to time, he would get to his feet to wave excitedly. Otherwise he continued to do what he always did on the lake shore: digging little holes in the sand, which he filled with herbs or wild flowers, then covered with stones, turning them into miniature graves.

In the kitchen, Ilse was making lunch with the previous night's leftovers, and Klára had left very early to return to the city, leaving a little note, so as not to waken anyone. Ilse told me this as soon as I entered the room, even before placing in my hands a cup of tea sweetened with honey. The note read:

I hope that the fuel provided by my guardian angel will be enough to get me to a petrol station. If you don't see me within the week, give me up for dead. A big hug for all of you – perhaps the last ever...

Klára

PS: Ana, the swag bag is for you

The cheeky cow! But we were used to her black humour, and the old folk had long ago stopped complaining about her jokes.

In retrospect that note from Klára was very telling. Perhaps – I don't know – because it spoke explicitly of death. The hours went by. At least Nando's disaffection was over, after two great fishing afternoons, netting a haul of six trout and two good-sized tuna.

I could not help but conclude, this time in complete sobriety, that his "recuperation" was linked to Klára's absence. Nando was no less taciturn, but he was calmer, thanks to a routine that had restored his equilibrium: the lake, the old folk, the interrupted nights in my room. We did not, however, make love again. We slept together because we were used to doing that when he was in the house, but nothing more. Even then, he still got up and went to sleep in the study.

We did not speak about Klára and her morbid note, or the city, or his work. We limited ourselves to being part of the scenery.

Under Ilse's almost overbearing care, Lanz recovered from the attack. He certainly did not want to go to hospital – for what good would it do? Ilse thought that it was best not to unsettle him further; there would be no benefit in telling him what had happened that night. She insisted that there was every chance of him having another attack if he were faced with something out of his routine, such as a hospital. As she was the ultimate authority in all that concerned the old man, we decided not to press the point. I could not have guessed that he would, indeed, very soon be going to the hospital in the city and that the trip would be prompted by the arrival of Pedro at our house.

At any rate, this happened before Pedro arrived, on the 29th December 1975 to be precise, as the year was ending and everyone had finally accepted that General Perón was gone for ever.

That day was strange from the start: the temperature had suddenly gone up and the wind that obstinately beat against the rocky sides of the mountains had dropped just as brusquely. Nothing moved – not the most delicate leaves, nor the chrysanthemums, nor the yellow flowers on the broom. The wood behind us was also abnormally still. On the kitchen window sill, two swallows pecked with exaggerated delicacy at the grain that Ilse sometimes threw out for them, as if they were lifting gold dust in their beaks, making not even the slightest noise, not even fluttering their wings.

Ilse was stirring strawberries on the stove top, and the silky scratching of wooden spoon against the jam was the only thing to be heard.

"What's going on Mutti?" I asked her, perplexed, unable to make sense of the quiet that had so suddenly invaded the landscape around us, normally so busy with noise.

"Hush," she said, in her usual way of soothing people, honey-toned as if she were lulling a baby to sleep. "Go and take a look at the lake, but don't make a palaver – Lanz is still asleep."

Ilse loved to use certain words, and "palaver" was one of them. I suppose she wanted to warn me not to make a noise and, since it was difficult for her to pronounce "racket" – another favourite – she preferred to conflate the meanings and stick with "palaver". Her inveterate desire to feed anything that moved meant that she could not allow me to leave the kitchen without thrusting into my hand a tablespoon full to the brim with some of the jam, which was nearly ready.

Thinking that in this strange new landscape deformed by quiet, a "palaver" was precisely what was required, I took the shortest route down to the shore, picking out a way among the stones and the bushes of musket rose and burr, steadying myself by concentrating on the spoon in my left hand. The path was short but steep. Víktor had built La Pedrera on very high foundations, not only to guard against any future floods, but to leave room for a spacious cellar, a European essential that he was not prepared to forgo.

I was still unwilling to let go of the spoon, for fear of cracking my head open on the rocks, but when I arrived on the shore the extraordinary sight that greeted me enfeebled my muscles so drastically that I dropped the spoon and my jaw fell open. The stillness that I experienced beside the lake had none of that calm texture we had felt in the kitchen, or the abnormal peace of the forest: it was aberrant. The air had become rarefied with a kind of yellowish fog, shot through with vegetal suppurations, volatilized resin, fossils of microscopic insects that seemed to emanate from above like a divine punishment. The lenga trees around the lake projected a heavy, lumpy shadow across the entire Melancolía Sound: the sun could scarcely penetrate it, and the light had that lunar quality, heightened by the rancid vapour that shrouded the lake.

But the abnormality of the air and the light, the absence of a breeze, the silence, were nothing compared to the phantasmagoric appearance of the lake itself: there, in front of my eyes, forming a filigree made up of millions of brownish-red threads, scarcely distinguishable from the opal colour of the water in that unworldly light, were the algae. Like aquatic plants in a marsh, these were the same algae that had been described by the Indians, more observant travellers and my own father. They floated opaque and sticky, in a silence within an even more poisonous silence, as if they wanted to pass unnoticed by gods or men.

Two enormous fish landed on the shore, miraculously inflated by their air-filled bladders, reddened by the threads that blocked their gills. Swollen and unrecognizable, they lay dying at my feet.

When I look back on it, now that it is spring again, all that seems so far away, so unreal and improbable. The new shoots will be late this year after so much drought, and the rains

74

do not usually start until October. If it were not for the arid appearance of the landscape, and this Patagonian breeze which seems to have reached even to the heart of the forest, you could say that this spring has honoured us with unusually diaphanous and warm weather – the tourists from Buenos Aires will be grateful for it, since they come for so few days. Anyway, some little shoots are beginning to appear, and the shore, so funereal during the winter, is recuperating. The reeds will start to grow again, without a doubt. The course of nature is inevitable.

The divers disappeared a little while ago beneath the surface of the water, and now you can hardly see the platform under this slanting sun, more typical of winter. The whole lake seems to be covered by a film of iridescent oil, making it appear more than ever like a body, the gelatinous mass of a world within another world that pays it no heed. Empty, radiant, mercurial.

"What could possibly be going on under such a serene surface?" Those were Ilse's words as she watched, indulgently, the last of the men in black. The expression in her eyes was frank, almost naive. Things seem so straightforward the ways she says them, so heartening and simple… if only I could fall under the spell of her words, like the others.

Since the summer I have been thinking very much of Mary Anning, the English woman who discovered the first fossilized skeleton of a huge marine monster between the layers of sediment in the cliffs at Lyme Regis. What must it have been like to live in a man's world, passionate about nature, but believing in God, and so poor that she could barely afford to eat? What must it have felt like to sell the first calcified bone to a collector in London, the first of hundreds of fossils she would go on to extract from the ground with such diligence, using little more than wooden spatulas and brushes made from pig bristle, as well as her own nails and ravaged hands

– all so that she could pay for supper the next day? Did she feel like a prostitute? Or a monster, an even more atrocious creature than the one she had just exhumed?

And how did the cream of society react on discovering irrefutable proof of all that really had gone on, of all *that God had permitted to happen*?

Here was a woman who sold bones in order to eat. The first plesiosaur, and the best-preserved for more than a century, was discovered by a woman, delirious and poor, who sold the remains to scientists so that men who had the knowledge but did none of the digging could come up with theories to match them. She alone knew where the bones were. She could smell them, she could smell the monsters and their skeletons. She could exhume and construct them from instinct, even though she had never had any formal education in the subject.

Nando calls me "the bone collector" and when he does I feel that I can understand, in some way, the perplexed delight felt by that woman in the face of the monster. She had no idea what it was she had found, simply that something was there, lodged deep in the hardened mud. It was there, and that was enough. Mary Anning could enjoy her discovery without classifying it: that job she could leave to the boffins who bought up her specimens. In her modest house, on a cliff overlooking the sea, Mary Anning never kept so much as a tooth or a vertebra. Beneath her very feet were thousands of monsters, unnamed, unclassified, scattered in the sediment. It was the fact that they were unknown that made them monsters, rather than the formidable size of their skeletons.

Mary Anning's unquestioning acceptance was similar to that of Víktor and Lanz; I've been wondering if it explains why the monster has revealed itself only to them.

Classification is both an act of love and murder. Everything you classify ceases to be what it was, to become something else. It is an act of love, because it implies a passion for clarity, for knowledge of the subject's essence, for revelation. Yet that same subject disappears to an extent when it acquires a name, a class, an order.

According to a book of natural philosophy I found in my father's library, Carl Linnaeus introduced the word "mammal" to zoological taxonomy in 1758, including mankind, primates and all species with breast, hair, three small bones in the ear and four chambers in the heart. His monumental edition of 1776 covered 4,400 species in 2,400 pages. Curiously the queen of the mammals is "woman": that uneducated and lethargic creature, despised by Nietzsche, defines an entire order.

The world must have seemed very straightforward to Linnaeus: he christened everything that did not have a name. He gave each thing a name and a home, a family, a grave in which to be reunited with other similar things at the end of its life. A common space, a label, an origin, a purpose. In Linnaeus's world I could have been happy and perhaps even at peace. I may even have accepted God, at least as an artifice for naming unnameable things.

I used to be able to talk to Lanz about Nature, life, death and God and the compulsion that both of us call "human taxonomy". But I don't kid myself: the old man can no longer follow a conversation. Ilse has, as she would put it, a different " world vision", and sees no need to talk about these things. Nando finds it boring, and Klára isn't here. Pedro, from his silence, was the only one who listened. Perhaps Nature, life, death and God meant absolutely nothing to him – but I'll never know now.

For three days, until New Year's Day, a strange calm covered the lake and everything around it like a great cloak, so vast and other-worldly that it was frightening to be there, and frightening to go away from it.

In his moments of lucidity, Lanz suspected a volcanic eruption. At other times, when he had fallen into one of those deep wells of memory – and he fell into them increasingly often – he would stand at the edge of the lake, now coated with algae, shouting that the bodies were there, that they had all been thrown in there, in the water, not underground, and that at last the blood could not be hidden. It was no use trying to calm him – for the space of ten minutes or several hours the old man would relive the horror of mass shootings in a maize field at Crvenka.

Ilse kept her own memories of the war at bay, but she too feared some apocalyptic event, some strange configuration of the planets. Nando went back to the city against his will, promising to bring a specialist from the institute, as well as the reagents that I needed in order to analyse water samples from the lake. I wanted nothing to do with the people from the institute. For years they had considered me "not academic enough" to be awarded a permanent post and also "too disinclined to interact with other disciplines" or "too disinclined to interact" full stop. One fine day they had thrown me out, with crocodile tears and assurances that they defended my "astounding intellectual capacity" to pursue solitary and sterile projects.

I did not protest when Nando suggested calling them, although I was annoyed by the prospect of having them snooping into one of those solitary, sterile projects which they so disdained. At any rate, I needed the reagents and, more importantly, I was counting on Nando's failure to persuade them to lug their equipment all the way down here.

From the morning I had first seen that web of algae and the fishes choking on the shore, I had decided to survey the surface of the lake with Víktor's old camera, a Leica with a metal body and lenses that, even today, are a wonder of optics – a luxury considering the difficulty of obtaining most things in this corner of the planet.

I mounted the camera on an old rusty tripod, another of my father's treasures, at an angle on the shore that took in the length of the Melancolía Sound, keeping the house on my right. In the evening, when the sun was already hidden behind the mountains to the west, the luminosity on the water was perfect, so much so that it was not necessary to use any artificial light. The tripod was firmly secured among the stones, standing like a monument to my longing to capture an image of the monster, or of whatever it was that had pursued my father so pointlessly throughout his life. Thus I could be sure of a fixed point from which to compare the photographs, which I took at the same time every day, whether or not I sensed the shadow of some creature lurking in the lake.

Mine was a methodological approach, a scientific, rational response to the slew of sightings that had been registered over the years. For reasons which I had never been able to understand, those eyewitness accounts – whether on the part of keen amateurs, Indians, expeditionaries or tourists with no knowledge of the mountains – had been systematically discarded as proof of the existence of a monster. Why? Surely the starting point of all findings, scientific or otherwise, is observation. Why then the insistence on considering sightings as secondary evidence, tainted by ignorance or subjectivity?

Of course, observation with the naked eye is not enough: one sees what one wants to see (though not in the case of my father, who was able to see the reality of things, even when it went against his own interests). So I decided to use the camera at that time of day pinpointed as "dusk" by travellers, Indians and Onelli himself. I took five photographs each time, separated by regular three-minute intervals, covering the dying of light on the lake and the moment the Indians described as "night's awakening".

And that went on throughout the summer.

Evening after evening, while Ilse went to the kitchen to prepare for us the little glasses of liquor that substituted for vermouth, I went down to the shore with the Leica. Lanz used to come with me, sometimes oblivious to our enterprise, at others repeating the story of the 1922 expedition in which my father had taken part, which I knew word for word. Some evenings he was completely caught up in a recurring cycle of thoughts about monstrousness, as if the physical monster for which we were searching were no more than a simple allegory of all monsters in humanity.

As for me, after the appearance of the algae I felt as if I had been completely taken over by the ghost of Víktor Mullin. But that probably had less to do with the algae than with the letter that I had discovered two months earlier, in October, when I chanced on an old moth-infested filing cabinet that all of us had believed was empty and only good for firewood.

The letter was a carbon copy, and quite faint – but it was still legible and even dated, a strange detail coming from my father, who seemed to live in a perpetual parenthesis within which time was almost meaningless. It was significant, then, that he had put a date on this note: 14th April 1955. I was struck not so much by the presence of a date, nor by the use of carbon paper – another anomaly, as my father hardly ever kept a copy of anything – but by the content, which was as enigmatic as the circumstances in which the letter had been preserved in the filing cabinet.

The letter was addressed to one Dr E. Guzmán at the Museum of Natural Sciences in Buenos Aires, and it said that, two days earlier, my father had dispatched to him a box the contents of which, as one might imagine, were of capital importance, and for that reason he earnestly requested that the greatest care be taken in the handling and conservation of the "sample", and that, again, he earnestly requested that it first be fixed in position and then evaluated. And that he would anxiously await any news, and that, for the benefit of them both, he would be grateful if nothing were divulged about the content of the consignment, even if the news were negative, until he (my father) had arrived in Buenos Aires. The letter was signed with his usual scrawl, which, set against the ashen face of the carbon paper, looked more like a random slash than a formal rubric. That was also strange: why should he sign a copy that he was going to keep?

There was no seal – my father had never used anything like that – nor a return address, nor any details of the sender: just that laconic signature beneath a text that concealed the secret of his discovery within vague circumlocutions that were very well constructed, especially for a man as uneducated, and even boorish, as Víktor Mullin. That is, if he was the true and sole author of the letter.

Attached to the carbon there was a tiny proof of postage from that era, a little stamp that must once have been red, on which nothing could be made out, other than the tariff in centavos.

When I showed the letter to Mutti, she recognized my father's signature with a smile, but she said that she knew nothing about the content. She thought it was strange, she said, that Víktor would send something he had picked up on his travels to anyone, unless it was someone within his intimate circle: Lanz, old Windhausen, some Indian associate or gringo cattle rustler.

Lanz read the letter a few times, with curiosity. Round about October, before the attacks he suffered at the end of the year, his ability to retain information was still quite good, or at least consistent. If you wanted to worm something out of him, all you had to do was wait for the most lucid moments in his day, then during these times repeatedly show him something, or ask him a question; it was worth persisting. During the course of one day, I repeatedly showed him Víktor's letter; at times

Lanz looked at it with confusion, but no interest, the way he often looked at me, or he recognized Víktor's signature with a discreet, sad smile, as Ilse had, or he returned to the subject of Frey's expedition.

Then, all of a sudden, when I was just about to give up, I got what I had been hoping for: Lanz, frowning, tore the letter from my hands.

"So it was true," he said. His voice sounded both thoughtful and perplexed.

"Lanz, I need you to tell me what this is about. Please don't get distracted: tell me – Víktor wrote this, didn't he?"

"Víktor, of course, it clearly says so here: Víktor. It's his signature. Who else would sign his name in such a, such a…"

"It's all right, never mind that. Do you recognize the person to whom he sent this letter?"

"Guzmán. But it's strange, Víktor probably knew the first one, the one who went around in the mountains – I think his name was Felipe. Here it says 'E', which could be for Esteban, Enrico, or…"

"Was Felipe Guzmán a friend of my father?"

"Friend? No, no. He was a naturalist, or something like that, who had been right-hand man to someone on the Ameghino expedition when they made that discovery at Última Esperanza."

"The Megatherium?"

"The gelatinous bones. That happened before the expedition, that was why Clemente Onelli was so interested in sending people to look for the animal. He believed that it was still alive in some place in Patagonia, way down south, protected perhaps by…"

"Lanz, look at me: that's not important now, neither is the expedition. This letter is dated 1955. Do you remember anything that may have happened at that time, anything to do with Víktor?"

"Of course. That was the year they chucked out Perón."

"Anything to do with *Víktor*, Lanz! Anything that Víktor may have told you, anything in connection with the monster – do you remember?"

Lanz looked back at the letter and at the minuscule receipt stuck with glue to the very bottom of the wafer-thin carbon paper.

"Guzmán went mad," he said very slowly, as if it had suddenly become a great effort to express himself intelligibly. "Guzmán went mad and he disappeared, and Víktor went after him. No: not after Guzmán, after the monster. Víktor wanted to know why Guzmán had disappeared. But I don't know if he's the one in this letter. That man was a mystery. Guzmán died in... in... I don't remember now, but it was afterwards."

"After what, Lanz?"

"After what he had seen. Perhaps Víktor saw the same thing. I don't know."

"Víktor brought something to this house. He found an object, or some sample which he brought to La Pedrera, and then he sent it to Buenos Aires from the city. Do you remember?"

Lanz turned towards me with a stupefied expression.

"The three bones?" he asked.

That caught me completely off balance. One bone might be expected, but three? Here I made a mistake in letting my incredulity get the upper hand for a second. It must have been reflected in my eyes, and Lanz, even when ill, had always been sensitive to signs of suspicion in other people.

"The what?" I asked, before I could stop myself.

The old man watched me for a few seconds with apprehension. Then I knew that the window of opportunity had closed. I took his wrinkled face in my hands, I made him focus on my eyes and slowly, clearly modulating the words, I made one last effort:

"Tell me, Lanz, what the three bones are."

But bewilderment was settling on the old man, like a shroud on a living body, and I realized that he no longer recognized me.

In fact, for a few days after this episode, he would not even let me near him; like a petulant child who does not remember the cause of his own annoyance, he refused to speak to me.

During the two months leading up to Christmas, I tried periodically to delve into Lanz's memory to recover some new information about the letter, about the first Guzmán, or his son, or about the mysterious bones – but all that I gleaned were increasingly fantastic versions of the 1922 expedition. Later, after New Year, I would not even be able to count on those, but then again, Pedro's arrival took all my attention.

In any case, the lines my father wrote about the "specimen", about the preservation of the specimen before its evaluation, *even in the event of this being negative*, made me think that Víktor had indeed found something connected very directly to the beast in the lake, and that he had turned to the only person he could trust at that time, at least among scientists. It was more than likely that Guzmán had had a son, and that in 1955 this son was working in some state organization. But to solve the mystery of the letter, we would have to go Buenos Aires and track down the recipient of the famous consignment my father talked about – if that person had not also died in the intervening years.

From that moment on, I found myself toying with the idea of going to Buenos Aires in hazy half-asleep moments; I planned the trip without making up my mind whether to rope in Nando or go ahead alone, and I spoke very little about my intentions. As the days went by, I began to feel unsure about how much credence to give the letter, and how much to regard it as another of my father's eccentricities, and gradually the incident came to seem like the fragment of a dream.

And so it was that I almost forgot about the business of the letter – especially, as I said, after bringing Pedro back to the house – until one day it struck me again, with all the potency of a revelation. For suddenly I did not have one vague reason to go to Buenos Aires, but two urgent ones, on which my whole life seemed to depend.

But I am getting ahead of myself again: Pedro still did not exist, for me, at the beginning of the summer, nor really did Guzmán – it was much easier to think of him as dead and buried, and forget about the matter. Then, two months after I had found the note in the old filing cabinet, the algae appeared. And if Víktor had always been a presence during my investigations, after the algae it was as if he had returned from the grave – or worse, from one of his trips – with all his demons still in hot pursuit.

Now that everything is so quiet and, as Ilse says, so "deathly calm", it is hard to say what it was I was ever expecting to find.

I had always thought of myself as a kind of naturalist, carrying out experiments in the field, a rationalist who sees the world through the pristine lens of deduction. Before the appearance of the algae, if someone had asked me if I really believed in the existence of a Pleistocene oceanic creature, supposedly extinct for sixty million years, I would probably have said no, allowing a margin of doubt for Lanz's whacky theory, or that one about the caverns under Loch Ness in Scotland. I respected the accounts of travellers, for sure, and those of my father, and the Indians – but that is not the same as believing that the fathomless depths of that lake harboured a plesiosaur like the one Frey and his team had gone after. I was intrigued by this entity, animate or inanimate, that had been drawn on cave walls, and that had obsessed my father all his life. I was intrigued, also, due to my own ignorance, by the fact that there was something happening in front of my own eyes, with an undefined, yet undeniable regularity, suggesting a pattern, a regular phenomenon with a cause and effect. It was something that troubled the depths of my own being, quite apart from the depths of that lake I knew so well.

In my neatly defined, rigorous world, the creature was an anomaly, a destabilizing element. I simply could not comprehend it, I could not *imagine* how something like that could have survived to the present day. I questioned whether it might be an amphibian, a freshwater devilfish, a mermaid, a mammal that was sometimes able to swim – like a deer – an inorganic manifestation of algae, gas or bubbles, a collection of branches, or all these things together, combined with a westerly wind, and waves that seemed able to gather themselves suddenly from nothing in the middle of the water – as though moved by a force other than air, a whirlpool, or a meddlesome god intervening from on high.

Lanz used to say, laughing, that mine was a metaphysical quest, and even more wrong-headed than my father's – because at least he believed in the monster. Whereas what I wanted was to apply a scientific method: to find remains, teeth marks, a piece of skin to classify, to give a name to the unnameable – and then rest easy.

But you could say that it was thanks to my method – an unexpected side effect of the method – that Pedro arrived, or rather that I first met Pedro, on the afternoon of 6th January 1976, on the high road that runs along the only passable side of the Melancolía Sound.

That road, via a hidden short cut that only the town's inhabitants know about, leads to the very foot of La Pedrera, my house.

3

Pedro

That afternoon, and nearly every afternoon, as if his illness were obeying some secret and predetermined ritual, Lanz was particularly disturbed. Like someone following the demented rhythm of a uroboric serpent that coils around its own tail before devouring it, in order to regenerate it, he kept telling the story of Leviathan – only to start it again as soon as he finished it. And almost every day, since his attacks at the end of December, he had retold the story of Víktor's expedition (he would always think of it as "Víktor's expedition", not Frey's), each time with some colourful variation in the story or a new addition that seemed to flow, invented, straight from his unbridled, demented mind. And if Leviathan and the expedition were not enough, he would also wake up every so often in a wartime era, speaking Hungarian, or sometimes a language that Ilse identified as Serbo-Croat.

For the people who suffered the old man's deterioration with him, the worst of it was knowing that he would never escape from that labyrinth. Events in the here and now were spontaneously lost to him: they evaporated, leaving no mark, no aura, no perfume, absolutely nothing. He was no longer able even to marshall two consecutive minutes of memory regarding the present; in fact his memory seemed to be withdrawing ever deeper into the past. Time, for Lanz, had ceased to have any meaning beyond the meaning of death and war, which now became the sum of all times, of all horrors.

That afternoon when they went down to the lake, he returned yet again to the theme of Leviathan, unravelling it, rolling it up again and starting once more at the beginning, linking the last and first words in the story, like a record playing on one of those old phonographs.

"Leviathan, monster of the seas, has the head of a serpent, the mouth of a dragon and the body of a fish, but it is also a mammal: its offspring suckle from two enormous breasts sprouting from its swollen flank – not udders but bestial breasts, a woman's breasts. That is the true, unique essence of the monster. Leviathan occupies the water, Behemoth the land. One swallows, the other chews. They are the same thing, and the antithesis of each other. Leviathan is not a fish. Leviathan is not a mammal. Leviathan is a sphinx, a gorgon, a harpy, a griffin, the lamia that devours its children and its lovers the same. Leviathan is a salamander that lives in the flames and also a dragon that produces fire in its guts and breathes it, and a unicorn, and a mermaid. Leviathan has the head of a serpent, the mouth of a dragon, the body of a fish. Leviathan..."

There was no way to stop the litany. On the steepest part of the path, Ana had to help the old man, gripping his shoulders from behind, as one might guide a child rather than an adult. In the darkness she felt a stab of sadness at this reversal of roles: Lanz was, even at his age, a strong man, and his reflexes, in contrast to his memory, were as sharp as ever. Why was the amnesia that was eating away at him so cruel, so inhuman?

The monotonous discourse on Leviathan continued, like background music, as Ana placed the camera on the tripod that was waiting behind some bushes on the path, firm as a flagpole, well-entrenched among the stones on the beach. The Leica, robust but obedient in her hands, clicked easily into its place on the tripod – so much better than the new, screw-in models. Ilse said that in recent years German industry had lost some of its inveterate passion for perfect mechanisms. She had made the remark while examining, with dismay, the ham-slicer Klára had bought her for Christmas, brand-new from a market in the main square of Osorno. "German industry!" Klára had cried as she tore off the wrapping paper, and her eyes shone with an almost childish pride at the sight of the burnished steel. Ilse had thanked her – she was always very grateful for anything Klára brought her – but, alone in the kitchen with Ana, from whom she was less inclined to hide her feelings, she oiled the handle disapprovingly. The primitive mechanism that tightened the cutting disc had already begun to fail, and the slices that fell into her hands were uneven, translucid and grainy.

"That's not right. That doesn't look good," Ilse tutted quietly, examining with distaste the slices as they crumbled up in her hands.

It was 6th January, Epiphany, and Ilse had wanted to show off, not so much her new German slicer, but a cured loin of goose which had been hanging for months in the thick and fragrant gloom of the larder, like a body left swinging on the gallows by some negligent executioner. Ana had the job of keeping Lanz out of the way – and especially out of the kitchen – where he kept distracting Ilse with the jumps and snares of his memory, making her lose her own train of thought and testing her patience.

"For the love of God, take him away, Ana," Ilse had murmured to her furtively in a corner of the kitchen. "Take him down to the lake and, if you can, put him in a boat and get him to row for a little bit. That way he'll be tired and have a sleep before dinner."

Lanz was fiddling distractedly with the dark goose meat and the handfuls of herbs that Ilse had arranged around it on the board to perfume it.

So Ana had taken him away, and now she dared not take her eyes off the old man, who was apt to start suddenly behaving like a child, then just as suddenly to revert to his old self.

"Leviathan is not a fish and neither is it a mammal. Two great breasts protrude from its side, where it suckles its young..."

"Vati," said Ana, interrupting. "Would you do me a favour and bring the filters that I left on the other side of the quay last night, please?"

"Leviathan... What filters?"

"The ones that I put out last night to collect new specimens of those algae that appeared on the lake."

"New specimens, of course..." Lanz said, adding coquettishly: "What did you say your name was, miss?"

It was only a few days since the last and most serious of the attacks, but Ana was used to the periodic forgetfulness of the old man, who paid absolutely no attention when she answered him.

"Ana, Lanz. Ana Mullin, daughter of Víktor. You remember your friend Víktor, don't you?"

Sooner or later her remark would prompt yet another account of the expedition, but that no longer bothered Ana. She had stopped listening to him some time ago.

"Ana, yes. Of course. Poor little thing..."

That bit still stung. What was the source of this deep pity that Lanz felt for her? Some day, if there was an appropriate moment – which seemed increasingly unlikely – she meant to ask him.

The old man's illness was marvellous, in a way. After a period of horrendous delirium, sometimes brought on by his imagination and at others by real memories, there usually followed very brief periods of an almost supernatural lucidity. These might sometimes be no more than an instant. At other times they occupied a few minutes, during which Lanz's mind

90

seemed to explode in a welter of theories, ideas, analyses and anecdotes. Lanz's erudition had been exceptional in any case. Ilse had complemented him, in the years of their youth, with an equally fine intelligence, though hers was more elastic, more artistic than Lanz's.

It was a shame that Ilse no longer played her clavichord, which had once looked fit to burst under her fingers. Ana had learnt to love Bach, because he was Ilse's favourite composer. But one day she found an old book of Bach scores in the waste-paper basket. It had been torn and crumpled with such hatred that it was impossible to recover it. She had not asked Ilse about it: they all knew that her arthritis bothered her, affecting her wrists and elbows more than her hands themselves – and it had been a long time since she had been able to play a piece right the way through. From then onwards Ilse had not played at all, nor did it give her pleasure any more to listen to the recordings Klára brought her every time she visited.

Ana saw that she had three exposures left, counting the two bonus ones at the end of the film; if she forced the wind lever there might even be one more. She decided to change the roll there and then, but, rather than waste the last few centimetres of such expensive film, she thought she would take some photographs of the old man, who was still walking towards the filters. It was this chance decision, plus her desire to focus very clearly on Lanz, that prompted her to select her most powerful lens, and so to pick out the car that was climbing the road on the hillside, in shadow and barely perceptible to the naked eye, against the dark-green backdrop of the forest.

As she switched from the panoramic mode she used every day to the manual mode, Lanz's dignified grey head appeared in focus so clearly that when he stopped and turned to look up at the house, Ana saw from the movement of his lips that he was still talking to himself. She wondered what he might be saying. He was not talking about Leviathan any more – that could be deduced not merely from reading his lips, but because the usual rant came accompanied by certain movements he made with his right hand, like the gestures of an eccentric professor trying to coax an audience of invisible students towards an understanding of something very mysterious or difficult.

No, it was not Leviathan, because his right hand was motionless, gripping the waistband of his trousers in a strange way, as though he were holding his breath. The old man's profile, with that light that burnished his eyebrows, making them two black bridges suspended over nothing, was strong and perfect, of an almost Hellenic beauty. Ilse always said that in his youth, Lanz had been the most beautiful man she had ever seen, or ever would see in her life. So Ana wanted to take the photograph for her, to show her that, for all his quirks and funny turns, for all the time that had gone by, Lanz was still the same beautiful Hungarian as before, and more than beautiful – imposing.

But the old man, oblivious to her plan, had put his hand to his head, shading his eyes, and was now looking towards the forest. Almost by a reflex action, she followed Lanz's effortful gesture with her lens: a vehicle, blue or black, or perhaps a very dark green, was quickly approaching, appearing and disappearing between the tops and the trunks of the lenga trees and the cypresses that covered the hillside all the way down to the lake.

She wondered who they were. Tourists? They didn't usually come this far...

Ana tried to follow the course of the car through the foliage, but with the sun now so low over the mountains, she knew that she would lose it. Even so, the lens of the Leica seemed to want to reach further, and Ana finally forced the magnification and the focus to the full. Now she could see sections of the car quite clearly: it was one of those big blue sedans, maybe a Ford Fairlane, with tinted windows reflecting the last orange rays of sun that were still available at that level of the hill. The speed at which they were travelling, the proximity of trees and especially the light, which was striking them full on, would have made it impossible for the car's occupants to see the shore from their vantage point. In fact it was likely that they did not even know that a section of the lake ran along below them, so close to the road.

It was clear that Lanz was looking in the same direction as her and, although his eyesight was unusually good for a man of his age, it was also evident that following the movement of the car was an effort for him.

Suddenly, in a gap between two of the oldest cypresses lining the road, as if everything were happening in a black-and-white film, Ana quite clearly saw the back door of the car open and some kind a bundle being thrown out over the side of the ravine.

It was over in a second or two, in the blink of an eye.

Now the car was climbing upwards, and seemed to have accelerated – even from the lakeside you could hear the engine protesting against this sudden uphill effort. Before disappearing completely from view, the car gave a series of starts and jolts, almost as if a tyre had blown... What kind of lunatic would drive like that?

But there was no time to find out: after satisfying herself that the car had not taken the turning that led to the house – access to which from the perimeter road on the hillside was obscured by a profusion of broom and musket rose – Ana trained her lens once more on the spot where the mysterious object had been thrown from the back of the car. She took two photographs, one focusing on the road between the two trees – deserted now – over which a cloud of dust still hung,

93

and the second centred on the wooded area directly below it in the ravine. Then, lifting the camera off the tripod, she ran to Lanz, who had been gesticulating impatiently at her for a few seconds.

Lanz's eyes were bulging so much that Ana feared the imminence of another haemorrhage. From his appearance, she reckoned his blood pressure must be through the roof, but, to her surprise, he appeared to be completely lucid. Not only had Lanz looked her straight in the eye without wavering, but as he pointed urgently towards the ravine, he had called her by her real name. His whole body was shaking with a violence which at the same time immobilized him. Until Ana reached his side, he had been rooted to the spot – only his arms moved wildly, like the sails of a windmill.

"They're here," stammered Lanz, unable to contain himself. "They threw him out of the car, that man, they threw him down the hill – did you see them? They threw him out like a dog!"

"What did they throw, Vati? Please calm yourself…"

"A man – what else would it be? A man. I want to go and see. Let's go and see. Help me up again, and we'll go and see."

"Lanz, we can't get up this way and anyway we don't know… How do you know that it's a man?"

"Because I know. I saw him."

"It could be dangerous to go up there now. Let's wait until the car is out of the way."

"They've gone, take it from me that they've gone. Come on!"

"Vati…"

"We can take the *chata* down the little path, and get down that way. He can't have gone very far down."

"We don't know."

"At this rate we'll never know."

* * *

94

Time was ticking by and Ana was going to miss her only chance to take photographs at the lake.

Dusk was the crucial time, not just for methodological reasons, but above all because of the light. Dusk is a double-edged sword in the mountains, a simulacrum of the sun, a false sunset. The mountains create a ghostly effect whereby – even though the evidence of a cloudless sky promises many minutes before the sun disappears below the horizon – in the hollows between their outlines, in the cracks between those monumental grey embraces, the sun quickly dips behind white peaks of permafrost, of ice, or behind a supporting cast of lower grey summits.

In the precise moment that the sun illuminates their backs, the mountains turn translucid, and then a dense violet colour. Each hundredth of a second they change colour.

The mute air in the valley witnesses this phenomenon day after day in the midst of an age-old silence: at the exact moment of the sunset, the air becomes completely still. When it moves again, the movement may set off a nocturnal breeze or a storm, but for an instant the mountains seem almost to disappear, or to become nothing more than a metal sheet facing the sun, the tenuous memory of accidental geography. Then the air becomes silent and so still that anyone paying attention – minute attention – could conclude that here is the place and this is the way in which eternity reveals itself.

But Nature also makes fun of the observant and, as quickly as the illusion has begun, so it ends. Then there is wind again, and the mountains, still warming their backs against the Chilean sun, become once more opaque. The sky darkens to an irreversible blue and one hears the sound of animals and insects, what the Indians refer to as the "waking of the night".

This fleeting display of the sun's trickery contained exactly the quality of evening light that Ana was looking for, as she obsessively fine-tuned the timing of her photographs. More precisely, she was looking for the way in which the landscape was transformed beneath that violent, chromatic grey in a few split seconds. It was the one moment in which the real world disappeared beneath the naked gaze of the lens, a moment so ephemeral and yet so undeniable that it was essential to capture it. And there was more: it was impossible to think that the monster – whatever it was – would not choose this mathematical parenthesis in time to emerge, to cast an eye on the planet that had disinherited it millions of years before. And perhaps to make fun of it. For all her rigour and methodology, Ana secretly favoured the second version of events.

She led the old man by the hand – or perhaps he led her, because Ana still did not know if she wanted to investigate what had just happened or to return to the tripod – and made for the truck that was parked by the house. This was a kind of souped-up tractor, a Citroën grafted onto the frame of a tractor, known to everyone as "*la chata*".

Lanz had suddenly fallen quiet, perhaps because of exhaustion, anxiety, or because he was on the brink of another episode. For Ana that meant at least ten minutes of peace, while she manoeuvred the truck round to take the gravel road leading to the hillside. What could the incident have been about? They could not have thrown a man out, as Lanz claimed. *A man*. But perhaps a piece of furniture, a suitcase? A bundle of clothes? It had been too big to be any of those things. *A man, Ana, what else would it be?*

Even before they reached the top of the ravine, Ana knew at heart that Lanz was right, that from the car a body had been thrown out into the void: a dead body. A corpse.

But why down into the ravine, and not into the lake? Ana was sure that if anyone unfamiliar with this part of the mountains approached La Pedrera by the hillside road, unless he had a very recent map to hand and – even more unlikely – really knew how to read it, he would never guess that further down the road ran parallel to one part of the lake, a dark, extremely deep inlet, inexistent, as far as official topography was concerned, after a point at Cuyencurá, which was several kilometres back.

This inlet did not figure on any signposts. The lake, as a body of water, was nowhere indicated as a place to sail or fish. Unless the people travelling in the car had stopped and ventured into some overhanging part of the gully, right among the thorny bushes of the forest, they would not have realized that the lake recommenced in this area. There would be no reason, therefore, to throw the body into a lake which, as far as they were concerned, did not exist. Or perhaps they did know of its existence and preferred anyway to leave the body to be devoured by animals, by worms, horseflies and wasps. By a monster.

Ana wondered if perhaps they had thrown the body into the lake as Indians, in their time, threw in goats, to placate the monster's fury.

Now they arrived at the junction where all thickets of bloom were. Ana had negotiated the hill like an automaton, lost in her own thoughts.

She stopped the *chata* at a point where it was concealed by bushes; the road ahead was empty. She could not even make out tyre marks on that mixture of loose earth and rubble.

Suddenly it occurred to Ana that it had all been a collective illusion, and that they had both got carried away – impressionable souls that they were – though for different reasons, and were now courting ridicule on the side of the road, like two private detectives who were bored to tears with a lack of mysteries to solve. Holmes and Watson in a world of myrtle, with their tuppenny magnifying glasses and their little checked hats.

"Drive on, there's no one here," said Lanz, and his voice resonated with such authority that Ana suddenly accelerated, sharply turned the wheel and swung the *chata* onto the hill-side road.

"It's there. There are the cypresses."

The edge of the mountain curved inwards, then the road lost itself behind a wall of greenery, all the while hugging the mountain's concavity and following a gentle downwards incline, so that, from where they were, they could see the silhouette of the trees in the gully, illuminated now by that ghostly and crimson light that Ana had been missing out on for her photos at the lakeside. There, so high on the hill, the light had yet to acquire that crepuscular red that made the air stand still.

When they reached the spot where the trees were, they left the car pointing away from the road towards the slope, then followed the distinct zigzag marks printed on the road by the car – which had veered dramatically to the right at that point – until they came to the spot where the supposed body had struck the ground at the lip of the incline. They must have meant to throw it right over the brink of what they supposed to be a precipice.

Ana and the old man climbed slowly down, holding on to the lowest and most prominent branches, sinking with each step into the thick and muddy mattress of leaves and rotten matter that rain dragged in waves towards the lake, in pursuit of tracks that had already become invisible. Whatever it was that had been thrown down from the road could not have remained intact in that tangled thicket of thorns and trunks lashed by wind and split by lightning, those branches sharp as knives in a medieval iron maiden.

Ana thought that Lanz ought not to be there, but one look at the old man, as he groped his way down the hill behind her, convinced her that it would be futile to ask him to stay away.

Besides, although Lanz's head was a problem, his wiry body was much stronger and more flexible than it appeared. The bulging veins, visible even beneath the loose skin of his neck, were the only indication of the tremendous effort Lanz was making to control his progress downhill.

Suddenly, however, the ravine opened in a clearing that dropped urgently towards the lake, a clean space in the undergrowth, covered by nothing more than greyish moss, which first struck Ana as bare rock, almost maritime rock. She gestured to the old man to stop before he set foot on that slippery chute – and it was at the same moment that she discovered the body, at the very bottom of the clearing, on their right, caught in the net of some creeping plants that had taken advantage of the rare absence of shade to grow unhindered. On top of the plants, one arm was flung back in such an artificial way that – unless this was some expert contortionist – it must be fractured at the base, almost to the point of being separated from the shoulder.

Then began the light display that Ana waited for so patiently each evening. The air turned a transparent magenta, then thinned and became completely still; the sun's rays penetrated the guts of the mountain, as coruscating as a noiseless explosion of fire, of carmine silence. It was in the midst of that crepuscular haemorrhage, above the oily, almost phosphorescent baldness of the incline, that they saw Pedro for the first time: Pedro's dislocated arm, his twisted body cradled by the plants' soft touch; further down, Pedro's head, bearing the small indentation of a stone; a pool of red blood that reverberated for a split second in the thick elasticity of the air.

Bright red blood. For Ana, that arterial bleeding was incontestable proof.

However, before she took action, this awful, still scene was shattered by a scream: it was Lanz, who had started to bang his head against the only tree trunk that stood between him and a drop into the ravine.

Then Ana felt acutely the black humour of Ilse's jokes about the delights of living in the last corner of earth, the atrocious charm of their life clinging to the edge of the world. There she was alone, or rather with two geriatrics, one of whom might die there and then, bashing his head against the tree, shouting like a lunatic, at the mercy of a haemorrhage, an attack, a psychotic episode or perhaps some terrifying memory that made him want to knock himself unconscious. Meanwhile the other one was at home, lost in her own thoughts, oblivious to all that had just happened and unable to be of help because she was too old, too far away and would get here too late.

As she sat on the wet and slippery ground of the clearing, Ana frantically weighed up her options: she was not sure about retracing her steps to rescue Lanz, even assuming she could reach him before he lost consciousness and fell to a possible death beside the other body. Meanwhile the man lying further down the hill was still alive, but he would not be for much longer. For the moment it was easier to keep going downhill on her backside, as though sliding down a chute, then later...

The drama in the ravine would have ended quickly and disastrously, if it had not been for Ilse's insistence that Nando come to try her wild goose conserve to celebrate Epiphany. Ilse marked both Jewish and Christian festivals without distinction, as had been the case in her family. In fact it was her extravagant habit to celebrate every episode in the Old and New Testaments, the Torah and whatever other holy book came to mind, for the exclusive and deep satisfaction of cooking for others.

But now it was drinks time, when everyone gathered to carry the table out onto the porch – if it was summer – and to pour little glasses of liquor, while Lanz and Ilse got to work in the kitchen, clucking over their pots and pans like the ridiculous pair of old foreigners they were. At least on this occasion they must have been grateful for Ilse's obstinacy, for all her whims and social graces: Nando, driving his own truck, and in spite of the fading light on the hillside (then again he knew by heart every tree and curve of the way to La Pedrera), had spotted the back of the *chata* among the bushes and brambles at the side of the road.

Ana later remembered only sketchy details about the events as they unfolded: to bring up the body from the bottom of the ravine had meant going back to the house to fetch ropes. As soon as they got to the hospital, the old man was given an intravenous sedation. He was so agitated that it proved difficult even to check his blood pressure, to rule out a "cerebral vascular episode", as the duty doctor put it. At any rate, by the time they arrived, Lanz had calmed down, although he was still talking about blood, blood and mud, and he had returned to the business of the yellow notebook and the corpses strewn along a country road in Serbia.

Doctor Marvin, an old friend of Nando's, came immediately, although by then the duty doctor had already given Lanz a tranquillizer, and settled him on a stretcher bed.

Lanz was not the problem: he would recover. The problem, as Marvin said, was "the other one" – who was fading rapidly beneath the surgeon's white lights.

Nando had had to leave before Marvin could complete his first aid, and Ana was secretly grateful for that. Someone had to take Lanz back home, or there was a risk of Ilse causing a "palaver". So Ana stayed on alone, with a cup of coffee courtesy of a half-asleep nurse.

"The other one" – that is how they had referred to Pedro during the first few hours in the clinic. It was only when the body was laid out on the stretcher, only then that Ana could calm down and take a good look at him: a young man, his body destroyed. How much of the blood that covered him was caused by his fall, and how much by his final injuries? Apart from a yellowish liquid running from the corner of his mouth, and the large clots forming in his black hair, his was a dead body, limp and lifeless, without any reflexes. As she sat in the waiting room, Ana's thought was simply that she had been present at the demise of a stranger, that she was doing no more than waiting for someone to come out of the operating theatre with a death certificate.

But for whom? To whom would she give it? Another nurse, rather more awake than the one who had brought the coffee, came down the corridor towards her, holding a dirty bundle in her hands.

"Are you a relative?" she asked, with a gentleness that was more professional than heartfelt.

Ana did not know how to respond, or indeed whether she wanted to say anything. Fear had taken root inside her and it sharpened whenever she remembered certain details about the car: the back door suddenly opening, the body violently pushed out, the zigzag marks on the road... The terrible, unreal calm of the scene was sinister, and instinct warned her to say as little as possible, and otherwise to keep quiet. Later she was very pleased to have followed that instinct, though at this stage she could not have explained it.

So the only response Ana made to this question was to cover her face with her hands, and the nurse, believing that she was crying because she was the man's girlfriend or sister, simply said that she was going to leave the clothes of the "casualty" there, because they would need his documents for the hospital's administration, and also for the police when they arrived.

Thankfully, the sympathetic nurse left her alone again: someone had appeared in the corridor leading to the operating theatre and called her urgently away. But before she disappeared through the swing doors, Ana asked if he was still alive. The nurse replied that he was, as far as she knew, but that she would come back with more information.

As soon as she had gone, Ana set herself to examining the bloody and torn clothes that the nurse had left on the chair. The remains of what had once been his trousers. A tattered T-shirt. A long-sleeved shirt, or light jacket. One sole moccasin. That was all. A bundle of rags that smelt shockingly of sweat – in fact more of sweat than blood. It was as if they had been worn for a long time before the ravine...

Before the ravine... who was he? How old might he be? Why had they done that to him? And who were the people in the car? Ana patted the clothes: there was nothing, no wallet, no ID card, nothing. Just rags, blood and earth and sweat, nothing more.

The moccasin belonged to a surprisingly small foot, or perhaps it was just that she was used to Nando's feet, which were enormous and flat with big, rounded toenails, typical of generous men. At least that was what Ilse said: to find out the essence of a man's character you must look first at his nails, on both hands and feet. Small, bitten nails on big fingers were the mark of an egoist, mean and evasive. Small nails on small fingers signified equilibrium and reserve. A large, rough nail with a hard edge, white and round as a clam: a sensitive and generous man. A yellow nail: narrow-mindedness – and possibly a fungal infection. Never, never go near a man with yellow nails, said Ilse. She was much worse with her astral phrenology than Ana was with her classifications.

At the other end of the room, the nurse decided to switch on the television on her desk, and fiddled with the tuning knob. On one of the channels there was a tuning signal – black and grey vertical stripes and a disagreeable buzzing.

"The aerial needs to be adjusted," said the woman, tilting her head, as she fiddled with the two arms of a ridiculously long antenna, while tuning into another channel from Buenos Aires. A fuzzy picture appeared, intermittently subject to a grey drizzle, showing a man who must have been the newsreader. Dressed in black, like an undertaker, he was talking about some atrocity that had taken place that very afternoon at a house in González Catán.

Ana wondered where that might be. She knew Buenos Aires, but only some of the neighbourhoods – Barrio Norte, where the German Hospital was, the centre with Calle Florída, Calle Lavalle, Avenida Corrientes with all its bars, Avenida de Mayo, the Plaza del Congreso and some parts of Palermo and Almagro. She had only been in Buenos Aires a couple of times – during holidays, on her way from the boarding school to La Pedrera and once to meet her father. The German school was somewhere close to the capital, but she was not sure where. In fact, she did not want to know. There used to be a bus that went from there, collecting the girls who had permission to go out and taking them to the centre of town. From there on, they organized themselves. To get back, they took a Chevallier bus to the nearest town. Ana could no longer remember the name of that sinister place, where every face had seemed cast down, and no one said anything, as if God were following their every move. But where was González Catán?

"This thing is really heating up," said the nurse, with a look of concern. And she added, with an arch expression that struck Ana as artificial, or perhaps copied from someone:

"Looks like the party's over."

Every time she saw the trouble that televisions caused, Ana felt profoundly grateful that at La Pedrera they only had that old heavy Grundig radio, on which Lanz sometimes managed to pick up even European broadcasts. She preferred the radio stations in Buenos Aires or Uruguay. Recently she had been listening to a Brazilian station, for the bossa nova more than anything else. Ilse, on the other hand, preferred Radio

Nacional, and its endlessly repeated programmes of classical music. In fact Ilse was quite happy with the record player, and only liked the radio for a change, or because it was something she could take to the kitchen or the cabin and listen to while she did other things.

Nando had a TV in his flat, and had threatened on various occasions to buy them a second-hand set – but Ana opposed the idea. Given that they were surrounded by mountains on all sides, it was very unlikely that they would be able to pick up a signal. Nando brought them the newspaper once or twice a week, and that was pretty much the only contact that the inhabitants of La Pedrera had with the outside world. And whatever came their way from Chile, by radio or print, was as good as nothing: since the fall of Allende, they could no longer rely on news from the other side of the Andes.

People said that colour television was only a few years off, and then they need have no recourse at all to their visual imagination. What a waste of time.

"When this country comes crashing down around you, you people are going to carry on oblivious," said Nando, in his usual way of predicting catastrophes.

"This country fell apart a long time ago," Lanz used to say, before his attack.

And he would add an observation that was as invariable as the "poor little thing" he reserved for Ana. "It's Perón's fault. They'll see that once he's gone. So long as he doesn't make a pact with the Devil and come back. They'll see!"

As far as the old man was concerned, everything had always been, and still was, totally and categorically the fault of General Perón. One of the few pleasures left to him was to hear, time and time again (because he kept forgetting it), that Perón had actually died in July 1974 on a day of interminable rain.

The thing was that, even when he had not been ill, Lanz had thought of Perón as immortal; he could not let him die, because someone had to carry the blame for all that had gone wrong in Argentina. If not Perón, who else? Unlike the radicals, who detested populism, but not necessarily the right, his own background as a poor Hungarian, an immigrant, turned away at borders and in universities, a secular wandering Jew – as he called himself – placed him firmly against the "new global fascism", which was more subtle, less pretentious in the short term, but so much worse as an enemy precisely for that reason: there was no possible alternative to the insidious power of its tentacles.

"You get a better picture when it's raining, don't ask me why, but it seems to be the same everywhere. These stupid machines…" said the nurse, suddenly satisfied by the clear picture she had managed to coax out of the television set.

Ana wondered if all nurses knew as much about politics and technology as the one who had been working the antenna. For a few seconds the screen achieved the clarity of a black-and-white photograph – such perfect contrast that Ana thought momentarily that this was something almost agreeable to watch. However soon some horizontal lines appeared and could not be eliminated by the duty nurse – or so it would seem from her strenuous attempts to reignite her old romance with the television set.

Ana looked at her watch: it was nearly 11 o'clock at night. She could not stay to sleep in that little room, but neither could she go off on her own. Nando had taken the truck to La Pedrera, and she did not have a key to his flat in the town, so she was obliged to wait for him in any case.

She looked through the clothes again mechanically, without expecting to find anything among the disgusting rags, when suddenly she felt in her hands the rustle of a different texture, something that at first she thought might be dried blood, a brittle crust of hardened blood on material. However, careful probing revealed that the inside of the jacket – she knew now that it was a light-weight jacket, not a shirt – there was a small pocket, probably for loose change. There, flattened and stuck against the material, was a scrap of paper. Ana took it out, being careful not to break it: it was a rectangle of paper folded over four times, minuscule, like the ones children make to play guessing games. Except that children coloured the four faces different colours, or wrote on them their friends' names or the names of flowers, and this dirty rectangle did not evoke anything so innocent or childlike.

She unfolded it, and for a moment she saw nothing more than dark stains and sticky ochre marks. But on one of the corners, in a Lilliputian hand, someone had clearly written:

PEDRO GOYENA 963

Ana felt her blood quickening again, as if those rags had contained a secret that was even more horrible than the current circumstances afflicting the man who had kept it. She still did not know if he was alive or dead, or what would happen in the doubtful case of his surviving the night – but at least she did now know that the man from the accident had carried, hidden in a pocket, a piece of paper with the name of what was probably a street, and a house number. A name! Even if "Pedro Goyena 963" did not suggest very much, it was a way to narrow down the almost infinite possibilities.

And here was a name: better than nothing, better than "the other one", better than "the body".

However Ana had no time to delight in her discovery because, at that moment, Nando's doctor friend Patricio Marvin came out of the operating theatre with another doctor and the nurse who had given her the clothes.

Marvin alone approached her. His expression was tired and strained, and it seemed that he was not bringing good news. Ana immediately thought that Pedro must have died. And that was the moment – when she first thought he had died – that she began to call him "Pedro".

Without preamble, Marvin asked: "Ana – do you know him?"

It was clear that the doctor had not had a chance to speak to Nando.

"I've got no idea who he is. All I know is that he was thrown out practically at my front door."

"It was an accident."

"An accident? How, exactly? They opened the door so that he could get some fresh air, and he fell out? Patricio, please..."

"Ana, I mean it was an accident that they threw him out right there. I'm sorry about what happened to the old man, but that will get better."

Ana noted that Patricio had stressed the second part of this observation: what happened to Lanz – *that* would get better.

"And the other one?"

"It's touch and go. That blow to his head really did for him. He has no reflexes at all, beyond the basics."

"What does that mean?"

"That if he survives – and that will be a miracle – this guy's going to be in a coma. Anyway, we have to tell the police."

"And what will the police do? Start searching for a kind of blue or a kind of green car that probably went west and is probably already across the border?"

"The problem..."

The problem was that Marvin was too tired. He had spent the last few hours literally bent over a dead man, with his hands deep in a dead man's guts, defibrillating the living heart of a dead man, performing cardiac massage, sealing arteries, suctioning blood from the wounds of an unknown and damaged body which, in spite of everything, had survived against the odds.

At least his blood group was not rare, and they had stocks in the hospital... but Marvin knew that the man was brain-dead. The extent of this was something they could determine the next day. On the other hand, there was everything else... Because what concerned the doctor were injuries unrelated to the ferocious concussion he had suffered, the fractures obviously caused by his fall. These were injuries that had been incurred *before* the man had fallen.

"We can't do anything else for him today. I can take you over to Fernando's, if you like."

"And if he dies during the night?"

"He's stable. Anyway, he should have died before now. Long before."

Ana did not ask how long. She did not know Marvin well, but well enough not to push him when he was clearly already absolutely exhausted.

"I'll wait here for Nando. He was going to take Lanz home first, then come back."

"OK. I'll see you tomorrow, then."

"See you tomorrow."

Doctor Marvin said goodbye to the nurses, and went out with the other surgeon.

The only sound that could clearly be heard now was the penetrating sound of the tuning signal: it was midnight.

That night she slept in Nando's apartment – a rarity. Apart from the few times they had decided to "go out" – to eat, to the cinema, to the theatre, Ana never stayed over. There was a symmetry here with Nando's dawn flights from her bedroom – except that Ana would leave even earlier, before any intimacy could pass between them in the context of Nando's house. Rooms by the hour were a better bet – although there were not many to choose from in this area – or a room in a normal hotel, just for the night. But they almost never slept together in Nando's home. Ana felt strange and claustrophobic in that little sitting room with its smooth white walls, a leather sofa and books overflowing the shelves of a bookcase, a green bouclé pouf (the legacy of an aunt) and not much else, because there was simply no space.

The apartment was in one of those modern blocks that had sprung up in the capital in recent years: an ill-judged mix of alpine style with the worst aspects of the American vanguard. "Mishmash" would be the correct term for it, although in the magazines, interior designers insisted on calling it "modernist". These modern buildings depressed Ana, and Nando probably felt the same way, but then his sole aesthetic criterion was functionality, and the apartment, albeit small, met his needs.

In the bedroom there was a divan, the only virtue of which was to allow sufficient space for a table that could serve both as a desk and somewhere to eat, as well as obliging Ana to bed down in the other room on the sofa, and not with Nando. That was why she usually left early, but the first night that Pedro spent in the hospital she stayed until the next morning on the sofa.

They hardly spoke at all. Ana thanked him for having arrived in time to help, especially with Lanz. She was grateful that Ilse knew little about "the other thing" – everyone, even Nando, insisted on referring to Pedro as "the other one", "the other thing" or with similar euphemisms – and grateful also that they would celebrate Epiphany together the next day.

"So long as the *cuero* doesn't suddenly appear in the lake, or the plesiosaur, or Lanz's atomic bomb carrier, just as they're sitting down to eat," said Nando, from the divan.

"A what carrier?" asked Ana from the sofa. Both of them were dozing off, and their conversation was incoherent at best.

"Atomic bomb," said Nando, yawning. "Lanz thinks that Perón has had a submarine made which is a Trojan Horse for the hydrogen bomb. He'll use it to declare a world war, and become the first Argentine super-villain to get to Hollywood."

"Where did he get that from?... He's pulling your leg."

"Without a doubt. Who would think Lanz was ready for a straitjacket... Did you speak to Patricio?"

"He said that they won't be able to give a full diagnosis until tomorrow – but that, in any case, Pedro will stay in a coma."

"Who?"

"That other thing."

"So they found out something about him."

"No."

"But you said 'Pedro'."

"No."

"You said 'Pedro will stay in a coma'."

"That's what Marvin said."

"Do you want to come here with me for a bit?"

"I'd rather go to sleep."

Nando did not say anything else. Neither did Ana, but during the night she kept waking up. She dreamt that she was rolling down a slope carpeted in soft green grass; as she fell she was thinking that this was not all bad – it was child's play to roll downhill without being able to stop, but also with no sensation of vertigo. The dream was gentle, almost pleasant, until Ana saw the lake at the bottom of the slope, a swamp that was as thick and black as petroleum, a yawning mouth that was swallowing the hill from below, as though sucking it through a gap in the ether.

At six o'clock in the morning Ana woke up, exhausted, convinced for the second time in twenty-four hours that Pedro had died.

He spent three days suspended between life and death, dangling like a child's mobile attached to a cot. Sometimes he stopped breathing, and a nurse would come to connect him to an artificial respirator. On other occasions, his heart failed momentarily. The catheters in translucent plastic, bearing yellow, ochre and some blue liquids were part of the intricate web that sustained him in the world. The veins of both his hands bore needle marks, and the forearms too.

He was young, far too young to languish for ever in that horror. How must he be feeling? That was something she would often ask herself over the next few months: how did Pedro *feel*, what would it be like to feel nothing, not to be. But of course his organs were still functioning – the heart, liver, lungs – each of those orphaned organs had a kind of consciousness, an iron will to surmount the ruination of his brain. "Devastated" – that was the word the doctor had used: "his brain is devastated and some internal organs are damaged, but *not as a result of the fall*" – those were his words. At that time the clarification "not as a result of the fall" had meant absolutely nothing to Ana and everything to Nando and the others. Ana had heard only the word "devastated" and pictured a beach after a tidal wave, a forest fire, a dried-up lake, a hillside running with lava, a lunar landscape pitted with craters.

Anything, but not Pedro's mind.

For every hour and minute of three days, he lay in limbo. His body had a will, and that was the other word Ana often thought about: "will". How could you have a will without consciousness? Was such a thing possible?

Ana saw him properly for the first time the morning after the accident, after the nurses had cleaned him, taking great care not to disturb the tangle of plastic tubes. Even with the inflammation, you could see that he was a young man, almost a boy. His head covered in bandages, the oxygen mask obscuring his face, his body covered with gauze and soiled dressings, his skin violet and ochre from bruising.

Ana could not stop looking at him – was it his fragility or the opposite that attracted her? Was it the body's extreme battle to survive and to recover? And, in that case, to survive or recover to what end? This visceral survival was a marvellous refutation of Darwinist theory, an unnatural act of faith, a madness, a waste of time – but she could not help but feel a compassionate tenderness that went far deeper than mere pity. It was something that Ana might on occasion have felt for herself, or for Lanz, but not for anyone else. Not even for Víktor, at the end, when he was dying. It was a feeling as close to humility as it was to perfect altruism. Perhaps it was the nails, those markers of character, as far as Ilse was concerned, along with a person's date and time of birth, his fingers and the bridge of his nose. Pedro's nails on his hands, and on the one foot that was not bandaged – remaining majestically aloof from the injury done to the rest of his body, as though preparing a solitary bid to escape – were white, rounded, big and flat, reminding Ana of a painting by Picasso. Generous, as Ilse would say later on: "They speak of a generosity without limits."

And there was something else Ana found hard to lay a finger on: Pedro seemed to create a tension around himself. In those three days, Marvin's exhaustion had increased a hundredfold, even though Pedro's condition was improving, relative to the early diagnosis. Yet suddenly he seemed dangerous, not only because he was unidentified and there was no one to claim him, but because of all that which, as they said, was "unrelated to the fall". Some pieces were beginning to fall into place: his hands and feet had been tied very tightly and for a very long time, to the degree that one of his feet showed the beginnings of gangrene. There were marks consistent with blows having been delivered to the area of his vital organs; there were burn marks; his nasal septum had been ruptured.

It was clear that Pedro had been done over, inside and out, before the decision was made to kill him once and for all by chucking him into the ravine. They had done him a favour, in a way, because the poor bastard must have known pain, real pain, long before he was thrown over the edge, and somewhere on the journey – and this was something he should be grateful for, at least by virtue of the loss of senses – he had lost a large chunk of his brain.

By 10th January, four days after they had brought him to the hospital, Pedro had come off the respirator and was breathing slowly but steadily on his own. But he was still in a coma – or, according to the doctor, in a state that was moving towards an irreversible vegetative condition.

The days spent in hospital since the incident in the ravine and the nights at Nando's passed in a haze. Ana vaguely remembered a meeting in a bar close to the hospital at a table covered with green baize, like a billiard table, with Nando sitting opposite her, and Marvin, the three of them draining a bottle of whisky in three enormous measures, which only served to worsen her already muddled recall of events. Marvin was saying – a tone of justification in his voice – that Pedro could not stay there, that if they did not want to report this to the police they would have to take him away as soon as possible. On Ana's instructions, he had personally signed an admission form for one Pedro Goyena, but he could not keep him any longer, especially not in his current condition. All the staff were speculating about the story behind his "accident" and it was only a matter of time before someone blabbed, and then they would really be in the shit, and there would be no averting the disaster.

Nando, from his corner of the table, nodded his agreement.

Well then they will come for him again, she had said, and this time they won't throw him into the lake, but God knows where. He's stable, Marvin said, without looking at her, but he is not going to get better. He's going to die, sooner or later, it's a question of time. For various reasons, we can't keep him in the hospital. It's too dangerous. But he can't hurt anyone, said Ana, what threat can a man in that condition represent, and that was when Nando had lashed out, as if someone had put a red-hot cattle brand on his back, but don't you realize what sort of a country you live in, what's going on in this fucked-up place, or did you really think you lived in the Tyrolean mountains? This guy had even his balls burnt, Ana, they fucking beat him with sticks, they fucking hit him, and when they were bored with fucking beating and fucking hitting him, they put him in a car and chucked him over a fucking precipice. Then Marvin said – without sounding overly concerned, probably because the whisky had hit his sweet spot – that they could move him for a few days to the dispensary on the road parallel to the south circular. In the dispensary there was all the equipment necessary to support him, even in the case of a cardiac arrest – but he wouldn't be able to stay there long either. How long, Ana had asked, when Nando interrupted her, slamming the palm of his hand down so hard on the table that Ana's glass toppled on the green baize, leaving a dark stain that spread, slow as mercury, like an omen of something calamitous. And indeed it was an omen, because just then Ana jumped to her feet and, in a passion of fury, slapped Nando hard across his face, knocking his glass off the table in the process.

A noise of breaking glass accompanied the dry sound of the slap.

Before anyone had time to react, Ana was once more on her way to the hospital, quite prepared to take Pedro, or Pedro's corpse, to the dispensary, and then, somehow or other, to her own house. At no time did she stop to give serious consideration to Nando's words, or to the significance of becoming guardian to Pedro's sleep, the jealous watchdog of a man in a coma who was, moreover, a complete stranger.

* * *

115

The old people had closeted themselves in the cabin behind the house. Since Ana had come back from the hospital, Lanz was more fragile than ever. "A bundle of nerves," said Ilse, who was keeping him to a strict regime of infusions of valerian, with two drops of absinthe, which she said was a natural sedative. Lanz drifted in and out of his stupor. The absinthe, perhaps, or the presence of someone unfamiliar, or his own fears and memories, so sensitized him that he would speak for hours without pause, passing from his usual periods of lucidity to confusion or delirium, then he would fall into an attentive aphony, a sort of enforced meditative state. Then he would sit beside the window looking at the mountains with his eyes wide open and his hands fluttering in his lap, until he suddenly fell asleep, and they would have to carry him to bed, sometimes dragging him like a deadweight.

But Lanz was not dead: Pedro was.

"He needs round-the-clock care. He needs a nurse," Marvin had said, the last time they saw him. "And it's not just a question of watching him, but of constant work – to prevent his skin cracking, or bedsores on his back, to prepare the feed, the liquid that goes into his stomach, to wash him, change him, attach the catheters…"

"Can I do it?" was all that Ana had asked. Nando had not been around for the last two days, and she was taking the decisions, for she felt a mysterious right of ownership over Pedro's body, as if the fact of having discovered him gave her first refusal on whatever happened to him.

"You can, if a nurse shows you, especially the catheters for urine, and how to look after the nasogastric tube – but you're going to turn yourself into a slave. A comatose is a tyrant without knowing it, like any gravely ill patient, but worse. Think about it… is it worth it?"

Was it? Ana glanced at Pedro lying face-up on the bed beneath the window, the same one in which Víktor had died.

Víktor had also needed to be nursed on the ground floor, where the kitchen and living room were. They had had to inject him at regular intervals with morphine for the pain. At least they had left him a line permanently in the hand, and the ampoules of Temgesic could go straight into the serum. As with Pedro, everyone had known that he could die at any moment.

The young man seemed to be sleeping peacefully at that moment, but it was not always that way: Ana had learnt in a few days to detect a constant agitation in Pedro, a tremor, a few small, almost imperceptible spasmodic gestures, such as knitting his brow, or moving the corners of his lips, something that Marvin had warned her would be common, along with involuntary reflexes that did not depend on his being conscious. Her father had been a different story: whether agitated or calm, he could always talk, although everyone would have preferred him not to do so. Víktor, under the influence of morphine, was not delirious – he said whatever came into his mind without scruple (not that he ever had had scruples, it was just that he had been too far away to impose on others that brutal right to truth-telling that was now, on his deathbed, the only thing left to him). It was a nightmare that everyone in the house, Ana, Ilse, Lanz, Nando and sometimes Klára had learnt to bear, in order to secure a dignified death for Víktor, after the aberrations of a life that had been full of mistakes and failure.

Had it been worthwhile, for example, to do everything possible to allow him to die with his delusions intact?

Víktor's last nights were marked by furious outbursts of cruelty, by crude and heartless words, exhaled on a thread of breath that seemed about to fail him at any minute; it was the superhuman effort he made to voice them that made the

117

comments particularly perverse and wounding. Ana often wondered if it would be better to leave him alone among the rocks to die like a sick animal. Like a dog – that was what she thought. She wondered if it was worth wasting her compassion on his death, when he had never felt compassion for anyone.

No, of course it was not worth it, not worthwhile to accompany him in his final hours, nor to continue his mad obsession with the monster, to live in the middle of the mountains like a hermit, to study shadows on the landscape in the hope of finding some answer, some element that, after much rummaging among earth, bones and time-hardened matter, might one day find its place on a table of names that meant nothing – beyond the work it had cost her to assemble it.

"He is a human being who has no one, and it is just as worthwhile for me to do this as it is for me to do anything else," Ana had told Marvin and, since this was her last word on the matter and there was nothing else to discuss, he had agreed to show her what schedule to follow at La Pedrera: the procedural steps, the manoeuvres, the changing and cleaning that would be practised systematically on Pedro's body.

During Pedro's last night in hospital, Marvin had taken him secretly, in the early hours, to encephalography, on the second floor, to determine the extent of residual damage, and re-evaluate his prognosis of coma.

From a yellow machine came a profusion of tangled cables, some open-ended, others ending in old copper connections or flat electrodes that Marvin carefully smeared with a clear gel. This was a small seismograph capable of registering minute tremors in a human body. Beside Pedro's head, a machine that was like a sort of miniature reproducer of maps suddenly came to life with a groan that could have been confused with some utterance of the patient. Ana, who could understand the graphs, but not their significance in the diagnosis, watched the reams of paper issuing forth from the printer with bewilderment. A thin needle, indifferent and parsimonious, traced slow waves, as if drawing blue hills that were occasionally interrupted by some irregularity that caused the equipment to shudder. These interruptions seemed so significant that they made the line jump to the edge of the paper, prompting Marvin to explain – as if Ana needed confirmation – that what appeared to be a strong indicator of life was in fact no more than "electric noise".

Anyway, the true line of the graph-maker was too meek and constant – if one can attribute character traits to machines – reflecting, above all, the elegance of death, rather than the untidy activity of a living brain. Could identity and consciousness really be reduced to these ink marks?

It was raining.

It was an unnatural rain, without wind or the slightest breeze to alter the leaden appearance of the water. The sheet of rain traced an almost perfect perpendicular against the earth and bored mercilessly through the surface of the lake. She wondered what such a violent tattoo must sound like in the depths of the water. What was the experience of rain like in the monster's lair?

The lake was still as congested as it had been during the first days of January, except that now it appeared even redder, and the temperature had dropped a little.

Pedro was lost in a dreamless sleep on Víktor's bed, just under the window. Water that had gathered in the old metal gutters fell in a splendid torrent, glancing off the wooden benches on the porch and battering the window panes in a vain attempt to waken the sleeper. Ana looked at his profile: the swelling was gone now and hair was growing again around the scar that circled his head from one eyebrow to the nape of his neck. It was a scar to no purpose, as useless as the

119

sound of rain on the glass, because there had hardly been any surgery beyond an emergency draining of the most superficial clots. Apart from that scar – a heavy purplish seam with a black crust forming above the sutures – Pedro's appearance had improved considerably. The initial inflammation that distorted his features, the bruising on the skin of his torso and arms, were gradually disappearing; even the foot, which had been miraculously saved from a serious infection, now resembled its partner, the foot that had reminded Ana of a sketch by Picasso.

She had cut his nails now. That had been Ilse's first suggestion, on seeing him arrive at the house; after examining him conscientiously, like a jeweller spotting unexpected quality in a knick-knack, she had pronounced: "This man's had no one to look after his nails."

Lanz had already completely forgotten the incident in the ravine, and how deeply affected he had been by the sight of Pedro's bloody body (or possibly by having witnessed the brutal event preceding that). For the most part, he treated this prostrate man as if he had always been in there. On occasion, he would ask who the "young chap" was, and then they all answered the same: a stranger. In some corner of Lanz's old, faded brain, Pedro's sudden appearance must have seemed a great leveller, because, for once, the others were no better equipped to know Pedro than he was. Pedro was the same for Lanz as he was for the other inhabitants of the house, and the old man seemed to be aware of that at heart.

For a few days now, he had made a habit of sitting beside Pedro's bed in a leather armchair that had belonged to Víktor, and speaking to him as if the other man could hear him. He talked non-stop, a ceaseless babble, but Ana let him go on. The window above where Pedro lay opened onto the best view from the house, displaying the bay and the entire inlet with its two banks. It was the same window from which Víktor had watched out for the monster on the few occasions that he had found himself at La Pedrera. Placing Pedro in the bed in which her father had wanted to die was a way of complying with Víktor's own desire to be there, awake, present and alert, whenever the monster surfaced.

The only reason Ana had to be down by the lake now was to take the evening photo, at the moment when the line of the wood threatened with its shadow the animus of that blood-red light that was a signal for predators. Everything else – the sampling of water, collecting algae and poisoned fish, and especially studying her father's papers – were things she could do in the moments that Lanz was with Pedro, or even when she was there herself, with her papers and maps, keeping watch. Ana had brought her walnut desk down to the living room and placed it beside the window, so that she could watch the lake and Pedro at the same time.

At night she went alone to her room. Nando had not returned to La Pedrera; she had done nothing to make amends after that scene in the bar, and neither had he.

The 25th of January was a Saturday. Ana knew as much because that was the first day since Christmas that Klára, who was only able to visit on Saturdays, had reappeared at La Pedrera. Moreover, she had seen the newspaper on the kitchen table, open to a foreboding headline from which she had picked out the words "elements possibly disruptive to order", before averting her eyes to the top of the page, and the date: 25th January.

Later on, she thought, she would try to read the newspaper with Lanz, and follow the Angola question, but it was still early, and Pedro needed her. When she entered the living room, Klára was sitting on the edge of the bed with Pedro's hand between hers. There was something more than maternal in her attitude, a spontaneity and affection that were typical of Klára, and also a protective quality that Ana lacked, and was always agreeably surprised to find in her. Klára was like a sister, and was someone who possessed qualities Ana could cultivate as though they were her own, a bottle from which she could serve herself without asking permission, savouring it without claiming ownership. Now, however, for the first time, that mixture of tenderness and understanding provoked nothing more in her than cold anger – to the extent that the only thing that prevented her starting a scene she would later regret was her surprise, her genuine amazement that something which once would have delighted her now filled her with rage.

Because it suddenly occurred to her that *perhaps Klára had known Pedro before*. And it struck her that she knew Klára as little as she knew Pedro. The two people whose hands she saw there, interlaced, shared an indefinable characteristic, a trait that united them in spite of her, and which she could not recognize. What was it that separated her from them?

"He's changed, hasn't he? You can see his features now," she said, standing behind Klára, who started and let Pedro's hand fall back on top of the sheet.

"He's handsome," answered Klára with a smile.

Ana looked at the lake, opaque with contamination, and it seemed a perfect reflection of her own state of mind. *Why could she not ask her about it?*

"Did they know anything over there?"

Klára turned to look at her, confused.

"About this?"

"About Pedro."

"Ana, that name's nothing to go on."

"What name shall I use, then?"

Klára turned away from her to take Pedro's hand between hers again. Ana could not meet her eye when she said, slowly and sadly:

"None. That's the point."

She could not ask her about it, and now jealousy pursued her, treading on her heels as close as a shadow.

It was true, besides, that Pedro's appearance had changed, as though illustrating that deceitful quality of time which had allowed Ana to fabricate a false memory, hazy but sufficient to justify her devotion. Pedro was another person now, someone different, who had nothing to do with that victim in the ravine, that beaten and swollen wreck that they had taken to hospital barely alive. The marks on his body were irreversible, but now they were covered with clothes; his mind was permanently marked too, but now it lay calm against the white pillow. Pedro's head was the repository of a secret that peace and silence had transformed into something benign, something that no longer stood for horror or pain.

The only troubling element was his expression beneath the half-closed eyelids. His eyes gazed insistently towards one side, as though envisaging the spot where the crime had been committed. Ana could not get used to Pedro's eyes. She could not look at him without her own eyes following his, as if, guided by their implicit entreaty, she might finally uncover the enigma that Pedro wanted desperately to reveal from his imprisoned state. But perhaps he did not even feel desperation any more.

Of his previous reality, apart from that skewed urgency in his eyes, all that remained was a sense of calm, like the still scene on a lake shore when flooding abates. It was clear, abstract aphony, with no past, like the blank forgetfulness of a cemetery. What history can a cemetery have, what memories, if its occupants are all at rest? In this new reality of Pedro's, appearance spoke for nothing, because there was nothing to say.

Ana had fallen in love with Pedro's aura of calm, which felt, not like an absence of reaction, but rather a pause in time. Perhaps it was because of the way Lanz treated him, or because of the reassuring presence of his body, wrapped in sleep: whoever he was, in less than a month Pedro Goyena had become another member of the household, one who was neither living nor dead, but floating between what he had been, what was left of his past, and what each one of them wanted to make of him.

She washed him daily, without fail – although neither Marvin nor the nurse had specified such a rigorous regime – and on each occasion Ana spoke to him, as did Lanz and the others, even Ilse. But Ana was the one who talked most to him, because she was in charge of his care and she had made the decision to bring him to La Pedrera. Every day it was necessary to check the tube that went from his nose down to his stomach, and detach the plastic container into which they would pour a kind of pap, two different concoctions, one for morning and one for afternoon. Apart from monitoring the feeding tube, they also had to turn him over twice a day, massage his back and the back of his thighs with camphor and take his temperature; for four hours during the night he had to wear a mask that delivered air mixed with oxygen, and that meant getting up at dawn to remove the mask, administer an antibiotic and drain the urine that had accumulated in his bladder with a catheter.

On an improvised bedside table there were syringes and capsules at the ready in case Pedro suffered a convulsion, and everything necessary for inserting a tube to remove the liquid which accumulated over time in his lungs.

Ilse's main job was to prepare the relevant pap for the morning and afternoon feeds, and to disinfect the feed bag in between times. In the evenings, Ilse watched over Pedro, or Lanz did, subjecting him to one of his tireless monologues, while Ana went down to the lake to take her photographs and samples. The rest of the time she was the one who stayed with him, sitting at the foot of the bed, or beside him at her walnut desk.

Marvin had said that half of all coma patients die within the first twenty-four hours, and after forty-eight hours, two thirds are dead. Ana wondered when Pedro's coma had begun. Marvin and Nando asked themselves the same question; the difference for her was that this was simply a figure to help her calculate his chances of survival after those critical forty-eight hours. These had probably transpired during his stay at the hospital, but they could have been much earlier, before he was thrown down the bank. Ana knew that Marvin reckoned Pedro would die soon, either as a result of pneumonia or a cardiac arrest, and that this was why he had undertaken to visit La Pedrera every week.

It was two weeks after the scene in the bar, and the slapping incident, before Ana and Nando spoke to each other again – and that was on a day that he dropped round with some shopping Ilse had requested from him: semolina and powdered milk for Pedro's liquid meals.

Ana was washing Pedro when Nando arrived.

"Rumpelstiltskin," she was saying, "is the story of a dwarf who wanted to possess something living, to have something of his own for company because he was ugly and horrible and rather sly. It's also the story of a poor miller – that's the version Ilse tells, the original story by the Brothers Grimm – who has a very beautiful daughter, and, in order to impress the King, claims that she can spin gold cloth out of straw. When the King hears about these qualities, he calls the girl to the palace and locks her in a room full of straw so that she will turn it into gold, threatening her with death if she does not comply. So really it's a story about the greed of the King – who keeps locking her ever into bigger and bigger rooms, each one full of straw, so that she can make more and more gold – and about the misery of the miller, who handed over his daughter for nothing. The only one who comes out of the story well is the dwarf."

"It's a thoroughly disagreeable story," said Nando, from the doorway to the kitchen. Behind him came Ilse, with the feed ready to be loaded.

Ana looked at him over her shoulder. She was using a damp cloth to clean Pedro's armpits, rubbing them gently, as though they were made of old china.

"How is he?" asked Nando.

"The same. Have you found out anything more?"

"Nobody's said anything, not to the police or anyone. He could be any one of those people that you read about in the papers. The address that you found doesn't mean much, either. There is a street with that name in Buenos Aires, but then it could also be in any other town or city in the country. Although Buenos Aires seems more likely..."

And suddenly, four months after having found Víktor's letter in the old filing cabinet, the words "Buenos Aires" registered forcefully in Ana's memory, revealed as a clear manifestation of what she should do. It dawned on her that she had not even bothered to call the Science Museum to find out if Doctor Guzmán, her father's famous correspondent, was still working there – or even still alive. Now she discerned a common denominator linking Pedro's presence and her own search for the monster. All the events, past and present, seemed magically to have found a connection through one place: Buenos Aires.

What Nando said was true: Pedro Goyena could easily belong to some other place in the country, but Ana sensed that that was not the case. She felt that there was a generic nucleus, an original reason for all the things that had happened to date – and some that were still to come. There was no point in trying to explain it to anyone, no one would understand. This impetuous presumption of links between events and objects

126

was very unscientific, very out of character for her. But then, wasn't she also the girl who believed in monsters?

After a silence that seemed to last a few minutes, Ana decided not to beat about the bush.

"We'll have to go then," she said.

"Where?"

"To Buenos Aires – where else?"

"You're mad."

"She's not just mad – she's barking," said Ilse, and she disappeared into the kitchen carrying the used container.

"It can't be done, Ana."

They were beside the lake again and Ana was getting ready to take her photograph. There had been a hiatus during the days that Pedro had spent in hospital, but otherwise Ana's plan to capture the impossible with the lens of her camera was still going ahead. In that time there had been no sightings, nothing to note except for the algae, the density of which seemed to be diminishing a little, though it was still far from disappearing. In the city no one had reported any changes in the principal part of the lake. No algae, no preternaturally still air, no dead fish or anything like the eerie calm that had stultified the atmosphere around the Melancolía Sound since Christmas. The strange thing was that so far there was no sign of any "specialists", suggesting that they had not heard about the extraordinary phenomenon. It must be completely limited to that area, to the deepest inlet, the one best protected by mountains. The prefecture controlled fishing, but this was not allowed in the area anyway, because of dangerous currents that sometimes lurked under the surface, thanks to the steep gradient of the slope forming the walls of the inlet, and temperature differences in the water. That, added to the inaccessibility of the place, meant that, unless someone took the trouble to report the change, no one from the prefecture was going to bother coming out so far. The people at the institute did not seem to have registered these goings-on, nor had anyone in Buenos Aires, so the matter was entirely in the hands of Ana, the old folk and Nando. But Nando did not believe in the monster, and the only regret he felt about it all was that he could no longer hop in a boat and go fishing a few metres from the jetty, which was something he used to do when he had time on his hands.

His relationship with Ana had now deteriorated to the point that neither were prepared to apologize or back down, let alone talk about "the other thing", as Nando still called Pedro.

Yet "the other thing" had integrated well into the La Pedrera household, and even proved useful in getting Lanz to sit still for a long time by Pedro's bed. He talked to him as if he were an equal, someone who may even have shared some of the same experiences.

Lanz would speak naturally, and sometimes with a lucidity that lasted for a long time, as if daily life constituted confusion for him, while his memories gave him focus and stability. Against the advice of the last doctor, who had treated Lanz at the time of Pedro's accident, Ilse had decided to continue the regime of herb liquors and absinthe drops while Ana, Nando and Klára despaired of reasoning with her because, as the old woman herself said, there was no better alternative for Lanz.

"It's not an option, Ana. It would be crazy," Nando said again, as Ana took the first photograph.

Ana gestured to him to be quiet. The lake called to mind that famous biblical description of the Red Sea, when Moses placed his foot among the waves, and the sea parted for him and his followers. If God had caused such a great miracle so long ago, why not repeat it now, and add this rebellious servant to his army of believers?

"Because the Bible was a story written to maintain the morale of persecuted Christians. That was then. Now it's a manual for idiots," said Nando. "Aren't we going to talk about 'the other thing', then?"

"He's called Pedro," said Ana, looking him in the eye for the first time in days. "And yes, you're right. It's crazy to go to Buenos Aires. But the whole thing is crazy, because I'm not going just because of Pedro. There's someone I have to go and see. Someone who had a lot to do with Víktor. I don't know if he's still alive or what I'm going to ask him. I just know that I have to go."

And she went up to Nando then, as she used to do, and embraced him.

"I'm not asking you to understand. I'm asking you to come with me, nothing more."

"I can't."

"Yes you can."

"I don't want to."

"I know."

The trip was fixed, in principle, for the 15th February. They planned to take the bus from La Estrella direct to Retiro, or even Zapala, then carry on by train. At the last minute Nando would insist on travelling by bus, because it was safer and more direct, and Ana would accept, unable to impose any more conditions on such a favour. In any case, that evening by the lake, neither Ana nor Nando could have known that before they could set off from the villa other things would happen, things that had something to do with the appearance of the monster and with certain black-clothed men who had begun to haunt Lanz in moments of sleeplessness. These things would definitively change the plans that Ana had finally managed to seal with an ambiguous and half-hearted embrace.

4

Lanz

It is a still and humid afternoon, with no breeze. The sky is clear, which is very unusual in the mountains, and especially so in this place, sheltered by rocky walls, which Ana likes to call the Melancolía Sound, even though Víktor was the first to call it that more than forty years ago and Ana usually makes a point of doing nothing that her father might have done. Her respect for this baptismal name is an exception – that and her pursuit of the monster.

You can barely hear the habitual murmur of the lake: it is a chimera. The surface of the lake is glassy; the edges of the ravine are cloaked in a fog that has been fitting out the trees in new garb.

There is a ghostly stillness, a lethargy that does not belong to this landscape, a toxic decay that is out of place among trees that are usually windswept, and water that is regularly whipped into rebellion by the currents of air. You can find no roughness on the shore either, not even among the rocks, which are so slick and glossy that they are crying out to be used in a game like Chinese chequers or hopscotch – that game that schoolchildren used to play in corridors when it was too cold to go outside. That was what they played in the town near Tisza, where Lanz was a boy.

The old Hungarian remembers his childhood very well. His most distant recollections still stand, solid as a forest of oak trees on the dry plain of his memory. But he does not want to remember his childhood, his homeland, his family or his brothers and sisters – not even Sashenka. He does not want to remember the bare minimum that is available to him because, thank God (it's a turn of phrase, because Lanz has no one to thank), he does not know that his memory does not encompass all his life but simply a small fragment that diminishes with every imperfect beat of his heart. He also remembers his youth, though less clearly. The last of the doctors described it as "fragmentary memory", a body of recollections that will gradually disintegrate in a process that affects the most recent memories first, then reaches for those further back. Like a deaf musician who has a tuning fork pressed against the bones behind his ear, his life no longer depends on exquisite sounds, but on a rustic vibration, un-specific and primitive.

Sitting in Víktor's old armchair with the window wide open, his forehead is pressed against the frame, and he looks ready to fight a duel with the afternoon – one of them may vanquish the other before sunset.

A new wave of fog lifts suddenly above the last, like a sentinel, and that means there is not long to go: the sunset is quick, and darkness falls suddenly, with no great preamble, in these latitudes. Or perhaps it is simply that the eye is ac-customed to seeing the mountains' shadow as night, mistak-enly fathoming a starless night sky out of that great mass of splendid, steely graphite.

It is already nine o'clock in this lost inlet of the lake.

For Lanz, however, the word "night" is an ironic way to test the weight of light: although it is late, the walls of stone still gleam, as though their perpetual grey were giving up the fight after a long battle.

On the shore, a shadowy figure, slightly obscured by the fog, ought by now to have steadied the tripod among the stones close to the water's edge, and on top of it she ought to have placed Víktor's old Leica. But Lanz does not think about that, he probably cannot think about it, because the same scene has been rigorously repeated every day – with the exception of the four days that separate Pedro's "before" and "after" – and each time it vanishes from Lanz's mind, just as steam evaporates over the lake when the first chill of night moves the air. His mind is disintegrating backwards, like an old film running in reverse – although he does not know that either.

This – the woman on the shore and the ritual of the photographs – is usually another cue for nightfall, but today that seems not to be the case.

Another mystery.

Another delirium.

"If they can make you believe in absurdities, they can make you commit atrocities," he says aloud.

In this case, speaking aloud was not a symptom of illness: Lanz had always spoken aloud to himself, like a madman. Or did he start that after the war? Ilse said that he had been that way at least since the war.

"The philosopher Voltaire said exactly the same as me," Lanz continues. "Voltaire? The name doesn't ring a bell, but it could be him. Because man is simply the sum of his beliefs. I don't know who said that. Perhaps no one said it, perhaps I said it and perhaps I once even knew it. I once knew, I have that mystericordious sensation all the time... Mysteri... ous, I once knew, perhaps because I once believed more, in more things. No, that's not it. I knew because you know things when you are young. The Greeks were right: youth is the only thing that matters. One does not learn more with the passing years, one invents more, which is different. One invents in order to compensate for the things one no longer knows because one is no longer young. And then all that about experience... excuses. Old people read more – what else is left for them to do? – and they see the same things again and again. Forgive me, but I don't call that 'wisdom', it's more like a capacity to predict. Real wisdom belongs to the young person, who knows no patterns, has no plans, has no compass, does not assume that he has lived everything and seen it all. None of that: life takes them by surprise, and the young, in contrast to the elderly, are permeable. That is what I miss, not remembering what Voltaire said... but living in the knowledge that people can make you believe in absurdities."

On the divan, the man moans slightly, as though he understood the old man, and his need to agree or disagree were strong enough to lift, for an instant, the heavy veil of lethargy.

"This night could be the night," says Lanz, looking outside, but making a warning gesture towards the interior of the room, which is now, thanks to the orientation of the house, in semi-gloom. "And if I did not know that this was a special night for other reasons, I would almost say, sir, that you are waking up."

There is a long silence, involuntary for both men. Then Lanz speaks again, without lifting his gaze from the lake.

"Perhaps you are waking up, sir, after all this time."

The man who is lying there, however, makes no further noise, and Lanz thinks that it must have been his imagination, or the murmur of leaves in the forest in that strange air.

"You are a poor devil who has fallen asleep, I see that very well. If you woke up now, if you woke up at this precise moment you would find the world very in... incon... incongruent. But a man... some man, probably myself, used to think that being strange was the only way to be in the world. I mean 'To Be', with capitals. Attaching yourself to things, belonging to them, clinging to them means conquering their identity, not your own. Let us say: one should 'Be' floating in a perfect vacuum, in the ether, in that chimeric viscosity of which both physicists and romantic poets have spoken. Suspended, like an atom of argon, hanging off the edge of the world. An automaton, programmed by God or, even better, by another automaton. You are a poor devil who has fallen asleep and cannot see for yourself, which is why I'm telling you. Perhaps you have fallen asleep in order not to see – because you do not want to see – or in order to forget. There are many ways to forget, but none is as effective as closing your eyes. To sleep, perchance to dream. To close your eyes. Making a journey doesn't work – I'll tell you now, in case you think of trying it when you wake up: you take your landscape with you and the nightmare does not recede, it goes with the traveller, accompanying him. He lives it. On the other hand, close your eyes and sleep. I also sleep, awake. I sleep, awake. I sleep, awake. I sleep, awake. I'm telling you this so that you don't feel so bad in that bed. I can also tell you what I see through the window, for example. If only you could sit up just a little. Or have a cup of tea. Wouldn't you like one? You are ill. I do not know who you are and, to be honest, I don't care. I'm not interested in you, but in that woman who's on the jetty, moving the boat. She must just have arrived because she wasn't there a minute ago. A minute ago... She seems to be wet, as if she had fallen into the water. And it isn't all that easy to fall into the water round here. Víktor says that this stretch of the lake is the most dangerous because it is the deepest in the whole mountain range. He says that the bottom of the lake does not exist. What nonsense. Although it would be interesting, a lake bed linked to a channel crossing the land from one side to the other. That would be in the Antipodes... but I'll tell you something: in reality the bottom does not exist, because it is connected to the sea on the other side of the mountains. That ocean. That ocean. The Baltic. No. The Baltic. No. The Baltic. No."

The old man's singing a sort of lullaby, a childish song based on this word that sounds completely new to him and which has begun to reverberate inside his head like an image in a room of distorting mirrors. The old man sings, and rocks himself gently in the reclining armchair. Sometimes he resists the rhythm, which disconcerts him, but most of the time he yields to its soporific effect. He finds that it is an enormous relief to abandon oneself, and that way the reverberation goes away on its own.

On the bed, the man suddenly throws out an arm in an uncontrolled epileptic movement, uncovering himself in the process. Usually he is covered up to the chest. At Doctor Marvin's suggestion, Ana sometimes doubles over a large sheet, tucking the fold deep under the mattress and in this way securing the man on the bed. To tie him down. Ana hates to see him tied down. The doctor has told them that there is no intention behind the movements and that sometimes they may be sudden enough to move his whole body so that he could even fall to the floor. The straitjacket improvised from sheets has never served much of a purpose, and in recent days Ana has stopped making it.

Lanz, with a sigh of tedium, switches his gaze from the window to the man.

"Your arm has fallen down, young fellow."

...

"So you're not all that asleep."

...

"Perhaps you're too hot."

Lanz scratches his ear, a little disorientated, perhaps. His curiosity quickly evaporates. It has not occurred to him to help the man, to cover him up. (Empathy, Dr Marvin has told them, disappears very quickly in these cases; it is the first human quality to be lost.)

"The girl on the mooring is called Sashenka," continues Lanz in a clearer tone of voice. "She's an angel sent from heaven.

136

She's very unusual, shall we say: she hardly speaks, and when she does she makes these guttural noises that can give you quite a start. Some people say that she is deaf, or deaf and dumb, and others that she's weak in the head. But she is so beautiful that it doesn't matter. I am in love with her, sir, but I'm telling you in confidence, because I know that Mutti's on the warpath. Mutti is my wife. Sashenka always was my wife, although nobody knew, not even her. Sasha's family are of Russian origin ('Sashenka' is the diminutive form, not that you would know that if you've never met her.) She used to be the owner of a parcel of land, good for growing maize. They weren't gentry, or anything like that, but the problem was not what they were but what I was. And I was poor. I always knew that I was poor, but not that I was a Jew. Poor people have no religion, and if they do it's of no interest, and if they change it or abandon it – who cares. Let me correct that: the Jews, perhaps, are an exception. That is why Hungary is full of people like that: Protestants who used to be Catholics, Catholics who used to be Jews, married Lutherans, Orthodox Greeks, atheists, theoretical Calvinists... all of them poor peasants, some of them comfortably well-off like Sasha's parents, but peasants at the end of the day. And then the Jews, who used to be Jews, who are Jews, Orthodox, neologists, secular, atheists, converted, renegades. In any case, if they are poor, it matters much less. I did not marry Sashenka because I was poor and because Russians take a very particular view of things. They hate the tsars because they are aristocrats. They love the Bolsheviks, but they detest the proletariat life. There she is now on the shore, watching the lake. It is a shame that you cannot see her too, my friend. She is a very slim young girl, with that paleness typical of Russians, a complexion as white as death, a stern expression, as though she were often annoyed. Russian soldiers never laugh – have you noticed that? And they are tremendously hairy. Now that I think about it,

I never touched a hair on Sashenka's head, and I never heard her laugh."

From the kitchen comes the sound of breaking glass, and immediately a quiet voice muttering words in German or Hungarian. Lanz smiles:

"That was Mutti breaking something and saying her piece. In Spanish that would be something like 'the bloody host on that shitty tabernacle'. It doesn't make sense, does it? Even in Hungarian it doesn't make sense. But that girl is getting the boat ready to go out again. The lake looks like the Sargasso sea. The Portuguese gave it that name: a mass of red algae, quite capable of bogging down a boat. Víktor used to say that the Indians died because of the algae, that they were poisoned. No, that's not what Víktor said. He said that drinking the water from the lake caused an infection in the brain. Delirium. In the worst cases they committed suicide by banging their heads against the trees. The bodies rotted, and were filled with worms and flies, alongside the rotting trunks of trees, all by the lakeside. Red blood, red tree trunks, red bodies. Red water. Red sea."

Suddenly, apparently animated by a burst of curiosity, Lanz turns to look at the man on the bed.

"Who are you?" he asks.

In his voice there is neither fear nor suspicion, but simply an intrigue that has suddenly roused him.

"Don't you get bored, lying there so still? Don't you tire of it? Your sideways eyes scare me a bit. Please forgive me if I don't look at you very much. Why are you looking over that way? What is over there? You remind me a little of Miklós. Yes, you do, because Miklós was a bit squinty. He had a bit of a squint. But I haven't told you anything about Miklós, and you have told me nothing about yourself. Who are you? Clearly you are not asleep: you have died, and are saying nothing so as to pass unnoticed. We pretended to be dead too, to escape, but they processed the dead too, just like chicken meat; the bones, the entrails – there was nothing they could not use. We escaped that time by faking our death. Miklós had a squint, like you, and as he lay on the ground among the corpses, I bet he had his eyes open, like you. He could not help looking to one side. The dead cannot help doing certain things. Death takes away their free will. Later come the warts… the worms, or the gendarmes or the Gestapo. They all come later and each one does his job, though the worms are the most honest workers. Have I already told you that there are some men outside watching us? They are wearing uniforms of a very dark blue, or black, standing at the edge of the forest. They are pretending that I haven't seen them. They camouflage themselves among the trees, the shadows, and when they step out, they do it on purpose so that I can see them. As if I couldn't recognize them anyway."

The man lying on the bed makes another sudden, automatic movement, which this time does not end in stasis, but in a light, continuing tremor. Lanz is too lost in thought to notice.

"Mutti will go round the bend if she finds them. They are the same ones as always, the ones who come to see if we are still alive. In order to kill us again, without a doubt. So you have taken the wise course. Very wise. Just as you are, they would take you for dead. But let me tell you something: be on your guard. If they notice so much as a breath, a twitch… I speak from experience. Miklós was no good, he did not have the nerve for these things, but I did. I could have convinced the Devil that I was dead, I was so good at controlling the fear. But them… what they smell is life, not death. Because they snuff it out every day, they know it better than anyone. So don't get distracted: you can pretend to be sleeping for as long as you like, but if they catch you out, they'll shoot you in the head."

Outside, down by the lake, Ana signals towards the house. She is in the boat again and she waves her arms as though asking for help, or trying to convey something, albeit not with any urgency. Ilse shouts something incomprehensible from the kitchen and Lanz gesticulates a kind of long-distance greeting. After a few minutes, Ana seems to give up, because no one helps her. She gets out of the boat and loosely ties it up. Bewildered, she makes her way to the other side of the shore, where the tripod is waiting, secured among the stones.

"I wonder what the girl can want with all that clobber. Poor Sashenka! She makes those signs because she doesn't know how to speak. Or because she cannot – I don't know, because I've never been able to speak to her. Can you speak, sir? And if you could, would it be any use to you? I wonder if it would be of use to her. Perhaps she has got this far precisely for that reason: because she cannot speak. Do not be alarmed, I am like a Sírkö: a tomb... Like Sasha, I mean like Sasha: Sírkö. After all, do I know anything about your life? I know about persecution, I know the marks that it leaves, and your body is marked in the way that war marks bodies. That is something Klára does not understand. She insists on defending the truth the way Víktor used to defend the monster in the lake. And truth does not exist. What is truth? The only principle governing the universe is that of indetermination – look no further than the physics of Heisenberg. Are you interested in physics? No? Let's leave that then. What a shame. But negation, in contrast to truth, certainly is absolute: one can only be sure of all that is not. The creature, for example: the monster can only be defined in negative terms because, if you were to use positive ones, it would no longer be monstrous. It would be God or nothing. For that reason, 'the truth about the monster' is an illusion that is ill conceived from the start: the truth does not exist, or at any rate, it is a statistical phenomenon. A probability. An electron in a cloud of orbits.

Like Leviathan. Leviathan is not a fish. Leviathan is not a mammal. Leviathan is not, and yet there he is, in the lake. Sometimes he appears for no more than a few instants, but he does appear. He is not a mammal. He is not a fish. He is not a whale. He is not a seal. He is not a deer. He is not a tree trunk. Nor is he a bubble: he is Leviathan. Now look at that girl: she looks as though she's taking photos of the algae. Who is she? What does she hope to discover from the photograph? Leviathan is under the algae, not on the surface. Almost never on the surface."

Ana hesitates beside the tripod, as though unsure whether or not to attach the camera. Finally she replaces the camera in a cloth bag she has been carrying, and returns to the boat.

"She's changed her mind," says Lanz, smiling. "A good thing. A very good thing. Do you think a surface reveals anything of what is going on underneath? Look at that swamp: it seems to be rotten, but I assure you that Leviathan could appear there today. Tonight. In the midst of that filth. There is something perverse in the roughness of this place. Life in the mountains is unbearable, particularly around this part of the lake. Perhaps it is the desolation. There are no lights around – have you noticed that? And it isn't just that there are no houses, no windows or roofs; there aren't even any of the birds associated with people – swallows, doves, nightingales, mockingbirds. Apart from my hens and goats, there is nothing domestic here. There is no kindness in this landscape. These stones, the shapes of the trees: it is all as monstrous as Leviathan. Nature is immodest by definition, and amoral too, like an empire at its apogee; when man finally manages to dominate her... she recovers and reasserts herself, with the same sly expression a whore makes after a public whipping. I can picture the biblical creation story: a furious, sullen God forging the world with blows, with hatred and with compassion too, and a vanity about his

task. And when he finishes it, he decides that the world has
not come out exactly as he was hoping, and because he is
a perfectionist, or capricious, he takes from the folds of his
tunic two stones, rubs them together and burns everything
without explanations; he decides never again to turn his gaze
on this insignificant and damaged corner of the universe, and
he forgets it. But this unloved planet does not fall apart. On
the contrary, it delights in its banished status, in the same way
that Lucifer would. No one detests or observes it. A kind of
bestial mould grows everywhere on it, not a mark of decay, but
of luxuriance. Moulds like forests, where the only limit that
is enforced is that of time. My homeland was like that world:
unloved by God and by everyone, except that in Hungary the
space felt more alive. It is not: it simply seems that way. Like
the cauldron of an alchemist who tipped in all his mercury, all
his sulphur and salt, and made of it only dirty gold. Hungary
was a land through which all the religions travelled, ever since
Kurzán and Arpád settled their seven tribes on the plain and all
the religions came together in the common man, the peasant
and the aristocrat, the intellectual and the pauper, even the
pagan rites of sacrifice and the cruellest tortures known to
mankind. She was a country seduced by Muslim merchants,
invaded by Mongols and Tartars, crushed at Mohács by
Süleyman the Magnificent, besieged by the Ottoman empire
for one hundred and fifty years and recovered after one of the
bloodiest battles in history, seventy-seven days of horror in
the name of Pope Innocent the Just. She was decimated by the
governments of various cretinous, inbred kings, humiliated
by the lust and megalomania of the Habsburgs, manacled by
the Red Army, raped, robed and bled dry by failed rebellions,
whether on the part of peasants or parliamentarians. She was
dismembered and torn into pieces along the borders of her
mountains and rivers, as though Churchill had wanted to
rip into her in the only places where his rotten fingers could

find some land to fasten on. She was occupied by Fascists, from within and without, but especially the insiders. She suffered massive exiles, because the Hungarians have never been big on borders. She was extinguished in gas chambers so perfect that she may have been ashamed to dirty them. Saint Stephen's crown was sacrificed for the empire, the empire for the monarchy, the monarchy for the double monarchy, double monarchy for the constitution, the April laws for the republic and for the parliament and everything that was left was sacrificed, in the end, for the great saviour: Stalin. What has emerged, you will ask yourself, from this cauldron of madmen? Hungarians."

Lanz falls silent at his vantage point by the window. Far off, Ana places Víktor's Leica in an improvised box and prepares the vials for water samples. The tops of the trees have acquired that forest silence that will soon be broken by the noises of insects, the diminutive hummings and buzzings of hunters and their prey at twilight. However, the old man's eyes are not focused on anything in particular. The communion with Pedro is more profound now that each is submerged in the lake of his own consciousness.

"Sometimes I dream that I am home again, and all I see is the fragility of man. Exquisite synagogues, imposing cathedrals with their chapels and sacristies, their statues, coffers, libraries and galleries, the collections of art, the frescoes, the marbles, the columns. All Europe is that: man is omnipotent, man is God, musical, refined, artistic. But I'll tell you something – when bombs are falling, all it serves to demonstrate is our human fragility. The aesthetic mask, if you like, merely disguises a wild animal that is out to destroy everything. Man is an imbecilic machine. Michelangelo himself attacked his own Florentine *Pietà* with a club. Why? Because he conceived it to be fragile. A contaminating stone in the marble plaque, and the whole thing is ruined. And believe me, there is no justice in fragility. Weakness does not guarantee understanding or special treatment. They are coming for us now, though once it was other people: the destroyers may be beasts, or someone like Michelangelo. It is in the essence of man. Nothing of what we see or do is destined to last, except for this banal life that we lead. Men everywhere are unthinking machines, and those who live in countries dominated by sub... jugation of any type end up behaving in a similar fashion. The difference is that, in war, the reasons why people disappear are clear: buildings blow up, there are bombardments, open shootings, brutal beatings, badly ventilated cellars, exploding mines, all those things. I mean that during war, death has its explanation. It is a logical consequence: the human body cannot resist starvation, thirst, tuberculosis, bullets, shells, aerial bombardment. It can resist the misery of war, yes, but not the paraphernalia. In normal times, you may see a person in the street and, even if he is unknown to you, make some friendly gesture. If it is a beautiful woman, you may even smile with no consequence. That is the word: consequence. Tiny gestures in daily life have no consequence in normal times; I want to say 'peacetime', but I cannot, it is as if I no longer believed in peace, not even as a word. It is obvious that you will not see that unknown man again, isn't it? And yet that certainty is not painful at all. In a war you know that you will never see people again, and they know so too. What is so striking about that, you may ask? Are you going to ask me? You don't have to ask me anything. You are also unknown to me. I do not think that I am not going to see you again, but I do think that you are going to die, and before I do, which is a paradox because you cannot be more than thirty years old. Perhaps you are younger than that. That is another aspect of war: you develop an intuition, a sixth sense, let's say, which lets you guess which people you are going to survive. It is enough to look at their faces to know. Take Miklós. When I first met him, I knew that he was going to die first, because Miklós was a poet, not a warrior. He knew it too, that is why he offered me the yellow notebook which he hid until the last moment in his sock. And the first time I set eyes on Mutti, I knew that she would survive me. In fact Mutti will outlive us all because that woman is made of in... consumable. Incombustible – that's it – incom... bustible material. Anyway, it doesn't matter."

Finally, dusk covers every inch of the Melancolía Sound, ending with a scattering of violet particles in the corners of the landscape. Behind the fog that serves to soothe the eyes of those spectators of the crepuscular display, on the other side of its compassionate curtain, night is giving free rein to battle once again.

"People don't come to this part of the lake any more. They're alarmed by the way the mist comes over so quickly, mimicking nightfall. Have you ever seen such a phenomenon? It is as if the air were pushing it down onto the water, like a mass of cloud that takes away all visibility. It is curious how all the things we cannot see terrify us, isn't it? They should not keep you here. It looks as if you have come back from the front without your uniform, or from a field hospital. Perhaps there is another war going on out there, and we don't know about it. Why would we know? After all, war is as stealthy as the monster. At the beginning it was like that: one would hear on the radio that the army had arrived at some place or another, that some people were fleeing and almost no one was putting up any resistance... but the radio is no more than a voice, a metal apparatus, a little box with some lights and two knobs, and one listens, one stops what one was doing for a moment and listens, and then one carries on drinking one's coffee. And the army was definitely coming through Austria. In Voronezh they had used one hundred thousand Hungarians as human... as human shields. While our people were killed by the cold, or the Russian cannon, they... they went. I was not there, but I could have died right there in Stalingrad with the others. The 'contingent' – that was the reserve army – filled up with young Jews of fighting age, but I got sent to work in a sugar factory and then down the mine. That was where I got to know Miklós, during the transfer to Bor. I had left my house, which at that time was in Vécses. We were among a group of casual workers who went wherever they needed us, so we all got accustomed to itinerancy from the start. While other people were herded about in trains and trucks, we used to go home, and a few days off would give us the illusion of still belonging to a city or a country, when in fact we had never been part of a city or a country. Uncle Dezso said we had, that during the monarchy things were different. Before you could get migrant work during the harvest, or you could rent land to cultivate grapes, maize or cereals, oats, linseed, those things. That was why the house in Vécses was not mine: it belonged to Uncle Dezso, who harvested for landowners on the outskirts of Buda for two years, while he was planning to return and sow his own land. That never happened: before the invasion the rules had changed again. But at least the work was still there... and now it is nearly night. Didn't I tell you? Night does not fall here: it crashes down on us."

Very little, and nothing, can now be seen from the window. A warm breeze has started to move the curtains, which ripple above the divan, gently caressing the man lying there, as though they wanted to wake him. But the man does not move, and the sheet that was covering him still lies on the floor. Ilse has just come in from the kitchen, with a flowery dishcloth hitched onto her waistband in the style of an apron. She is carrying a lit kerosene lamp, one of those old ones in the shape of an elongated tulip. She has always loved lamps, candles, firelight and glowing coals, and always detested electric lights.

"It's dark," she says, approaching Lanz, "and Ana still hasn't come back from the lake."

From his place by the window, Lanz looks blankly at her.

"She hasn't come back from where?"

"From the lake."

"Who?"

"Ana," repeats Ilse. "Ana, Víktor's daughter, from the lake. She went out a long time ago in the boat, and she still hasn't come back."

"What about dinner?" asks the old man, in a jovial tone.

Ilse ignores him and goes towards the divan, where Pedro is shivering, though not from cold – and she knows that – but all the same, she picks up the sheet and covers him up again.

"What shall we do now?" she asks quietly, as if she were talking to Pedro, as she tucks him in. "Don't you go worrying, you already have enough on your plate. Ana knows the lake better than her father, I can assure you that she isn't going to get lost. I'm just an old worrier, that's all. Now then," she says briskly, "it's time to close the windows, because it's dark and this poor chap could get even more sick than he is already."

"No! Not yet, Mutti, I'm keeping watch."

"But you can't see anything outside. It's dark…"

"I'm keeping watch over the night, Mutti."

Ilse strokes his hair, and kisses the old man lightly on the top of his unkempt head.

"*Az, az éj már vissza se jö soha többé,*"[1] she says.

The words sound strange in the candlelight, but Lanz does not seem startled – on the contrary, he smiles gently and shrugs his shoulders as if to say "who knows, perhaps it will come back after all".

Outside, the lake can be seen only as a reflection of the moon – on the rare occasions that this emerges from behind the clouds. Neither Lanz, Pedro, nor Ilse, her expression alive

1. "That night will never return." (Hungarian)

with worry, would be able to detect a movement in the gloom on the shore. A shadow walking among shadows, something stealthy and perhaps human, its sleeve of a colour that merges with the forest, its cheek pockmarked with acne. Nor would they be able to pick out the strange point of light, small and darting like a bat, on the black body of the lake. None of them would be able to say, if they could see it, whether that light came from Ana's torch, or the phosphorescent reflection of an enormous pupil. As this mysterious luminosity approaches the shore, so Lanz's eyes grow accustomed to the dark. His mind is still lost in the past, but there is a part of him that physically catches sight of the change that is taking effect down by the water. The animal noises – that nocturnal cacophony that has only recently replaced the bloodthirsty merriment of dusk – have changed all of a sudden. Lanz knows it with an absolute certainty: he has risen from Víktor's armchair and is leaning against the window, straining his eyes to see a little more, a little further. He knows something instinctively – he would not be able to explain with which of his senses he perceives it; perhaps it is that sixth sense that used to tell him which friends he was going to survive during the war. It is a sense linked to the perception of death, or of those things that are on the limit, such as this light which is drawing closer, tracing an uncertain zigzag out there on the Melancolía Sound.

"I can't see you. But I know that you are there waiting. You are lying low. Sometimes you are furtive, like elves or spirits. Sometimes, like now, you hide. At other times you carry on for all to see. You know that, don't you, sir? Right? Young man? There's no need to play dead now, they aren't coming for you. They are soldiers, they're trained for this. Not all of them, mind, some of them are normal people like you or me, but with a great deal of hatred or need. In war you should never underestimate the power of need. It's terrible, but it's a fact, believe me. I used to argue with Miklós about the causes of war, of any war. He was cautious, and a little naive. He had faith in human beings, in words and in what words can transmit. I had lost that naivety, and I told him that words are worthless at times of war. What counts is the degree of strength separating the victor from the defeated, because that minimal difference signifies power. Listen to this: in Niš, in the south, the bombardments were starting to lay waste to some German bases. Bombs were falling beside the train – because the train itself was an object – along with an encampment that we could not see, because the windows of the compartment were sealed from the outside with wooden boards, and only a few cracks allowed us to see out at all. The train suddenly stopped and the Hungarian guards – our compatriots, our own brothers – got out and made a run for it, hiding in the mountains before continuing to the station. They left us there, locked in the compartments, at the mercy of the bombers. Later they came back, although all that mattered to us – once we were sure that no compartment had been bombed – was the news that the Allies had arrived, and that there was no way out for the Germans, and that there were therefore two courses of action for them: they could withdraw, or kill all of us. Many months later we learnt that they had done both these things, but at that time, the presence of the Allies meant that Germany was definitely beaten. And it really was, there was no doubt about that. The ones who had not been beaten were those on the inside among us, the gendarmes, the militia: they were more alive than ever, and in charge of almost everything, except perhaps supervision, which fell to some Nazis from the Gestapo who had decided to remain in Hungary in spite of the Russian tanks. Our people meanwhile had their own project to carry out, and a unique opportunity to free themselves from the race that was contaminating the kingdom...

Where'er Danube's waters flow,
And the streams of Tisza swell,
Arpád's children,
Thou dost know,
Flourished and did prosper well.[2]

There you are, a verse from the hymn. And I assure you that Arpád's children took it very seriously."

Without realizing it, the old man is now leaning right out of the window and no longer addressing Pedro, but a sort of auditorium of ghosts, moving among the shadows. He still cannot see what he is sure is there, lurking, palpitating, in the thick night, nor can he see Ana, though if he could, it is unlikely that he would recognize her. Close to the water, the algae are shining with a pale pink phosphorescence.

"Listen, everyone, to something really disgraceful: Heidenau[3] was a paradise. Yes, a paradise set in the most beautiful mountains in Bavaria. It was May, the middle of spring, and the hills were full of flowers and grass covered the slopes as though someone had gone and planted it, blade by blade, a few weeks before. The cliffs were throwing down ravines the colour of turquoise, thanks to some shrub the name of which I don't remember, and, if it had not been for the posts nailed down in front of the barracks – we saw them there, and others in front of the quarry for showcase punishments – if it had not been for those posts for hangings (a repugnant and medieval punishment the gendarmes called "suspensions") and for our primitive living quarters, work at the Heidenau camp could almost have been pleasant, at least if you knew how to appreciate the surroundings. Miklós said the same, and he took the opportunity to write when we broke for lunch; the poor man

2. Translated by William N. Loew.
3. A labour camp for Jews in Bavaria.

said that his bunk in the barracks was too infested to write there and that the bugs would devour the little paper he had left. Anyway, inside the camp we were separated, because the pure Jews slept in the biggest barrack, and the ones who had been baptised slept in a kind of storehouse next to the kitchen. We knew that the gendarmes had orders from the supervisors not to kill anyone: every worker was worth what he could drag from the quarry for the construction of the tracks. They were only permitted to kill those who tried to escape, and then they shot them right in the act, in front of everyone. In the three months that we spent there, there were only two executions, and one of those was dressed up as a punishment for an attempted escape, when really someone had broken into the dispensary to steal bread. If it had not been for the gardener giving Miklós that little yellow notebook – risking his life, and Miklós's too – my friend would have died long before. He would have let himself die, as he later did, during the march, even if they say that they executed him because he couldn't walk any more... But listen to this! Listen to this! That Bavarian gardener was one of the few who took risks to give us things: a notebook for Miklós, a pair of shoes that were confiscated anyway by the guards and a small cheese for a friend who was suffering from typhus and died a few days later. Months afterwards, they took us across the countryside and through small towns, some of which were quite well populated – there were houses on both sides of the road. Sometimes we could glimpse into the gardens, through gaps in the high fences the owners had erected to shield themselves from people on the road. And there we were, desperately hoping that someone from behind this green stockade would throw us a bit of bread, or make some sign that they had seen us, that we were still flesh and blood, there in the middle of the road, in some neighbourhood where no one would have had reason to suppose that four columns of thousands of people, dressed in striped rags and clogs, were suddenly going to appear, as though through the curtains of some terrifying theatre.

But in Crvenka, very far south, in the middle of the country, before they shot half the prisoners and divided the battalion in two because they could no longer cope with all the ones who were collapsing, a little girl came running out of a country house, almost hidden by the maize crop, and she brought us pumpernickel and a jar of jam. Jam! Judging by the look on her face, she had managed to sneak it out of the kitchen. She came within a few metres of us – we had been trying to pull up roots to make soup, or young shoots to suck – left the things on the ground, then ran back to her house. She would have been twelve at the most, and she had tied a scarf in her hair; no doubt she was trying to imitate her mother, who would have been at that moment in the kitchen, distracted, thinking that wartime hunger was going to leave that year's maize harvest wanting. We slept under an open sky, and the next morning only those of us who could still get up carried on. The ones who could not were executed with a shot to the head. One shot, two, a hundred. We could not keep count of them, but that morning we knew that for each of us standing there was one man less. But all that was later, when we were marching. When they evacuated Heidenau it was the end of August. Miklós and I, and four hundred others, had managed, miraculously, to survive the whole summer. The transfers began immediately, and we already knew – because there were informers inside the camp, trafficking news, bread and cigarettes without discrepancy – that Romania had capitulated; that the caravans of civilians passing along the road beside us were fleeing from the Russians; that the Russians would arrive at any moment. Equally, we knew that they would take us on foot to the Berlin camp, and from there, we were told, we would be returned to Hungary. Finally we found ourselves walking together – the trains and lorries were not available to us because they were reserved for the gendarmes – hardly able even to hold one another up, from the Bavarian mountains to the Austrian border, where the gendarmes escaped like rats, and Miklós was left, shot dead, on the road.

"That was something else I found out about much later, along with the manner in which my friend had died. Before, when we had just begun the march along roads leading to Belgrade, we walked by day – if that floating can be called 'walking' – and at night we slept outside in the October cold, the rain, no matter what the conditions were. Miklós and I used to take turns in carrying a bundle of equipment, so that the other one got a chance to walk with a straight back for a while. Miklós would recite Lorca's ballads. He had learnt Spanish simply in order to read Lorca, and during those months with him, I also learnt to recite verses in a language that still sounded unfamiliar to me – apart from its obvious similarities with Italian, which I could speak – and to communicate in mangled fragments with other prisoners who had come from the West. 'Tell me, is there still a country in the world where people know how to use hexameters?' Miklós asked. How, I thought then, as I watched him writing, bent over the tree trunk that served as his desk and his dining table, and which nobody had dared take away from him, how can a man wonder about rhyming schemes when his feet are so deformed he can no longer remove them from his clogs? A man with rotten, perhaps gangrenous feet writes poems on yellow paper and in a perfect metre. How can it be? But Miklós would say again: 'Tell me gentlemen, if you can remember, is there a country out there where people still know about hexameters? Because I nurse the illusion that they do, and even if that is all that I have left, it is enough for me to know that I am going to go back.'

"Far from the watchful eye of the Germans, in Újvidék, the Hungarian gendarmes carried out executions with impunity. It was no longer a punishment simply for falling down, but for the slightest disobedience: for walking off the road; for trying to pull up a pumpkin to eat; for stopping. They did not want the civilians to see us, but thousands of men walking in columns are difficult to conceal, so finally they decided to reduce the number of men: a 'final solution' writ small. Behind us, a truck picked up the bodies, and from time to time they made us stop to dig graves far from the road. In such a crude fashion they hoped to make the evidence of their massacre disappear. Do the things we cannot see not exist? Is Leviathan not lurking beneath the surface? Do the dead not exist, in their tombs, in their mass graves, in the bosom of their ashes?"

He no longer feels anything, although his body is trembling, transformed into a muscle that has lost all coordination and shakes without achieving any movement. In the middle of the lake, a current has started to shift that cloak, shining with a reddish luminosity, of algae and tiny organisms. The current disturbs the water as much as air: a transparent wave, like ultraviolet sound, travels in all directions, and the old man feels it in the bones of his temple. All that he cannot see is about to become manifest in the instantaneous and fleeting world beyond the window, and in the agitation of his own memory.

"They separated us, and Miklós went on with a column bound for Sombor. I stayed in Crvenka and there I should have died with the others, but it wasn't to be: the Germans and the gendarmes ran out of ammunition after a night on the rampage, spent murdering men who were already practically dead. They made them stand at the edge of a natural ravine, but first they took out a group of twenty or thirty – those of us who were a bit stronger. The next day we realized that was because we were going to be digging graves for the corpses.

"Miklós, before he went, had wanted to entrust to me the notebook from the Bavarian gardener. Believing that we would all be dead within a few hours, I told him no, that I did not want it, that, in any case, neither he, nor I, nor any us were going to survive, and if by chance a gendarme found one of us with hidden papers crushed against our stomachs or our calves, that would merely merit a bullet between the eyes. Miklós looked at me with his sad, oblique eyes, not angry but rather embarrassed for having requested such a thing of me. I could not tell him then that I thought his poems contained more humanity, in the true sense of that word, than anything else I had seen during the war months. And even though I knew that those poems, written with such determination, justified his life, as much if he died the next day as if he were to continue living, I told him that I did not want them. On that note, we left each other and I never saw him again. Miklós was not among the prisoners who survived the walk towards Austria, at least not in the list that was drawn up in 1946.

"I barely remember the days after Crvenka, when a group of partisans burst into the barracks and the men shouted that we were free to go home, and all of us, without exception, agreed that the word 'home' no longer had any meaning, that we would not go back home but to the place where our own judges, our own neighbours and institutions were waiting for us, just as, up until now, our own gendarmes had accompanied us. And we fled to Romania without thinking twice, on a night that I have also forgotten. I do not have any photographs from the war, nor any sane memories. I mean memories that are entire, intact. No diaries, no documents. I have clothes from the sisters at a convent in La Spezia where we spent two nights before setting sail for Brazil. The sisters say that in Brazil it's cold, though you wouldn't think it, and they give us some coats. Ilse gets a grey woollen man's overcoat that reaches almost to the floor and a shawl to put around her head. Under the coat she's wearing nothing but a petticoat and three pairs of tights, one on top of the other, and some shoes that are also too big. When I see her on the dock standing in front of the boat, full of mistrust, I know that she doesn't want to get on, I know that she regrets the decision we have made and that that decision was merely a brief illusion. She does not want to embark and I know it, and yet I still force her to do it. I could count that image of Ilse in the port refusing to embark among a handful of other memories that are all I have, because, apart from the useless coats given to us by the sisters, we were allowed to bring almost nothing. Almost nothing. We were allowed almost nothing. Jews are not allowed – that sign was everywhere. Here we do not serve Jews. No Jews attended here. Jews live here. We burn Jews here, display Jews here, bodies of Jews, piles of corpses of Jews. Jews walk this way, because this is a Jewish walkway or what is left of a walkway. They are all signs that conjure images: a dead prisoner beside a railway line; prisoners behind an electric fence, circus animals, men who become empty under your gaze, so weak they look to be eternally in profile: "I am not a Jew! I am not a Jew!" shouts one who is kneeling in the mud, his eyes closed against the sight of three shotguns held by invisible hands; bodies lie scattered pell-mell in a field, but at the same time the group suggests a curious pattern, as if some tidy authority governed the place and ordained the manner of falling down dead; bodies are piled onto a truck, one body on top of another, and the symmetry of death is maintained, after all it is not death who decided on the order but the gendarmes, and their concern is not for aesthetics but to save space; bodies that spill out of a mass grave, and you can't see any more than that, something that could be bodies spilling out of a collective grave or perhaps vultures feasting on a skeleton or an unexpected stem of maize in a recently ploughed field.

No! They are bodies coming out of the lake, a black mass of bodies of soldiers that has risen up, that lifts its head because it has nothing to do at the bottom of the grave and it can no longer remain still and it is coming out so that others can see it and so that they remember all the bodies. They are there in the middle of the lake! Leviathan! Do you see it? Can you see it? It is here! It is here!"

5

Ilse

It was Lanz who was shouting.

He was yelling so ferociously, with such a vehemence, that Ilse stopped, paralysed with fear, in the middle of the kitchen. There was another clatter of breaking crockery and several seconds, or perhaps minutes, went by before Ana (where had she appeared from? When had she returned from the lake?) shot past Ilse in two great leaps, like an animal in flight or full attack, throwing open the door to the living room with a violence that made the wood splinter against the stone.

Both women, Ana and Ilse behind her, shuddered in the doorway at the sight that greeted them: Lanz was hanging halfway out of the window that looked onto the lake, turned back on himself, as if at the very point of falling or throwing himself out; he had suddenly changed his mind, and now scrabbled at the thickest part of the window frame in an attempt to regain his balance. He looked deranged, his eyes bloodshot, the veins on his neck and forehead writhing like snakes beneath his skin.

The area around him was like a crime scene in which one can still smell the perfume of fresh blood. Lanz had evidently tried to lift Pedro and carry him to his vantage point, because the young man's body was flung face down with his arms stretched out in front of him and his face pressed against the floor. The end of the feeding tube had become detached from the bag, and a trail of pap was leaving a dark stain on the sheets and ground. The rest of the tubing was squashed under his face and, thanks to the adhesive tape, was still attached to his nose.

The old man had evidently wanted to show him something, and he had dragged Pedro almost over to the window – or at least he had tried to do that – before returning to confront the night alone, armed only with his terror.

Now that the living room was no longer in shadow, the interior of that room illuminated by electric light eclipsed what was happening beyond the house at the lake. The rectangle of night filling the window became monolithic, as impenetrable as black quartz. No one inside the house was in a position to notice what was going on outside: it was over in a matter of seconds.

Out on the lake, the event to which Ana and Lanz had been witnesses ended now in silence, majestic as a shipwreck at high sea, observed by nobody.

It was impossible to determine what Lanz had seen, even for someone like Ilse, who was used to the rhythm of his monologues, the marvellous confabulations with which he filled gaps in the present, as each minute passed and evaporated, leaving him with absolutely nothing. Ilse was used to interpreting the quality of his every groan and whimper, to predicting the imminence of an attack that might randomly expunge a few vital remnants of memory, to differentiating his fantasies from genuine recollections. A black body bursting forth from the lake, a tarry amalgam of bodies emerging from a grave. Leviathan, a monster from the depths, perhaps.

But what had Ana seen?

That night was the 2nd of February. Ilse would always remember it because, that same afternoon, she had heard on the national radio that Heisenberg, the creator of the uncertainty principle, had died in Munich at the age of seventy-four. Heisenberg had discovered a whole new branch of logic, a new system in which man must reorientate himself, just as he had reorientated himself in 1915 with Einstein's theory of relativity. However, Ilse would not remember him particularly for that achievement, but because he had been the Nazis' physicist, and because on the following day, a Tuesday, a wave of rain and wind had been unleashed on the whole republic, as mighty and manifest as a divine funeral.

Those two events fixed the precise date in Ilse's memory: 2nd February, the day that Lanz and Ana had seen the monster – each of them their own monster – almost simultaneously, one from the window of the house and the other from the little boat that Nando used for trout fishing.

But was that what they had really seen? What had Ana seen? And how was it possible to know what Lanz had seen?

Ilse could only piece together what she remembered of the exclamations, at first excited, then violent and finally terrified, that had come from the living room. They were as wild as the cries of pain one used to hear during the war – not pain caused by injuries, but that other kind, the pain of a dead child, a home destroyed, a mother taken away, a father executed on the edge of a quarry in which the flowers would cover him with compassion. It is a kind of pain that surpasses that of the flesh because it never abates. For a moment, in fact, both Ilse and Ana thought that Lanz had tried to kill himself – but Ilse knew him too well to give more than an instant's credit to that thought.

And it was not because Lanz was not capable of doing such a thing, or had not thought about it on more than one occasion, no: Ilse knew that if he chose that path, nobody would be able to stop him. Lanz now was exactly as he had been in his youth: his determination knew no bounds. Had it not been that same determination that brought them here? The decision had certainly not been hers. Once they had both finally acquired the papers necessary to leave Italy, Ilse seriously considered returning to Hungary: Györ or Budapest struck her as no more terrible places to live than anywhere else. But Lanz was strongly opposed to the idea, and not without reason. To what would they return?

The end of the war might see an end to the bombing, he had argued, an end to round-ups in the train stations, perhaps an end to the camps, but no more than that, because men and women had lost the will to oppose their own destructive and absurd natures. It was a sign of the times for Europe, and Ilse knew that. But she did not want to admit it, that afternoon on the dock of the port in La Spezia as she faced her last opportunity to walk away from that ramp full of tired, frightened and poorly clothed people, carrying the few belongings they had managed to salvage from their homes.

To leave Lanz, abandon him in mid-flight, so soon after meeting him, would have been possible only at that moment, when all that united them was nationality and the war, and little else. Even then, in those circumstances and among so many others who were about to become exiles, it was too much to ask.

As Ilse stood on the ramp leading to a boat that looked elegant far beyond their means, something else contributed to her sense of mistrust and confusion – and that was her memory of Gyula, which was like remembering a time of horror. Gyula for Ilse was like Sasha for Lanz: they formed part of a history that both had tried to forget, two secrets that had allied to become one great secret, unique and indivisible, about which they did not speak and never would.

And perhaps, in the end, it was that image of Gyula, rather than Lanz's obstinacy, that had prevented her from turning heel, going back on their agreement and returning to her country. After all it was the country that had brought forth the traitor, and in which she had fallen in love with him.

Ilse could not forgive herself the humiliation of having loved Gyula with such a passion that she was blind to the evidence of his treachery, and of his indifference. Gyula, in Spanish, would be called "Julio". Perhaps here, in Patagonia, he would not have stood out among the ordinary people as much as Klára, with that red hair that one only sees among the peasants of the Balkans or the Caucasus. Burnished copper, it shone like a flame when the sun was on it. Gyula came from a family of upright military types, pure-blood Magyars, rebels to the kingdom. Like them, he had a dark, tanned complexion and gypsy black eyes, framed by eyelashes so thick that sometimes they seemed to be lined with a kohl pencil. His hair was as black as his eyes. She pictured Gyula in his gendarme's uniform. With any luck, he would have escaped the fury of the partisans and would today be just another citizen in that country to which Ilse, still standing on the ramp, considered returning. In any case, it was not very likely that he would have died after the war, since they had hardly tried – much less condemned – the last executors of the Final Solution. Besides, Gyula was not even German.

She had only managed to escape the country by chance: at the last minute she had tried to return to her house in Romania, the frontier of which was one of the few that resistance activists were managing to cross with the collaboration of local contrabandists and Yugoslav partisans. The methods of the Halutz[4] were more dangerous – but safer than trying to obtain one of the famous *Schutzpässe*, or "protective passes" issued by the no less famous "neutral consulates". No, for one of these you needed to have too many contacts of the kind that only someone like Gyula could call on – supposing that he wanted to use them to save the life of some Jew. Getting her the false German passport had been no more than a gesture to facilitate her passage across some European borders during the war, when the Reich's victory was still a possibility and Hungary was a favoured ally of

4. Clandestine Jewish Resistance during WW II.

the Nazis. And the consequences of that "gesture" had been rather surprising: thanks to Gyula and his natural ability to change adverse circumstances – even surnames – Ilse had become the owner of a German passport as artificial as her new name, but with all the corresponding stamps. Thanks to Gyula and that passport, she had been able to cross the southern frontier, still guarded by the SS, like crows in their black garb. But it had not been easy. The last days of October in Budapest had been sinister: there were rumours that the Jewish quarter and the area surrounding the synagogue were going to be enclosed to create a ghetto with its central axis on Wesselény Street (and this would soon be the case, but by then she had left the city). Not only had the night-time round-ups not diminished with the imminent defeat of the Nazis, and with the Russians in Poland since July, but they had become more frequent and ferocious. Towards the end of the year the capital itself was identified as a problem. At night, the gendarmerie began entering houses that had been singled out by paramilitary groups, or they carried out urban "sweeps" in which anyone still bold enough to wear a yellow armband paid the price. Those who hid, or refused to wear any identification, might be shot in the middle of the street, depending on the whim and origin of the gendarme. Generally, the Germans were not the worst, because there were not very many of them, and anyway, they were too busy carrying out last-minute exterminations to worry about the *Judenfrei*. The paramilitaries of Nyíla, however, had no scruples when it came to getting rid of bodies: they threw them in the Danube, leaving them to float until they sank, or until the ravaged corpses were washed up at Margarita Island in plain view of everyone.

And people continued to visit the theatre, billiard rooms, the opera. How could they dress up, wear jewels, style their hair, while the world around them was falling to pieces? Blue corpses appeared every day on the banks of the river. But death alone was not enough: they waited for the bombing, and only then, when everything really did start to crumble – the bridges, the castles, the thousand-year-old monuments – then they stopped going to the theatre because there was no theatre, only a blackened stump, splattered with gilded plasterwork and carmine velvet.

There has always been one sure route to terror. In all humanity's blackest epochs, the same effect has been achieved by creating an atmosphere of dangerous uncertainty: good and evil mingled in a simple but stupefying brew, so that passions that had once burned separately became one terrible passion – death as a universal solution. And in Budapest, in October 1944, death was certainly a solution.

But not for Ilse and, if Gyula's passport served any purpose, it allowed her to escape Hungary by the only route possible. There were borders that she could not cross: Austria, for example. The risk of ending up at the Mauthausen camp was too high. The north was also off-limits, and completely destroyed, and the east had been taken by the Red Army… only the south was an alternative – she could go back to her house in Temesvár, back to her family and try to get them all out through Yugoslavia…

That was how she had managed to get to Italy and had met Lanz. But when they arrived in Argentina – shortly after the country decided, belatedly, to enter the conflict on the Allies' side – something totally unexpected happened: her false German nationality made her *doubly* vulnerable to controls and suspicion. First, because she was showing the credential of a country she officially disavowed, and second because the Argentine government had, with a pragmatic clarity, revealed its true position by refusing Jews permission to disembark in their territory and denying them visas and political asylum.

How could she have guessed that that passport would end up condemning her in such a ridiculous way?

None of those who were crowded into the hold of that luxury liner – every corner of which was crammed with refugees – expected much from whichever country finally conceded some kind of asylum to them. Argentina was no exception. They had entry visas, but anticipated that these might be of no use when they arrived in the port.

And so it had proved, both in Buenos Aires and Entre Rios. Patagonia, on the other hand, was a strange land: it was as if laws made in the capital arrived there deformed by the echo of that desolate space; the trains were delayed by tracks that were destroyed by cold; the inhabitants seemed to live out of reach of an indifferent administration.

Correspondence for La Pedrera was received in a post-office box in the city – at that time more of a sprawling town than a city – and Ilse's notification probably languished there for several weeks before Lanz discovered it. At first he was bewildered by the content, then it made him furious. He had to persuade Ilse not to go straight to the district office and give them an earful (by then she spoke a mixture of Hungarian and Italian with a few ineffective but pretty Spanish words, learnt from the poems of Federico García Lorca).

She did not attend the summons that time, testifying in writing that her degenerative arthritis prevented her from moving around too much, after the major upheaval thrust on them by their exile. She trusted that they (they? Who were they? Oh – how alone they were, and how far from home!) could and would understand.

Of course the officials persisted and, when summoned a second time, she was obliged to attend.

A man with a stern expression requested her passport, asked her questions, took her fingerprints to compare them with the ones on file, and let her go. Lanz had been at her side all the time, and they went home together, she leaning on his arm, walking so slowly that it took them nearly half an hour to get back to the warmth of the little hotel they had rented so as not to have to travel back to the mountains at night.

The conversation with the official had been as brief as it was absurd:

"Come in, take a seat."

"Thank you."

"Do you understand Spanish?"

"Perfectly, and also German, English, French and some Balkan dialects."

"It is rare for a woman to speak so many languages…"

"I am European, sir. Europe is small and there is an excess of languages."

"When did you enter this country?"

"In March 1945."

"What were you doing in Germany?"

"I did not live in Germany, sir, but in Austria."

"What were you doing in Austria?"

"I studied."

"At the university?"

"That's right."

"And what did you study?"

"Benedictus Spinoza."

"He is?…"

"Dead, unfortunately."

The man looked up from his typewriter, disconcerted. He hesitated a few seconds before continuing.

"Forgive me, but I must ask you…"

"He was not the Fascist ideologue, if that's what you are worried about. He was a philosopher, a Jew, a great man who died very young. I don't know if you would like to know more."

"This is a delicate situation: you are German."

"No, sir, I am not German, because my husband is Hungarian and, according to German law, I take his citizenship."

"But you hold a German passport."

"Do you believe that I am one of Hitler's spies?"

"You could be."

"Do you believe that the German government could be so stupid as to send a woman with degenerative arthritis to spy on your government, or rather on the very little that your government does for its people in this wilderness?"

"Perhaps your husband..."

"Then question my husband, sir."

"But he is not German. And besides, he is Jewish."

"I understand. That puts him above suspicion."

The official did not pick up on her irony, nor did she have any intention of explaining it to him. He would have needed a profound comprehension of brutality, and, although the official was probably capable of understanding this, even of exercising it in some measure, he would always be a more modest version of the true brutes. Even now, so many years after the war, she was wont to tell Ana that human beings were instruments of good and bad, but especially of bad. Francisco de Goya had said that "the sleep of reason engenders monsters".

"Reason," corrected Ilse, "engenders all things, the good and the bad that lives in us and makes us all. That is why all we can do is impose on our own natures a will not to be bad and, just as in the myth of Sisyphus, we are condemned to keep pushing a rock up the hill only to see it roll down again. It means that one must strive to be good at heart: to have the will to live in opposition to one's own nature, not once or twice, or when the conditions favour it, but for all of one's life."

However, she had to acknowledge that the traitor had done something for her, even before arranging the passport:

knowing the brutality with which the Hungarian police carried out their round-ups, he had asked her on no account to board a train if she was ordered to do so. He had told her that, as far as possible, she must not take trains or go to the busiest stations. She had asked him why and he had said simply that it was "too dangerous for ordinary people". At that time it was still not obligatory to wear an armband with the star of David, or to hide away in ghettos. One could still stroll along the pavements, sit in the perfumed terrace of a café or buy bread, sold from great baskets by the farmers who made it themselves each day.

Yes, she had agonized over returning to that terrible and beloved country until the very last minutes before setting sail, until finally accepting that Lanz was right, that there was no reason to return – neither family, nor house, nor friends – because the truth was that her country no longer existed, and had never existed in fact.

Had Lanz decided for her, or was it her own iron will that made the choice for them both? It was certainly Lanz who had proposed leaving Europe, and he was either going to do that or kill himself: nobody would have been able to stop him.

For that reason Ilse knew immediately on 2nd February that Lanz had not intended to harm himself, or to harm the young man, and that, if he was hanging out of the window, clinging on for dear life, it must because he had witnessed something extraordinary – something that had happened on the lake, or perhaps in the wood.

Or even – she had to consider the possibility although it pained her – inside the war zone of his own head. But then how did Ana fit into the picture?

She could still remember every detail of that night, because she had mentally noted them and repeated them dozens of times for Ana, who, during the days that followed, had tried to extract some memory from Lanz, any fragment that could be salvaged from his mind. Ilse explained how she had gone into the living room because she was anxious and wanted to share her concern with Lanz – who probably did not even know whom she was talking about.

Ana had gone down to the lake to take her usual evening photos, and was late coming back. Ilse had seen her setting sail in the little boat with her camera and some objects she could not identify from the kitchen window – she only had a partial view of the shore. After two hours' absence, this was a delay that would have worried anyone: since New Year the lake had been dangerous and strange; too many things had happened that filled the hours with an anxiety Ilse found hard to control: the rotting lake, the saga of the monster, Lanz's attacks, the arrival of that young man who was sleeping on the divan beneath the window, Klára, who was visiting La Pedrera much less often, and who was much more circumspect, almost defensive, on the occasions that she did come. Yes, something was going on with Klára, but Ilse could not put her finger on the nature of the change. In short, since Christmas the world had become more uncertain for Ilse. Even Nando seemed to have been infected by the inexplicable malaise, and he no longer came to spend the night, nor to fish, at least not as often as he had in previous summers.

So when Ilse first entered the living room, she was already uneasy: she had come to feel that each new natural manifestation provoked some corresponding monstrous trait in the household.

While she went through the usual rigmarole explaining to Lanz who Ana was, Ilse had rearranged the bedclothes over the boy, as he lay inert on the divan. She had looked at his pale hands splayed on the mattress, long with fine fingers (although some of them were still quite distorted from having been broken), and the rounded, wide shape of the nails told her, once more, that this poor wretch had been a good man and a generous soul. The swelling in his face had reduced very quickly, so much so that even Nando's doctor friend had been amazed by this stranger's physical recuperation. Nails apart, the young man reminded Ilse very much of Gyula. Of course his skin, sallow from immobility, could have been darker; his expression less oblique. The hair which Ana insisted on combing back every morning could, with a little water, have looked fresher – he was still a lively young man – but even so, for all his pallid insensibility, his features brought to mind those of the traitor.

For that reason the boy provoked ambivalent feelings in her; all the same, when she entered the room, the first thing she did was to cover him up tenderly, before turning her attention to Lanz, who was scrutinizing the lake from the window at the foot of the divan, where the young man lay.

Ana's boat could no longer be seen from the window, but it must have been visible at some point, going on what she had heard Lanz saying a moment before. Needless to say, there was no point asking Lanz about it: he tended to invent fantastic stories for the sake of giving an answer. Anyway, Lanz's memory was caught up with events far from the lake and many years distant. Ilse had heard him mention Miklós, the man who had accompanied Lanz through much of his forced labour in the camp, as well as on the march towards Hungary at the end of the war. Recently Lanz had become ensnared by his memories of the war. His mind seemed to be retreating further and further back, locking itself in a room from which the only escape route was one of useless suffering – but Ilse could do nothing about it.

Lanz had spoken about the night, the night of war, and Ilse had answered that that night would never descend again. Lanz had smiled, and she had returned to the kitchen. Later – how much later? – Lanz had started raving about bodies and mass graves, and afterwards – but how long after? – he had begun to shout.

In the kitchen, two serving dishes, one with pieces of chicken marinaded in oil and herbs, had slipped out of her hands. Light from the lamp was reflected in the oil – a shining patch on the floor, like a broken mirror. Lanz's fearful cry brought back all the panic Ilse thought she had forgotten about, or at least suppressed. It was so sudden, like lightning or an electric shock that stuns and paralyses, destroying time, while simultaneously illuminating it with the most powerful of all lights.

Afterwards she could not find words fit to describe the experience, and when they were piecing together the sequence of events, that part of the night had to go unexplained.

When Ana passed by her like a shadow, a light breeze had skimmed her, resuscitating her, putting her in motion once more. Those impatient hours Ilse had spent needed to be accounted for and matched to Ana's story. She told it herself, some time after midnight, becalmed by the effects of the liquor, after they had managed to prise Lanz away from the window and put him to bed, return Pedro to the divan, use the sheets to fasten him to the mattress, and check that neither man had suffered serious injury.

Ana got to work with the precision of an automaton, with no consideration for her own energy reserves. Her hair was wet, dripping water like her clothes, and she smelt of the red algae, and some other substance, more sulphurous and penetrating. An oily secretion covered her completely, as if she had been rolling in the juices of some enormous viscera.

Ana had helped Ilse to carry Lanz to the cabin. They had to drag him a little, because once they had managed to haul him away from the window, Lanz had succumbed, as was usual after one of his attacks, to a sort of delirious drowsiness which would be followed by complete silence. For that reason, Ana tried immediately to coax information out of him about what he had seen, before it was swallowed up by the amnesia.

"What was it, Vatti? Was it something in the lake?"

Lanz inspected her with eyes that were half closed, though not distrustful.

"Anita. When did you get here?"

It was rare for him to recognize her spontaneously, but on this occasion, Ana had no time to take any pleasure in the fact.

"Just now, Vatti. I've come from the lake. You were shouting, you were falling out of the window and Pedro was lying on the floor. What happened, Vatti?"

"What happened? I was in Víktor's old chair, not at the window."

"Outside, in the lake, please think about it for a minute. In the lake, or in the wood, or on the shore. Did you see it?"

"The young chap too."

Ana had bent over him and now held his arms, as though he were a child, obliging him to look her in the eye. A drop of foul-smelling water ran down Lanz's forehead, disconcerting him.

"Mutti, this creature is dripping on me."

"Lanz! Look at me! What was there outside?"

Ana, without realizing it, was digging her nails into him, hurting him. The old man pushed her off.

"They are always watching us," he said, his hands covering his eyes.

"Who?"

"The dwarfs."

"What are you talking about—"

"That's enough."

Gently but firmly, Ilse moved her away from Lanz.

"No! Later it will be useless!"

"That's enough, Ana!"

And she had said nothing else.

Later Ilse had helped Ana to take off the sticky wet clothes and to fill the bathtub. The liquor she used to calm Lanz was poured into two glasses, and drops of cobalt-coloured tincture put into each.

As Ana lay, half-submerged in the camphorated water, her expression in the candlelight began to lose the frenetic worry of the previous hours.

The absinthe had dilated her pupils and Ana's grey eyes became two opals shining with a cloudy iridescence. She looked exhausted (later Ilse would make up a bed for her near to Pedro, so that she could keep an eye on them both) but she held onto her Ilse's arm, obliging her to sit down. So it was that, in a state of collapse alleviated by the alcohol, she began to tell Ilse what she had seen on the lake, a few hours earlier.

"Since the afternoon everything had been strange, even stranger than usual. The water was still stagnant. The algae were still there, and getting worse – redder, more puffy. There were insects everywhere – horseflies, flies, mosquitoes, bees, some orangey wasps. Everything was buzzing, and the horseflies were like vultures feasting on carrion. The birds were quiet, only the noise of insects filled the air.

"At seven o' clock in the evening, a westerly wind had got up and sharp gusts were rippling the water, so I hurried to get down to the shore. The tripod was still there, but water was lapping at its base. The level of the lake was too high for me to take photographs in the usual spot. Also, the smell was fetid, as though every living thing in the lake had died. There was a gelatinous substance, a kind of slobber on the surface of the lake, forming a brown foam. Everything smelt rotten, decomposing; the smell was so overwhelming that for a few minutes I had the impression of being part of an enormous corpse. The ravine was silent. The air had that strained, tight sensation that comes before something blooms or bursts out. You could sense it, you could smell that nature was looking for some channel through which to unburden itself, or the lake would burst open, up into the air, like lava. I don't know, perhaps I'm not making sense, but this place is never usually like that, this place is exactly the opposite. That's why I decided to get into the boat with the camera. I knew that Lanz and Nando had not finished caulking it; it still smelt of tar, and one of the oars had a split in it that hadn't been banded yet. But it didn't matter: at that moment even a raft made of reeds would have done the trick – though later I regretted being so hasty.

"From the jetty I had seen that in the middle of the sound, right between the two banks of the ravine, a current was being generated, something circular, suggesting a deep whirlpool… Did I tell you that? No, I didn't. Well, that was how it all started: there had been the odd atmosphere of the preceding days, the stinking algae and now that movement in the water. The shimmer on that circle of water was tangential, red, raised like a lip of water, and it never closed. But I could barely see it from the shore. I got into the boat with the camera slung on my back and I rowed inwards, towards the centre of that whirlpool, or whatever it was. To start with, everything was fine: I had the wind in my favour, the evening sky was lemon-yellow and bloody-mindedness gave me all the strength I needed to keep going and put the shore behind me. But time passed, and I seemed not to be getting to the place I wanted. That was when the westerly wind stopped blowing and was replaced by this up-to-down, centripetal version, like a heavenly wind, which seemed to push the water and sky in all directions. I wished I had brought the little motor, in case the oars proved to be insufficient. Anyway, it was too late for that. I kept rowing even harder towards the middle of the lake, even though the light was going and I knew that I should not go so far away in the dark, with no lantern and no equipment. You know what night is like here, Mutti. But before that, before it was really dark, when I had managed to row far enough to be equidistant between the two banks, I looked at the way the oars were entering the water and realized that it was not the wind that was holding me back, or the algae: I was traversing the wake of something that was sliding beneath the boat, towards the shore. That "something" was moving, and what I could feel in the oars was the effect of that movement in opposition to mine. Reflections on the water prevented me seeing it – and the density of the algae would not have allowed it anyway – even so, I took a couple of photos of the traces on the surface of the water. It won't have been any use, I realize that, but what other thing could be generating a current like that in a lake that was practically stagnant?

"Afterwards I took a few minutes to point the prow back towards the shore, to follow the trail of the eddy. Whatever was swimming underneath me had now gone past and was moving away very fast, so fast that for a moment I believed that mad idea of Lanz's about nuclear submarines. I knew that I could not catch up with it, not without a motor, and that soon I would be rowing in utter darkness, but I didn't care. I got the camera ready and, rather than put it in the drawer of the prow, I decided to keep it to hand, throwing a canvas over it for protection. I still could not see the house or the quay, and I did not see them until you put the light on in the kitchen. By then it was completely dark. I could scarcely make out the mountains against the sky, which had turned the same purple as them. The light from the window came closer and closer until I could also see the silhouette of the house, about two hundred metres away from where I was. I could feel that both sides of the ravine were nearer: sound reverberated on the lake in a special way, like when you hold a shell to your ear. I was entering into the narrower part of the sound, close to the quay. The kitchen light... I recognized the light from that kerosene lamp, because it looks pink from a distance. But I had lost all notion of time. I was rowing leeward to a capricious wind at night, on night, in the midst of night sounds. I was rowing as though in a dream. I had stopped feeling my arms, my hands gripping the wood, the oars' resistance in the water. I suppose that tiredness made me lean backwards without realizing it, because suddenly something – I couldn't tell you what, a noise in water perhaps, or the boat lurching – brought me to my senses, and I found myself not rowing, but lying face up, looking at the sky. I thought that the boat must have capsized some way back, that I was dying and that the last thing I was going to see would be the bottom of the lake. The air had the same filmy texture as the water... But the confusion didn't last long, because just then I felt it come up, burst out of the water at some point between the boat and the house. I managed to sit up – too much towards the stern, and that was a mistake – to try to locate it, to see what it was like. I don't know how to explain it: there it was, an indefinite mass of water, shapeless and black as onyx, which for an instant – just one instant – covered that single source of light. It was a glassy, crystalline shape... but invisible. It filled the air, it changed the sound of things, eclipsing the light.

"It was pitch dark by then, and when the light from the kitchen disappeared, I was scared... Part of me wanted to get out of there, the other part wanted to see. I suppose I must have tried to reach for my camera and the oars at the same time, but I only managed to do one of those things, and made a hash of it. The camera was at the other end of the boat, covered with the canvas. First I tried to pull the canvas towards me, to drag the camera over. Then, as the seconds were passing and I could not reach it, I moved my whole body towards the prow, holding onto the thole pin, but without standing up, edging along the side of the boat. At that moment a wave hit the side, the boat lurched and the camera fell on top of me. With what little balance I had, I focused the lens on that blackness and got ready to shoot. It wasn't very much: a mass radiating a black sheen, multifaceted like the eye of a giant fly. Even as I was taking the photos, I knew that nothing I was seeing through the lens was going to stay fixed on the film, because what I was trying to register was the *sensation* of a presence. It was everything around me: the wind that came from nowhere, the waves that were generated by some unidentifiable movement to starboard, the stench of the water, the massive, oily blackness of whatever it was that had emerged from the lake, my hands, rigid as hooks around the camera. It was hopeless. Then I heard Lanz scream and I knew that he must be seeing exactly the same thing, but from the other side. It was as if that scream had touched it: the thing began to move towards the left-hand bank and only then, I think, did the kitchen light reappear. When I got to the quay I hadn't even realized that the bottom of the boat was waterlogged, like the camera, and that my legs were freezing cold..."

"And that's all of it?"

"All. Or nothing. It's a disaster, Mutti. I don't even think I can save the roll of photos. The Leica is ruined. Lanz doesn't remember anything and nearly killed himself, and I could have sunk in the middle of the lake..."

"But there's no need to worry about Vatti," said Ilse. "I'm not certain that he saw the same thing, Ana. Vatti was talking about something else; maybe he did have some sort of vision, it's true, but whatever he saw was from another time, in another place. Believe me, Ana: that monster is not the same for you as it is for him."

Ana did not answer for a long time, and when she did, it was not to say anything about her experience on the lake.

"We can't leave Lanz on his own with Pedro, Mutti. Not any more."

Then it was Ilse's turn to say nothing. She knew that Lanz could not be on his own, either near to Pedro or far from him, and that the situation would get worse, as it had been worsening since the beginning of the year. But she did not want to talk to Ana about it.

The silence between them lengthened, and Ilse thought that Ana might have fallen asleep, or even fainted as a result of fatigue or liquor. Approaching the girl, she saw that that was not the case. Submerged in the bath, half-asleep, Ana was weeping silently, as she herself once used to weep. Ana had always had an adult way with tears – they fell, solitary drops, from the sides of her eyes – and a habit of wiping them clumsily away with the back of her hand.

Ilse waited patiently, sitting on a wooden stool with the towel ready. The candlelight on an enormous iron candelabrum flickered against the whitewashed wall.

"I'm so tired, Mutti."

"No one needs to make a palaver over this, poppet. Lanz is lost in his own world, and what happened to you was…"

"Madness? Agreed. A fantasy? No, Mutti. It's true that I couldn't see it, but I swear that it was there. It was very close to me. And Vatti also saw it."

"Never mind. If it really exists, it will appear again."

"It exists. It's there. It's… alive."

"That's not saying much. Poor old Pedro is also alive."

"It's not the same. Or maybe it is: I don't know what they are. Either of them. They are like orphans with no name."

"Not everything can have a name, my love. This place is a bit like that: no people, no God. There's nothing here – this is just a scar on the face of the earth. There was no Reformation here, no Renaissance, no World Wars. We are far away from everything and, for all practical purposes, we may as well not exist. What difference is there between today and ten thousand years back? There's electricity and antibiotics in that bathroom cabinet... but nature laughs at us, Ana. So that monster, if it really exists, is still living out there alongside us. If this place had a name, it would surely have ceased to exist. Nor would that boy have been thrown out here. Not having a name can afford you some protection."

"That may be the case, but I can't live with it."

There were a few minutes of silence, broken only by the dripping of the tap, or the candle guttering as wax melted. From outside, however, came the usual racket of night noises in the wood. Ilse still waited.

Finally it came.

"Tell me the story about Carmen," Ana asked, in a voice that sounded girlish and hoarse. Her tears had dried and she seemed about to fall asleep.

Ilse smiled: it was more or less what she had been expecting.

"But first of all," she said, "get out of the water, or you'll end up as wrinkled as I am."

"For your age? I'll stay in, then..."

Tenderly, Ilse enfolded Ana's long, awkward body in the towel. She was still her little girl, with the same slight frame, the adolescent breasts, boyishly slim hips, narrow calves. Ana embodied her mother's simple but devastating beauty. Her body was not made for clothes, but for walking naked outside, at one with nature. Klára, on the other hand, was small and white, with the paleness and black eyes of a Serb. She had always been attractive, since childhood, but seemed oblivious to the fact, disguising her wide hips with long Indian dresses and jackets that were three sizes too big. Ana did not even bother to choose her own clothes. They could not have been more different.

With the same care, Ilse took Ana to bed, tucked her in as though she were a child, and then lay down beside her in the quiet gloom of the house.

"'La Carmen' – everyone here, and there weren't many of us, called her 'that Carmen' – was a tall, slim Indian woman with the brown eyes of a Tehuelche. When the lonely man first found her, she was very little. She had been abandoned on a ranch; the poor little thing kept herself going for a few days by chewing on scraps of dried meat, sucking them dry. She would have been very young. Without thinking about it, the lonely man took her with him. There was no sign of the parents, at least that is what he claimed. There was no need to harm them: he took her with him, tied onto his back in an old poncho, not to abduct her, but because he thought perhaps she might be useful. The lonely man lived in the mountains, and there, in the middle of nothing, he brought her up with the same dedication he might have shown one of his goats. He called her Carmen, because that was the one word he could understand from the lips of this girl, who spoke another language and who, very, very soon would stop speaking altogether. However, the Indian girl responded to the name Carmen, because it was the only possession she had. La Carmen grew, her eyes became half yellow, like those of a puma. She could hardly manage all the household chores – she grew thin and supple, like a willow branch – she became a sort of maid. The lonely man didn't talk to her, unless it was to give orders or communicate essentials. She did not talk either. The man never knew if that was because she had been struck dumb, or if she simply refused to do it. What he did know was that Carmen perfectly understood his language. He no longer needed to make the gestures and signs that accompanied the first few years of those difficult lessons in naming things. The lonely man did not explain anything about life to her, but he maintained certain indispensable superstitions to prevent her from leaving him. La Carmen kept growing taller and taller. The colour of her skin and eyes showed that she was mixed race. The lonely man surmised – and gave her to understand – that this girl had been abandoned by her mother because she was the offspring of some shameful act. The girl was almost as wild as he was and showed no sign of knowing what the word 'shame' meant, and the man did not mind all that much: it was not the only weapon he had to keep her at his side. La Carmen entered into puberty full of fear and potency, like a forest animal. The day of her first menstruation, the lonely man told her that this was a fatal illness. She screamed – one of the few times in her life – and escaped to the mountainside. After two days, the lonely man found her, freezing cold and bloody. That same night, driven by hatred and frustration, he forced her to submit to him. Her second menstruation never arrived: Carmen fell pregnant, believing that the illness was following its course and now had taken root in her belly, waiting for the right moment to eat her insides. She was thirteen: her mixed heritage had bestowed on her slim hips, a straight back and the strong, lean muscles of her indigenous ancestors. Then her body started to swell inexplicably. At night she moaned in pain, thinking that she was going to die in her sleep, that she would never see the next morning. During daylight hours she rubbed the bones of dead animals over the stretched skin of her abdomen, to kill off her illness. Finally, one May day, she bore a child, a girl even whiter than herself, expelled by her own guts. Terrified, she thought she must have lost part of her body, the part that beats, that kept her alive. She thought she must be empty, and that certainty was so strong that it became self-fulfilling: the Indian girl emptied out, dried out. The lonely man put the baby to the Indian's chest, and the newborn learnt her first lesson in life: to suckle at an indifferent breast. The baby's persistence could not prevent what was always bound to happen: Carmen died six months later. The baby did not know, or seem to realize. The thing is, she had never had a mother, only a uterus which conceived then thrust her out. The bottle that replaced the mother, and from which she quickly learnt to suck, provided a much less bitter milk."

Ilse's voice had grown softer until it was no more than a whisper. Ana's breathing came slowly, with a light snore that disappeared when Ilse turned her on her side and drew the blanket up to her neck.

On tiptoe she went to check on Pedro, who was sleeping peacefully, and again she thought of Gyula. Later, exhausted, she sat down in the darkness of the kitchen. The pans and ladles of copper and tin hanging on the walls around her – her "clutter" as she used to call them – received her with indifference. The light of the moon, or perhaps the dawn, had transformed them into extravagant objects alien to their usual functions and to the room that contained them: rims and handles, lids, metallic interiors shone like a medieval artillery, or faintly threatening pieces of armour belonging to a giant.

There were two places in the house that Ilse loved, where she spent much of her time and found an inexplicable solace: one of them was the kitchen, that same square room, with its rustic wooden table and an iron oven that ran on firewood. The other place was upstairs on the landing, beneath a window that was oval, like a bull's eye, and always reminded her of the boat in which they had crossed the ocean, fleeing Europe. In this little corner was the clavichord – though really it was an older, simpler instrument, more like a virginal: a cedar box in the shape of a harp, which contained the strings, standing on three thin legs, roughly turned. Judging by the inscriptions inside the box, the clavichord had been made by a luthier in Santiago for a young lady called Magdalena. It was an extraordinary object to find in the middle of Patagonia:

the international renown of Polish harpsichordist Wanda Landowska had evidently reached this far. For her, the strings' simple sound, metallic and ancient, was the only true medium for a baroque score. If it had not been for Landowska, the clavichord and all its variants would have become permanent museum pieces.

Ilse had stopped playing years before: that box, though it looked so basic, required a flexibility in the fingers that her arthritis would no longer allow. The scores, for their part, required a loving sensibility, a gratitude that she no longer felt. All the same, she still sometimes sat down as though she were about to play, and caressed the lacquered keys for hours, without allowing the instrument to exhale a single note.

Yes, there were two cherished places in the house, but no more, and that night one of them had inexplicably made her a stranger, capable of construing weaponry in the meek arrangement of a set of pans, danger among the pots and the spatulas... Could it be Ana's account that had transformed everything? Or Lanz's despair? Or the memory of Gyula? Or perhaps the sad story of the Indian girl who had never been able to leave her mark in the unflinching hardness of these walls?

Outside, through the window, a zinc-coloured lake indifferently reflected the moon. Inside, the whole house sank into a silence that so precisely matched the night, one might as well have been out in the elements.

She spoke aloud, to coax a minimal echo from the walls.

"This house does not smile, it does not know how to smile. It's a shame, because that means it cannot be a home, but only a refuge. Like a cave in the storm."

She heard nothing.

It was hopeless: that body of stone completely absorbed her voice, and it was if no one, nothing had ever interrupted the dark silence.

She could not help but remember her own house in the outskirts of Temésvar, her paternal home defended by the River Maros to the north and the last foothills of the Carpathian mountains to the south, fighting to the death as they fell almost on Serbian territory.

The Treaty of Trianon had left all the region that was once Magyar in the hands of Romania: the entire Hungarian perimeter had been broken up in favour of neighbouring countries. They – the inhabitants, the people – had exile imposed on them without moving an inch. And that merciless exile stripped them from one day to the next of language, customs, religion, nationality. Everything.

In the area around their house there were more Germans than anything else, and that would not win them any favours a few years later, except in Ilse's case because, by then, she spoke German perfectly and had decided to go to Romania, to leave her house in the green hills, her white house with marble staircases and walnut panelling, with patios full of ferns, rooms hung with Turkish silk, her white house among the chestnut trees, at the end of a drive bordered by evergreens and yellow pots of lavender from the Caucasus. Everything in that mansion spoke of a cultivated, happy life, a Romanian life that spoke German, and Hungarian in secret, by the stove in the kitchen, when her mother wrapped herself in a woollen shawl and sat with her father to drink warm wine, arm in arm, with no servants around to wait on them, as if in a scene of country life. Ilse and her two brothers rollicked around them and each one recounted the events of the week. This ritual did not take place every day: if that were the case, Ilse would not still remember it as something special. It tended to happen on a Saturday, the day when nobody worked in the house, not even the domestic servants or the gardeners. There were never parties on a Saturday: that was a Jewish custom they respected, the Sabbath rest day, rigorously implemented by her mother. On those days, even the house, emptied of servants, sleepy in the afternoon sun, seemed to smile. With her parents in the kitchen and a fire burning in the hearth at night, it smiled. In the garden, among the ferns and the mosaics, it smiled. From inside the canaries' cage – Ilse kept dozens of these birds, yellow and ochre or orange like petunias – it smiled.

Not so Víktor's house! A grey stone house does not know how to smile. Stern and frugal, it cultivates the appearance of a retired schoolmaster, surrounded by haughty trees and the enveloping darkness of the lake beneath a sky that is perpetually overcast. What a world of difference there was between these twisted lenga trees, the red myrtle and cypresses dense as absinthe, and the graceful oak trees of Temésvar, or the almond trees in bloom, or even the humble elegance of the beech trees!

Víktor had striven to build his house here, deep in the midst of a wild vegetation, and, in spite of the many years they had spent living in the cabin and sharing the amenities with Ana, they had never managed to banish so much as a millimetre of its brutal and mute solemnity. Víktor, with his flinty obstinacy, his silences, his fits of rage and despotism, had built a house that suited him down to the ground, guaranteed to ensure the unhappiness of all those who tried to live in it.

Of course even Víktor had fled from there. The monster had always been a perfect excuse to escape the pain that La Pedrera caused him, the presence of Ana, the absence of Carmen, whom he had never loved, but rather controlled. It did not make much difference, because "love" for Víktor had always been a form of domination.

He was like Nimrod, the King of Babel, but instead of a tower, he had built an indestructible house. Here it squatted beside the lake, proud in its mountain stockade, defying God.

6

Nando

It was eleven o'clock at night. They had all been given a tray with a sandwich and a plastic cup of coffee. The Southern Star was half full and all the passengers were locals, some of them wearing gaucho trousers and thick woollen ponchos. They must have come from the ranches round about. Ana had made a pillow of her scrunched-up jacket and fallen asleep, fortunately leaning against the window. In fact he had taken the aisle seat for that reason: so that Ana could sleep and he could get up to smoke a cigarette at the back of the coach, or to chat with one or other of the two drivers. One of them, he had noticed, when getting on to the bus at the terminal, had brought his own thermos flask of coffee – much better than the stuff they would be getting. They deserved it, considering their long drive.

She had tried to fold over her jacket a few times (thinking that it was the best she owned, and would be completely inappropriate for the capital, and for the season) but there was no elegant way to do it, so she ended up crushing it against the window. Anyway, she did not want to close the curtain – she preferred to see the country: the gentle undulations giving way, at night, to the Patagonian wasteland, flat, barren, a bluish grey colour. Little clumps of *jarilla* and *coirón* were dotted about the land, although they had not yet reached the true plateau, the *meseta*. Nando was obviously itching to get up and go out to stretch his legs with the drivers. She could feel him beside her, huffing and shifting in his seat, continually checking his rucksack. Thank goodness he had not decided to put on the light and read a newspaper.

A newspaper!

What wouldn't he give to read a Buenos Aires newspaper!

At least that would stop him thinking about Klára. She had wanted to accompany them to the capital, and they had had their work cut out trying to dissuade her. Nando had argued that Lanz was weak, that Ana was determined to make the journey alone and that Pedro (or whatever the poor bastard was called) needed attention, and finally she had agreed to stay with the old folk, acting as housekeeper for three days. The role really did not suit her, poor thing, but at least she had stopped demanding to go with them.

Anyway he sensed, he had a foreboding that she would soon go far away. To put it more euphemistically: she would feel obliged to go, or rather *they* would oblige her to go. Where to? Chile? What a joke – nowhere in Latin America felt safe, although Klára talked about Venezuela or Mexico, even Europe. He had begged her to go to Europe, as far away as possible – to a quiet country, but Klára answered, as always, that there was no such thing as a quiet country – why could he not see that the world would never be a quiet place while inequalities remained, while there were injustices, diseases and hunger? It was the usual harangue, more or less, and by now Nando knew it off by heart. You can't solve it on your own, he would say wearily, for the sake of saying something, because no one could go against such a simple argument brandished so passionately by this girl, whose pale and delicate skin was flawless, save for the freckles that adorned both cheeks and the sharp bridge of her nose. Her black eyes shone with sincerity, and the brilliant copper hair illuminated her face, like a gilt frame around a work of art.

Besides, men could not stand up to a beautiful woman, and Nando was no exception.

Who said I'm on my own, Klára would say. She taunted him with her most innocent expression, as if she were thinking what a shame it was for such a handsome boy to be so dim-witted, or she brushed the very corner of his mouth with one of those kisses she had been giving him recently – except for on the three or four opportunities they had had to be completely alone. A light kiss, like one from a bee or a butterfly, and one that required her to stand on tiptoe to reach a few centimetres higher.

Where must they be now? In Choele? They had not stopped since the afternoon, and some people were beginning to get up, restless, more anxious to eat or to visit the toilet than to sleep. Nando's burliness seemed to exceed the limits of the narrow seat in all directions, but especially upwards. It was not discomfort that bothered him – even if he did feel like Gulliver in Lilliput. Nor was it a desire for coffee, or to go and chat to the drivers (two cheerful types, night owls by nature, whom he knew from the city) or to read for a bit. It was the journey itself that preoccupied him, and Ana's obstinacy – the consequences her pig-headedness would wreak in all their lives. Leaving Klára alone at such a time, for example. Lanz, who was deteriorating all the time. The poor half-dead man they were sheltering and who might be reclaimed (but by whom?) at any time. And the lake suddenly transformed into an indigenous soup, in which you couldn't catch even one miserable trout. What had happened in the lake? Recently he had begun to believe that Ana had seen something, after all, nothing to do with Víktor's obsession, or Lanz's hallucinations, but something secret, the product of some experiment, more like the nuclear submarine Lanz fantasized about than that ridiculous, legendary monster. He had never believed in the monster and, luckily for him, had never known Víktor. That, thought Nando, had been a determinating factor in his continued mental health.

* * *

Her father was, in fact, the last thing Ana wanted to be thinking about, but it was inevitable: if there was one place particularly associated in her mind with the image of her father, that was Buenos Aires. It also brought to mind memories of her school and all those years of silence and distancing – which brought her back to her father. No: she did not want to think of him or anyone else, nor of what she was going to find – if she found anything at all – by way of an answer or an explanation. She had already thought too much, chewing over thousands of possible answers and explanations, about Pedro, about the package sent by her father to this Doctor Gúzman, and the more time went by, the more they all began to seem equally wild. That was why, after the episode of that night on the lake, she had decided not to dwell on it any more.

But this night was going on so long…

Twenty-three hours or thereabouts. Never in his life had he undertaken such a long journey for his own benefit, let alone for someone else's. It had crossed his mind to use the intimacy of this situation to talk to her. He did not know what it was he going to say to her, but for a long time he had felt an urgent need to confess what was going on with Klára. It would be so much easier if he could simply slice open his chest or his head, physically open them to expose what he was unable to explain to Ana's critical, quiet gaze. She had always been able to see things that eluded him. Perhaps that was why they never really talked – conversation seemed sterile. However, they could not continue like this either. He, at any rate, was sure that he could not let it go on, because there was probably nothing left between them.

What was it that had changed? All of them had. Nando and she too had changed. But why? She did not want to think about that either. She wanted to sleep, and it seemed inconceivable that a landscape as soporific as the *meseta* could not provide her with at least one hour's shut-eye. Inconceivable, too, that they were already approaching Choele Choel on route twenty-two, with its potholes and lorries loaded with fruit.

And yet there he was: trapped like a poor huemul in a swamp, stuck in an uncomfortable bus with fifteen hours' travelling ahead of him. Beside him, Ana – as was her custom – pretended to be asleep. With any luck, she really was asleep. The ritual of Ana's sleep was a mystery to him. Klára's sleeping habits were also a mystery, but for a different reason: they still had not had a chance to sleep together or even near each other, nor to separate with embarrassment or fear at first light. They had not slept together, that was a fact. And yet it felt as though something had happened between them.

Now the coach had suddenly pulled into the hard shoulder, although the engine was still running.

Where could they be?

To the left of the bus there was a lit-up building. A terminal? Impossible: there were no towns, not even ghost towns, this side of Choele. Was it a service station? It looked more like a division of the highway police. Whatever it was, more than one of them was desperate to use a bathroom.

But the drivers did not open the door. And they seemed to have parked, not in the obvious place, but at some distance from the building where lights were on.

Ana had woken up. Why were they not opening the door? No one moved, no one got out to fix anything. The engine was still running, but none of the passengers who were awake got up to ask what was going on.

For nearly fifteen minutes, they waited in the dark.

When the engine finally stopped, with a long crackle from the exhaust, the passengers gradually became aware that there were more people behind the bus, out of view. They were wearing camouflage. There was a vehicle. Also stationary, with its lights off. Also camouflaged.

"Ana, wake up. Ana!"

"I am awake. What's up? Why aren't we moving?"

"Look outside and see if you can see anything. Behind the coach."

Ana pressed her face against the glass. The large windows could not be opened from the inside and there was no fresh air. As the atmosphere became suffocating, people began to get restless. Some, though, slept on, snoring lightly with their heads dropping onto their chests.

"It's a lorry. Its lights are off, there's not much to see…"

"The army."

"The what?"

"Have you got your ID?"

"I've got it in my wallet. Why, what's going on?"

"Take it out. Have it in your hand."

"But what's going on? Nando!"

The drivers got out of their seats and opened the door. Nando could see that they look worried, but not scared, and he wondered how often this had happened before. Then figures moved in the night quickly, like mountain animals. Suddenly they were at the door of the bus. He felt Ana's hand grip his arm.

"Nando!"

"Shhh. Be quiet."

Much later, after they had arrived at their hotel, they would piece together the different elements of that night: the soldiers in their ordinary uniform; the light automatic rifles that some carried on their backs and others pointed straight at the passengers (Ana would remember that those soldiers aiming at the body were very young, holding their guns with an unsteady hand, as if the simple act of making this threatening gesture could equip them with the indifferent calm of their more hardened colleagues, who aimed at the floor); the way they had been made to get out of the bus one by one, like prisoners, carrying their bags and jackets, and the untidy line they had formed at the edge of the road; the pitch-black night and the lights of that building which they were never able to identify; the drivers' concerned and subdued faces; the sudden nausea of one woman and the weeping of another; the sleepy or frightened or surprised expressions of country people; the meticulous inspection of their belongings and their documents; the photos checked one by one; the cold drizzle or the fear that made their teeth chatter; the return to the warmth of the coach, which no longer seemed suffocating but infinitely protective; the sighs, the questions, the whispers. The dark hours that followed before dawn.

They would recall all of this later, in a tacit agreement not to talk about it until they were in a safe place.

A safe place... the truth was that it was years since Ana had been in a place that felt so comparatively civilized. On arriving in Buenos Aires, in spite of her apprehension, she had felt a thrill of anticipation. They had taken a taxi from the coach station to the hotel, the driver keeping a suspicious eye on them all the time, in his rear-view mirror. During the journey they had not spoken, either to each other or to the driver, other than to give him the address of the hotel, and to thank him for the change.

The hotel was a big old town house, typical of the 1910s and 1920s, with wrought-iron doors and poor-quality glass where original windows had been replaced. Outside there were still some mouldings of flowers and women's heads adorning the windows, and the floor in the hall was a mosaic of burgundy-coloured tiles with a cream border. The design entranced Ana, who was so used to the crude, solid stone of her own house, the cypress wood varnished to within an inch of its life.

Behind the parapet of his counter stood the concierge, a man with tapering bejewelled fingers and the look of someone who cheats at cards. Without much of a preamble, he passed them the register and then a bronze key attached to a felt ball on which was embroidered the number "three". The marble staircase, with wrought-iron banister, led to a carpeted corridor smelling of cigarettes, along which there were four tall wooden doors. Their room was at the back of the building, and had a view of motley terraces and balconies on which washing was drying in the breeze. Nando sighed with relief: a window onto the street would have made him feel very nervous, after what they had been through.

Neither of them said anything about the double bed and its frayed counterpane. Nando took a quick look at the bathroom, which was dominated by an old bathtub with feet shaped like talons. Ana could not help smiling when she saw that and the enormous oval basin, with taps emulating swans, tinged with green. They were wonderful objects, even allowing for the rusty watermarks on the old porous tiles, and she forgot for a moment the gruelling events of their journey. Nando, however, was impervious to the charms of the anachronistic bathroom fittings, and suggested they get going. So Ana made do with a quick face-wash, rearranging her hair in a loose bun.

They decided that they would go out to get something to eat – a pizza – nearby, and come back soon. Nando did not want to be out and about for long. The arrangement made Ana feel uneasy, but she knew that Nando was right.

The pizzeria – which the card-cheat concierge assured them was the best in the neighbourhood – was on the same block as their hotel. They sat at a table by the wall, even though the place was empty, and asked for a jug of wine. Ana asked what the army was doing in Choele, and Nando answered that they were everywhere, and that it would get worse.

Ana asked why, and Nando said nothing, but he could not help thinking about Klára. Then their conversation moved on to the details of what had happened, though neither of them felt much like discussing them. The sequence of events that night had been so quick and precise, so effective that, the next morning, as dawn brought reassuring light to the pampas, people in the bus had looked around at each other with confusion, as though wondering if they really *had* been stopped on the road and made to form a line while guns were pointed at them.

That night, when they returned to the hotel, Nando closed the window and drew the curtains, in spite of the heat. They prepared to go to sleep, each one at his or her side of the bed, lying face up, as though awaiting some catastrophe, and Nando said:

"Tomorrow we'll go to look for that address, and the day after tomorrow to the museum, and then we're going home, right?"

After a pause that was uncomfortable for both parties, Ana agreed.

That first night was long and filled with strange noises unlike anything they had heard before. The voices floating up from the floor beneath sounded strangely shrill and nervous; the muffled noise of city buses, their horns muted by the closed window, was overlaid by gurgling in the building's old pipes. At three o'clock in the morning, when at least the hotel's noises had subsided, they finally fell asleep.

They woke up at about seven o'clock, Nando feeling stiff from the journey; Ana with heavy eyelids and limbs. From downstairs came the metallic sound of cutlery being sorted; the smell of coffee and croissants filtering through some unsuspected chink brought them fully awake.

While Nando showered, Ana stayed in bed studying the street map. They were not so far from the street the name of which had been Pedro's sole piece of identification. Provided Nando was not in a bad mood, they could even walk there.

Nando's moods preoccupied Ana, especially now that she had no choice but to put up with them. Usually, the rules of their engagement were strictly defined by desire, and Ana was not used to having to relinquish or alter her plans in any other sphere. It was going to drive her mad if Nando got too paranoid – but she had promised herself that this time she would accept his decisions without objection. Nando hated travelling and hated, also, to be afraid. Ana struggled to understand what that feeling of fear implied for him, because she had rarely felt it in her own life. Unhappiness, yes, apprehension, pain, failure, perhaps – but not fear. That was a quality she had inherited from Víktor.

"It's the continuation of Carlos Calvo Street," she said aloud, hoping that he could hear above the noise of the shower. "If you're walking it's about thirty blocks, or forty at the most."

But there was no answer, even though the bathroom door was open.

Nando felt the water coursing over his face and back. He would have liked to spend the day lying on the bed looking at the ceiling, letting Ana get on with whatever she had to do, without having to worry about her, Klára or anyone else. He would never abandon Ana and yet he would never, so it seemed, stop thinking about Klára. Here was the nub of his problem.

The episode on the road had made him feel more nervous than usual; he had the sensation that even the people hanging their shirts out to dry on their terraces were watching Ana and him. But it was not feasible to keep the windows closed for two days in this insufferable heat. He needed to calm down, to relax. Above all, he needed to forget. Ana was saying something from the bedroom about Carlos Calvo Street.

Knowing her – and he knew her pretty well – she wanted to walk there. She wanted to pace the streets until she found that spot marked "x". But perhaps that address actually had nothing to do with the guy in the coma, and this notion of Ana's was more the product of wish fulfilment than logic. Why would such a man, beaten almost to death, thrown over the brink of a ravine with the clear intention of drowning him in the lake or of making his broken, dying body disappear – why would this man be carrying in his pocket an address from the capital, written in minuscule handwriting, like a woman's, on a scrap of paper that had probably been saved thanks only to the sticky mess of sweat and grime suppurating from his body after the beating? Was it a safe house, the home of a some filthy-rich capitalist, or a trade unionist, or a guerrilla? What had this guy been up to for them to lay into him that way? Which group had he been with?

He would have liked to stay in bed *not* thinking about any of this and not thinking about Klára either. Just looking at the ceiling, resting his muscles. Forgetting. Simply not thinking of anything.

Nando turned off the tap, reducing the jet of water to a thin trickle which he anticipated – after strenuous efforts to stop it nearly took the tap right off – was going to frustrate his attempts to sleep that night.

"Carlos Calvo Street," he repeated automatically, stepping out of the bathroom with a towel wrapped around his waist.

"Do you know it?"

"No, but it sounds like San Telmo."

"We could walk there…"

He *knew* it! And he also knew that this neutral territory demanded some concession from him, and all the better if it were not an important one. It was an old trick, a favourite tactic of the Leopard in the film by Visconti.

"We could," he said, and Ana smiled.

197

After that they had gone down to breakfast, and in the restaurant they were greeted by the same concierge, his ineffable smile revealing a gold tooth.

"It's free for guests," he said, showing them into a kind of anteroom that looked onto the street. The hotel's bar was also open to passers-by who stumbled upon it, or who already knew it.

Three men wearing blue overalls with sleeves rolled up were drinking coffee and talking quietly. Nando and Ana sat at a table beside a large, arched window, the one they had seen from outside, adorned with plaster mouldings, and as they ate breakfast, they tried not to listen to the men's conversation.

"I'm telling you," said the one who was sitting across from them, "another bright idea like that and they'll blow all our brains out."

"But..."

"I'm just letting you know..."

Ana and Nando fixed their eyes on the street, uneasily remembering the incident on their journey. Every so often, however, it was impossible to avoid glancing at one of those animated faces.

"We should go," said Nando. "That street isn't very near and, if we're walking, we need to get a move on."

It seemed to Nando that all cities were essentially the same. For years, the old folk had talked to him about Budapest, so that now he felt that he knew it as well as if he had lived there himself. He imagined that the avenues of that city were like those of Paris, or the Cañada in Córdoba, offering an uncluttered vista that took in trees of a bluish green and houses fronted with white stone and marble. Lanz laughed when Nando described these impressions, and Ana looked at him pityingly. But Ilse would step in to say that yes, he was right and that Hungarian avenues had much in common with Parisian ones, and that, in general, they were not so different from the ones in the city of Córdoba. Not at all different, Lanz added then, staunchly. The intimate and shabby harmony of Rome, the monumental symmetry of Vienna, the perfect castles of Györ, the factories of Linz, the wonderful decrepitude of Prague, the rigidity of Brno and the hills of Temésvar, the clarity of Belgrade and streets of Kiev, the villages on yellow and green plains – as flat as the ancients had once believed the world to be – which the old folk referred to there as "*puszta*" and here as "pampas", the similarity between the peoples who inhabited those villages, all of them nervous of anything that was new or out of the daily run... Lanz was right: city streets were the same everywhere in the world. Perhaps there would not be an acacia tree in Europe, but a chestnut; there would not be perfect lime trees, but perfect oaks or beeches, and the paving stones there had seen a few centuries' more traffic than the ones here – but the essence, the core, the heart of cities was the same, be it Chile Street, or Corrientes, Andrássy, the Champs-Elysées or the Cañada.

For Ana, Buenos Aires was not like other cities at all. She looked at the big town houses on street corners, with their high windows of glass panes, imagining the daily life that went on behind crocheted curtains, that were as fussy and artificial as the women she had seen strolling along the pavements with handbags and hairpieces, wilting in the heat. Some of them lugged about plastic carryalls with cane handles as they hurried back from the supermarket with expressions of great anxiety.

Back home they had also felt the effect of price increases produced by the famous petrodollars, of which there seemed to be an endless supply – but the situation never got too serious. Lanz and Ilse had got used to providing certain basics for themselves. Lanz's goats were sacred, and then there were the geese that Ilse allowed to roam free, Nando's fish, which they pickled, green vegetables, fresh from the valley and magically conveyed to the jars which Ilse, with the greatest care, sealed with wax to prevent contamination. They could even do without alcohol, although Nando every so often brought them bottles of commercial wine.

When there is nothing around you, when there is no one, you do not need much more than the basics to survive. Here people had telephones, probably one in every house or apartment – although, judging by the number of people queuing to use two public telephone boxes they had passed, a private telephone might still be considered a luxury – and there were television sets, only in black and white, but at least here they had aerials that were better adjusted to avoid the disruption to the picture that they had to put up with in the country. Cars circulating in the streets were quite modern, not decrepit and with rusting panels like the ones back home, and surely not like the ones that you would find in any European city. But this city, with its florists and its scent of jasmine and bakeries, its graffiti on the walls and even on the pavements, its secret meetings and conspiracies, was a very particular place. This was no Budapest graced by the Danube: a bilious, ugly river spilt over its banks, a dirty bus terminal darkening its doors.

When Ana was younger and used to come into the centre to meet her father, the chaos of it all was monstrous to her. Her father, in such a context, seemed equally monstrous, or more so. The neon marquees on Corrientes Street both repulsed and fascinated her, but she did not understand them, she did not understand the bustle of the centre, that sophisticated, meaningless grime to which her father was apparently oblivious. All of which led her – as she walked beside Nando in the ambiguous tranquillity of Almagro – to a conclusion that was both sweet and sad: she was no longer the person she had been. She no longer loved the same people, and that city which she had once hated for its transient quality she now experienced as somewhere special.

Now they were walking – Nando quickly, Ana slowly – along Carlos Calvo Street. Nando calculated that they might be in the district of Caballito. They were definitely in the southern zone because Rivadavia – one of the few avenues he remembered well – was on the right, towards the river. The road sloped downwards, imperceptibly to start with, but as they walked on, the gradient became more marked. The shops and businesses they were passing were downmarket, quite shabby, mostly lottery-ticket sellers and workshops. A funeral parlour caught their attention because of its gaudy façade, and because it was the very first house on the avenue they had been looking for. "The dead deserve a little respect," said Nando, but there was nothing else noteworthy until, a few blocks on, they passed a monumental public building in the style of those they had seen in the centre, such as the Post Office, or the Obras Sanitarias, headquarters of the water company.

Pedro Goyena Avenue struck them as too wide, as if someone had removed the boulevard that should run down the middle, complete with lamp posts and flowers. After they passed that building, which occupied an entire block and was surrounded by iron railings and rubber trees, the street seemed to slope more steeply. The lofty *tipas* trees, weeping sap and parasites, became entwined over the asphalt, meeting in an embrace some twenty metres above the ground that transformed the street into a dense, greenish-grey ravine. The houses on either side were increasingly old and grand, tight-lipped beneath the *tipas'* shady embrace.

That bustling stretch of shops and pedestrians had given way to a more sombre neighbourhood. Silence rebounded off the sides of the great houses, each with pillars and porch, with front gardens hidden from view by exquisite ironwork from another era. Light glanced off the flat, shining leaves of rubber trees in stone flowerpots, and purplish mulberry trees darkened the passageways that could just be glimpsed behind the railings. As Ana walked on through the half-light of that opulent, residential neighbourhood, she was suddenly overwhelmed by a memory of the blood that had covered Pedro's body and the bruises on his skin, which were the same colour as those mulberries. There was almost no one in the street. The odd doorman, ensconced in blue uniform, could be seen polishing bronze statues in the few modern homes that interrupted the impeccable classicism of Pedro Goyena Street.

They continued down the hill, riding the silence, until they reached the number that had been written on the paper: 963. In fact it was a house positioned opposite the opening of a small side street. Perhaps for that reason, it received a little more light than the other houses, and Ana and Nando could get a good look at it from the other side of the road. It was square and solid, two storeys high; the upstairs windows followed hard rectangular lines and sported shutters painted in racing green. These were all closed and between the columns of a balustrade they could see two large tubs of dead geraniums. Downstairs, an imposing porch, surmounted by an arch, was closed behind a black iron gate. At the side of the house, they could glimpse a long white passage with walls that were covered in ivy. The rest of the place looked as abandoned and shuttered up as the rooms upstairs. The house was flanked by a strip of wasteland behind a thick wall that was in such bad repair you could easily see through it to the land beyond. On the other side was a house that looked older yet more lively, with succulent plants as green as lettuces sprouting out of pots in the garden and on the balconies, and lit-up windows in which long drapes were drawn open. Opposite, where Ana and Nando were standing, there was a traditional-looking school with doors and windows that came to sharp points, recalling Arab architecture, or the Gothic style of European churches. There seemed to be no classes taking place, but given that it was summer, there was nothing unusual in that. However, beside the door, on the pristine and embellished wall of that strange building, someone had stuck up a paper sign that read "Farewell *Sui Generis*".

Having failed to discern whatever secret the abandoned house might be trying to conceal, Ana made to cross the road, but Nando stopped her. "What do you think you are doing?" he asked, and Ana was not sure how to answer. It was true that no one was going to respond to the ancient knocker on iron gate, nor the doorbell – if that splendidly anachronistic stately manor even had such a thing. They would not find anything in the wasteland, and talking to the people at the house on the right might raise suspicion or even be dangerous. After fifteen minutes standing opposite the house, there was not much more that they could do.

So they walked slowly back up the hill, Ana pondering the meaning of that elegant and shuttered house, closed to the world, while Nando had the strange impression of having been buried for several hours and cut off from the rest of the city. It was nearly two o' clock in the afternoon. The sunlight hurt their eyes. They had already passed the enormous public building: only on their return had they noticed the combative graffiti that covered its walls. Those words, scrawled in red or black on a surface that was already obscured by the attempts of many previous graffitists, floated between them, in a silence that had been lengthening since a dark green and heavy mood had enveloped them a few blocks back.

When the silence was broken, it was not by either of them, but by a woman enclosed within a heavily barred balcony on one of the old houses they passed. "Do you have a cigarette?" she asked, extending one arm between the bars, the palm of her hand open. She was a young woman, with hair brushed back, small and untidy, wearing glasses with lenses that were so thick you could barely see her eyes behind the misty haloes. "Do you have a cigarette?" she asked again, insistent, and Ana took a packet out of her bag and offered her one. No sooner had she grabbed it than the woman put it in a pocket and stretched out her arm again, with the open hand. "Do you have a cigarette?" she demanded once more, this time of Nando. Nando watched her, but did not move. Ana, roused from her stupor, observed this scene with the lively curiosity of an anthropologist. Nando had an aversion to the mentally ill. For all his imperturbable expression, she knew that he was petrified, unable to walk on or to answer the woman. Gently she took his hand and pulled him towards the corner, waving goodbye to the woman on the balcony as she did so. Only after they had walked two more blocks did he murmur: "She was bonkers." And Ana replied that perhaps she had just wanted two cigarettes.

They made a long detour around the grand public building, then found themselves once more at the start of the avenue. On the street corner two puny *tipas* trees were fighting for survival, neither yet reaching the height of the traffic lights. At the demarcation line (you might almost say the "frontier") between one neighbourhood and the next, there was a small, sombre-looking hotel with an arched façade, an old house that must once have looked rather glamorous and quietly sure of itself. Behind ornate, orange balconies, the windows were draped with delicate lace curtains, hiding with genteel ambiguity the splendour, or deterioration, of the rooms behind them. Ana noticed the name – Hotel San Lorenzo – and the damp, cool breeze that blew, like a rush of fresh air, from its dark entrance hall.

For some reason she knew that she would return, and that it would be a good place to spend the night.

After that incident with the woman on the balcony, and their long, calming walk along Carlos Calvo Avenue, Nando agreed to sit down for a while in a bar. It was half-past two in the afternoon of their second day in the capital, and events back home, on the Melancolía Sound, were taking on the quality of a dream. While they had lunch – both observing with amazement the unfamiliar urban life around them – they tried to relate the strange new information about Pedro to all that they knew about him, from the moment he had been thrown into the ravine. Who might Pedro be? What was his connection to the beautiful, abandoned house in that very well-to-do part of the city? What was that grubby, carefully folded piece of paper doing in the inside pocket of Pedro's coat? Any conclusion continued to elude them, just as it had before they started their journey.

In the afternoon, they went to a cinema on Corrientes Street. That area, quite unlike the one through which they had walked in the morning, was strongly reminiscent of Víktor and the old-fashioned bars in which Ana used to meet him on matters of finance, or organization, but never simple affection. On the last occasion, for instance, Víktor had taken her to an office that looked something like the branch of a foreign bank, with three or four people who spoke German and very little Spanish beavering away behind wooden desks and typewriters. This office occupied one floor of an old building on one of the streets perpendicular to Corrientes, some way off from the excitement of the cafés and theatres. The air smelt of mothballs and cleaning products: Ana thought that all Germany – its streets, squares, roads and rooms – might smell like that, but she did not dare say so to Víktor. They had gone there to arrange for Ana to have access

PAOLA KAUFMANN

to Víktor's funds using her own signature. She never asked
him where the money came from – which account, which
business, which discovery, which extortion. Víktor would
not have answered her: after his death, when "that money"
had saved Ana from having to move from La Pedrera more
than once, she no longer cared to find out. She and the old
couple were largely dependent on it.

So Corrientes Avenue, associated as it was with Víktor,
and with secrets in general, made her feel uneasy. It was
as if all the businesses, the shop windows, the neon lights
conspired to hide the truth about themselves from her,
some significant detail that went beyond the fact of being
a theatre, a bookshop, a café or a fine-wine merchant. But
going to the cinema was something they had not done for
years, so that afternoon they bought two bottles of beer
and a bag of hot sugared almonds from a man who had a
barrow on the pavement outside. Then they plunged into
the darkness, to kill some time, if nothing else.

When they came out of the cinema, something changed for
Ana. It was as though everything unclassifiable, unnameable,
secret, impenetrable, incomprehensible – all this became
condensed, suddenly, in a city that was no longer the one
she had enjoyed at midday.

It had started soon after they emerged onto the street:
there was the dim noise of an explosion and the almost
immediate response of police sirens, followed by an urgent
wail of fire engines and, rounding up the procession, an
army truck. People on the street had hastily retreated into
the buildings, taking refuge in restaurants and bars – the few
of them that had left their doors unlocked. All of a sudden,
the street in which they found themselves had been deserted,
and Ana felt on her arm the damp but decisive pressure of
Nando's hand leading her to the corner, and then to another
street and into a shop that looked, at first glance, like an

206

old ironmongers or a small and old-fashioned general store. The door was unbolted. When they stepped inside, there was a tinkle from the delicate doorbell, similar to a wind chime. Inside the shop, on the walls and in display cabinets, hanging on ropes, cables, or piled on the floor, was a curious collection of tools and implements, relating to country pursuits, many of them obsolete. Enormous screwdrivers with Bakelite handles, monkey wrenches, tiles, pulverizers and spirit levels came together in a solemn scrapyard that conjured up a long-gone era of explorers and immigrants. It was a place that her father would have relished.

The man behind the counter, who had hair of a leaden grey in keeping with his peculiar tools, watched them closely for a few seconds, before asking what they were looking for. Nando went up to the counter and, quickly casting an eye around the hundreds of objects on offer, asked for a screwdriver.

Ana stayed close to the door, looking outside. The street was still empty; the sirens sounded more distant.

"What happened?" asked the man, returning from a back room with a red screwdriver in his hands.

"We don't know," said Nando.

So began Ana's sensation of having leapt into a parallel universe. From that moment, everything seemed unreal: the exorbitantly expensive taxi ride, the frugal dinner in the hotel's bar, the business of the locked windows. "We're going tomorrow," said Nando, before turning over in bed. Ana tried to reassure him with a caress that was devoid of any erotic intent, but she knew that it was useless.

At 2.35 in the morning she woke up, got quietly out of bed and dressed in the bathroom with the light off, fixing her hair with a clasp. Ten minutes later she was in the street, the night still and muggy, as dark as that time she had found herself alone in the middle of the lake.

She never stopped to ask herself what she was doing there. She only knew that she had to go to the hotel she had seen early that afternoon, the Hotel San Lorenzo. She had remembered the address and look of the place, and the best route there, with a precision worthy of a cartographer. It did not occur to her to wonder if this were some dream or hallucination.

She simply began to walk in darkness, retracing her steps towards that other hotel with the peachy-coloured balconies, and back towards the mysterious house on Pedro Goyena avenue.

Later she did remember that, after walking for five or six blocks, she had taken a taxi that seemed to float down the street, slow and solitary as a premonition. She would have sworn that the taxi driver was the very man who had served them in the tool shop, except that, deprived of his usual context, he could seem another person altogether.

By taxi, then, she had arrived at Carlos Calvo Avenue, at the point where it joined Pedro Goyena Street, a place plunged into mortal silence. The dawn light made a ghostly spectacle of what she had seen that morning in the sun: Carlos Calvo was like the entrance to a monastery, whereas Pedro Goyena, as far as the eye could see, was one big carnival illuminated by flaming torches and electric lights, the orangey tones reflected and multiplied in the canopy of the *tipas* trees. It looked like one long circus tent, connected to a mysterious voltage – exactly the opposite of the street she had been in a few hours before. That discovery, far from disconcerting Ana, filled her with a childish joy at the prospect of walking the length of the street again, and seeing once more the house which shortly before had seemed so lifeless.

The taxi drew up in front of the hotel. Ana recognized its façade, even though the sign that had been there in the morning had disappeared. In its place, a string of flowers and interwoven boughs adorned the upper part of the door frame like a rare garland. There was a light in the hall, and the balconies seemed to be illuminated by Chinese lanterns in different colours.

"Is this it?" asked the taxi driver.

"This is it," she said (she could not remember later how she paid for the journey).

Feeling no surprise at the transformation the place had undergone, Ana made her way through the hall to an outsized counter made of lacquered wood that was polished like ebony. The room was small, but with a ceiling so high that it was entirely lost in the dark upper reaches. It was lit by several old kerosene lamps. Ana thought for a moment that Ilse would like a hotel with no electric light, then suddenly she realized that this memory of Ilse was prompted not by the lamps, but by the woman who was standing behind the counter in an apron, slim and stooped, her hair gathered in a hairnet. Ana was startled to see her, and waited for some sign of recognition on the part of the old woman, but she received nothing more than a kindly smile.

"Good evening."

"Good evening," answered Ana, and she added, unable to help herself: "Mutti?"

"I beg your pardon?" asked the woman, raising an eyebrow but still smiling.

Ana shook her head. "It must be the light," she said quietly.

"Does the light bother you?"

"No, it's fine. Do you have a room for the night?"

"A room?"

"To spend the night. Only for today, not longer."

The woman looked at her with a kind of pity, just as Ilse did whenever Ana asked her about the past.

"You don't have one..." said Ana, guessing as much from the woman's expression.

"No, it's not that. The thing is, this is not a hotel, señorita."

"But the sign outside says Hotel San Lorenzo..."

"Hotel San Lorenzo? Where does it say such a thing?"

Ana realized then that the sign must have been replaced or covered by that garland adorning the door.

"That was what it said yesterday morning…"

"Yesterday morning we were disinfecting, señorita. Cockroaches. They get everywhere and the only solution is to fumigate with professional equipment. They're revolting!"

Revolting! That was also what Ilse said, every time she found a cockroach or some other insect scuttling across the floor or on the walls.

The woman was watching her now with a mixture of curiosity and irritation.

"So… you say that this is not the Hotel San Lorenzo," repeated Ana, squinting in a last attempt to reveal Ilse's true likeness.

"No, I'm sorry. Have a good evening, señorita."

"Yes. I'm sorry to have bothered you. I think I've got the wrong block."

"It must be that."

"It must be. Goodnight."

"I'll come with you, then I can lock the door."

Outside on the pavement, Ana looked back at the door, disconcerted. The garland had transformed the wall, with its balconies and windows, into a giant mocking face. She reflected for a moment on the black counter under the orange light, on the open hall and the illuminated balconies. But the decisive noise of a lock turning was followed by that of a heavy bolt, like the kind that might secure a vault, or the hatch of a submarine, and she moved quickly on towards the sloping part of the street.

The monumental public building was lit up like some ungainly and misshapen Christmas tree. What might they be celebrating inside? She could hear the murmur of people behind the graffiti-daubed walls. They seemed to be enjoying a party with great merriment and hoopla. But there was no entrance in the perimeter wall, no chink through which she could spy on them. The building was sealed shut, while the party raged on in its guts. Outside on the street a carnival atmosphere also prevailed. Passers-by, each one looking more outlandish than the last, appeared to have hijacked the neighbourhood and made it the setting for a masquerade. But this was not the usual sort of South American street party, with people in fancy dress costumes. Each thing had literally become something else, and there was a sense of people enjoying a rush of freedom and joy in a prohibited street. The apartment blocks, the frigid and imposing mansions, the bronze door-knockers and silent rubber trees: everything had been altered, without losing the enigmatic quality she had seen in daylight hours. That same quality, now at dawn, shone beneath the flaming dome of the *tipas* trees, in the flickering glow of the candles at every window, filtered through elegant shutters.

In the lower, darker part of the avenue, the school they had seen opposite the house was now glowing with a phosphorescent light, its arabesques so accentuated by their own shadows that the place resembled a small Gothic cathedral. Inside it people also seemed to be celebrating carnival, with music from a violin orchestra spilling onto the street. Ana glimpsed tables with red tablecloths and little votive lanterns, glowing like amber cocoons; a naked, pale-skinned man whose damp hair clung to his forehead, an old man with a long white beard throwing back his head in stentorian laughter... the smell of sweat and withered flowers, all tinged with a brothel atmosphere. Ana recognized – how would she not – the wild abandonment of the Hungarian dances Ilse had played when she and Klára were little and used to play at hiding her scores. She could almost feel beneath her fingers the yellowing staves, the name of Brahms in starchy lettering, presiding over that orphanage of notes that made no sense to them.

Very close, a block away, she saw a tram pass – the first she had ever seen. It crossed the entrance to the street in a hiss of cables, as weightless as if it were a whale swimming on the high sea. All around her was merriment and movement, but the house for which she had gone to look, in stark opposition to the music and bacchanalian revelry of the night, remained as silent as a medieval fortress. The porch was dark and locked up, the upstairs rooms cloistered like a convent, the plants were still dead in their pots.

Ana sat on the kerb and hid her face in her hands. Then, through the gaps between her fingers, she saw light filtering beneath a door at the side of the house. It was barely noticeable, a mere thread that could have been taken for the reflection of a street lamp.

Ana slowly approached the side door, to all purposes locked, and found that the heavy handle moved under her hand, with a gasp of oiled hinges. It opened only a crack, enough to reveal a passage: the light that she had seen from the kerb was coming from the end of that passage, filtering beneath another door, this time to the side, hidden by the wall's angle. On the white garden fence, a dense wild ivy absorbed any rays that may have permeated through holes in the whitewashed panels; the whole place possessed the density of a quasar, a voracious gravity. Ana opened the door a little more, and slipped furtively inside, before closing it behind her.

Without having planned it, she found herself, finally, on the other side. In principle, this "other side" consisted of that ivy-clad corridor and two thick lines of cobblestones separated by a flower bed. On her right, on a door protected by a domed porch, a bronze knocker in the shape of a lion's head invited her to poke her fingers in its yawning gullet. A milky pale light was dispersed now among the rubber trees' dark leaves, glancing off the teeth of that beast that was bidding her come in. Ana grasped the knocker firmly, undaunted, but then the lion's head came away from its clasp like butter. The shock made her drop it suddenly, and the head was lost in the earthy darkness of a flower bed. Then she tried to knock on the door with bare knuckles, but the sound simply vanished in the dense wood.

She retraced her steps and, following the wall of the house, she made her way to the end of the passage and the source of that frail light. At the end of the passage, the path turned left, forming the bottom part of an L-shape which comprised a covered gallery and the remains of a courtyard overgrown with tangled trees and vegetation.

Various doors led off the gallery, all of them closed but for one.

This tall door with open shutters, together with the window beside it, seemed to belong to a kitchen or a utility room. A weak light, bleached by curtains rippling at the window, trickled like water into the rest of the garden, bestowing a ghostly sheen, a lunar quality on the ceramic pots. In the dark, accustomed as she was to finding her way in nature's true night, Ana crept to the edge of the window, listening out for sounds and movement, and peered inside through a gap at the side of the curtain.

It was, in effect, the inside of a kitchen dining room, lit from a single ceiling lamp that focused a beam of light onto the centre of a little table. In the parts of the room that were not plunged in darkness, she picked out a row of cupboards, an oven, a kettle and little else. However, it was not the room's objects that caught her attention, but the extraordinary group that was gathered around the table, quietly playing cards.

There were four of them beneath the light, and a fifth who, head bowed, was sitting beside the oven, perhaps sleeping or warming his feet. To start with, when Ana saw how the skimpy tablecloth revealed several pairs of minute shoes swinging far above the floor, she thought that these must be children. But just then, one of them got up – or rather down – from his chair, so that his whole tubby body, with its brawny little shoulders, was suddenly brutally exposed to that torrent of light, as though he were standing in a spotlight at the circus. On his feet, the dwarf barely surpassed the height of the table. The other three, dressed identically in black, watched as he made his way to the oven, lit it with some effort, standing on tiptoe, then shook the fifth member of the group, who was, as Ana had suspected, fast asleep. But it proved impossible to wake him: the sleeper slept on without budging an inch.

Back at the table, the dwarf struggled to climb back onto his chair, and Ana noticed that the others made no attempt to help him.

With her back flat against the wall, watching the scene from one side and out of the corner of her eye, she followed their conversation with difficulty.

"...now they call it the 'thanatic impulse'" – this came from the one who had got up and then returned to his seat opposite the door. "Modern nonsense, psychoanalytic mumbo-jumbo. People just don't want to accept the truth!"

The one who was on his left, wearing thick glasses and a thicker moustache, put the pack in front of the little man Ana could only see from behind, in a silent invitation to cut. Then he quickly shuffled the cards, and started to deal them from his right.

"Blind," said the first one to have received a card, without waiting for his friend to finish dealing, and he put some coins on the table.

"And what is the truth?" asked the one who had his back to Ana.

"That man is an animal," said the other, beaming as he turned over his cards and arranged them in what he clearly imagined to be a splendid fan. "Now they want to tame him, they want to make him docile with culture and all that rubbish, but they can't disguise his true nature: he's a killer animal."

The moustachioed one concentrated on his cards without saying anything.

The last one, closest to Ana, with a wrinkled profile and a balding pate off which the light bounced, did not even lift his cards from the table.

"No animal is a killer by nature. Jacks open then?"

"Yes, two jacks. Who says that? Nature is the engine for everything: fighting, competition, killing, even infanticide. Take lions. Here in the zoo they're pretty dumb animals, but on the plains where they live in Africa, the solitary male will attack a female with young – you know, if she's from a different territory. They leave the lionesses alone, but they'll kill the young straight off, one by one. With no cubs, the female is ready to fall pregnant again by the very murderer of her own offspring."

The one who had got up before (and who, it seemed, was meant to be opening the game) thumped the table twice. The others eyed him warily.

"Don't get started..."

"He's a wily old fox..."

The balding one studied his cards, then placed his bet.

"I'll bet twenty," he said, and pushed a fistful of chips into the middle of the table. "I think that aggression between animals of the same species has to mean something."

"I call," said the one sitting with his back to Ana, and he added something that she did not hear, which made the others laugh.

The one with the moustache flung his chips down in the middle of the table.

"It's good that the winner takes all. It's better for the species, because his progeny will be stronger and better fighters, so they will conquer more territory and females and have more progeny and so on until..."

Then the one who had got up said languidly:

"I call your twenty and I raise you twenty."

"We should take out the seven to have a better game," said the one with the moustache.

"No!" chorused the other two, and the one who had doubled the stake smiled.

"...until they rule supreme. But the secret is that the real enemy of a species is not the one who can eat it, but the one who can take away its food supply. Most of the time the enemy is within, not outside," he said, casting a sideways glance at his emboldened friend.

The balding one scratched his forehead in a clear demonstration of scepticism.

"He's bluffing," he said.

"I don't know if that's the case," said the one with his back to Ana, "but without aggression, there would be so many animals that they would suffer twice as much, because they would either die of hunger or get eaten. You could say that aggression within a species ensures a better distribution of resources for all."

"I'll call your twenty. Not for everyone, only for the strongest."

More chips were pushed towards the middle of the table.

"I call," the one with his back to her said, and Ana heard the clinking of more chips. "Well in this case, it's the same: 'the species' are necessarily the strongest, because they came from strong stock, and they've been eliminating the weak ones over time. Besides," he added, "the pack mentality is not always bad: real hunters, carnivores like lions or tigers, cannot attack a pack. They can't concentrate when there is so much prey. So there is in fact safety in numbers. Even so, there's always one who wants to single himself out, act the hero..."

The moustachioed one said: "Pass."

And he added: "So packs are a form of defence... but why don't they kill each other then?"

"Cards, gentlemen?"

"Three," said the one who had doubled the stake.

"One," said the balding one.

"Going for a straight, eh? Even our dead friend could have guessed that."

"What's it to you? Mind your own business."

The one with his back to her ignored the change of cards for a moment, and addressed the moustachioed one's question.

"They don't kill each other, because Nature is wise. For example, do you know why turkeys don't kill their little chicks? Because their little chicks go 'cheep, cheep, cheep, cheep'... The chicks' chirping inhibits the turkey, but if the chick cannot chirp, or if the turkey is deaf, she pecks them all to death. In other words, all of us are murderers, the thing differentiating us is merely the kind of chirping that holds each one of us back."

A thoughtful silence descended on the players.

"Cards?" persisted the one with the moustache.

"Stick," answered the one with his back to her finally, and his little voice, mild and self-conscious, had the effect of a bomb going off in the middle of the kitchen.

"He hasn't got anything!"

"He's trying to keep us in the hand..."

The man with the moustache did not deal any more; quietly withdrawing from the game, he limited himself to watching, with great concentration, what was left of the round, while urging the one who had doubled the stake in the first round to do the same again.

This man had asked for three cards, but faced with the call of "stick", he passed. He did not even look at the cards that had been dealt him. He seemed to have decided that he would wait and see what happened with the others.

"Sometimes," he said, holding his cards between thumb and ring finger, then lightly plopping them on the table, "being another animal from the same species is no protection. Rats live in families and defend each other within these groups, but when a rat from another clan shows up, they tear it apart. They have family feuds, like the Mafia. What difference is there between a man and a rat? None! Why are you so proud of not seeing what's so obvious?"

When the bald one turned over his new card, he blew out his cheeks in disgust.

"Fold," he said, and he threw it down with the others on top of the table.

Then the enigmatic "sticker" piped up:

"My friend, if men were as proud of their digestive systems as you are of your brain, this species would have become extinct some time ago as a result of diarrhoea. And I'll give you another exclusive piece of information: if you want to see my cards it's going to cost you another fifty."

And lazily he added a fistful of chips to the shining booty in the centre of the table. Now two of them were left face to face. Ana could only see the face of the dwarf who had got up at the beginning. The one with a moustache now got down from his chair with exactly the same effort, and went to the fifth individual, who languished silent and immobile in the shadows close to the oven. He shook him a little. He moved his hand back and forth, wiggling the fingers. One finger remained at right angles to the back of the hand. There was a muffled crunch that made Ana's heart jump.

"Rumpelstiltskin! Is that necessary?" the balding one shouted with exasperation, but his attention was still with the two opponents still in the game.

Until that moment, hypnotized by the conversation, Ana had been oblivious to an obvious detail: the fifth member of the gathering, alone in his corner of the kitchen, was dead.

The two dwarfs who had got up had gone to check on the advance of his rigor mortis, and the second had broken his finger. Ana realized, too, that she had started to shake.

The one opposite her sighed.

"Oh dear... Are you going to make me pay to see them? This chat is so interesting..."

But his pitying tone evaporated when he saw the first of the three new cards. He laid it face-up together with the two previous ones, and he showed them all, so that Ana too managed to see the three aces that the dwarf was flaunting so smugly.

"With these three alone I see your grubby fifty and I'm all in," he said, and burst into sharp, disagreeable cackling.

The one with his back to her took his time. Ana could not see what it was he was turning over obsessively in his fingers, though, going by the sound, it was the chips he had left, slippery from the sweat on his palms.

Finally he answered:

"I'll pay to see the other two."

The other immediately displayed his hand in a perfect fan: he had the three aces and two nines.

"Full house!" whooped the one with the moustache, who had returned to the table.

The bald one clapped his chubby little hands together, waving his legs in the air.

The one opposite Ana was still looking expectantly, with eyes as black and smooth as tar. He still held his fan up in his hand. A shining thread of saliva trickled from the corner of his half-opened mouth.

"And?"

"They're better than mine," conceded the other, and he placed his cards face down on the deck.

The winner, with a hoarse squawk of triumph, threw himself onto the table and gathered up all the chips.

Ana was aware now of the physical effort she was making to keep her body flat against the wall. She could feel every irregularity in the bricks, their roughness, their temperature behind her head. Her hands ran with a cold, sticky sweat: if she had gone there looking for Pedro, she had to accept that the closest she would get was the dead man who was splayed on the chair in the gloom of the kitchen.

The dwarfs seemed to be preparing for another hand: one was busy shuffling the cards, another was collecting the chips, while a third handled the bottle of whisky that had magically appeared on the table. The fifth remained in place, immobile. By bringing her head a few millimetres forwards, Ana could see his arm hanging at the side of the chair, the hand with the index finger that was completely bent back, and finally his legs, extending to the floor, and the vague shape of a slipper, and she knew that the dead man was not a dwarf like the others. Once again she remembered the appearance of Pedro in the hospital, Pedro in the ravine with his arm bent back and broken, his head lying in a pool of water, moss and blood. She wanted to vomit. Feeling the retching begin in her diaphragm, she peeled herself away from the wall and stepped back into the shadowy area of the gallery, far from the window. She walked first, stumbling, then ran the few metres left to the garden door.

Once back on the pavement, she kept running back to the top of the avenue. After a few metres she stopped to lean against a stunted ash tree, daunted in the bestial presence of the *tipas* trees. The early-morning breeze swept across her face in a half-hearted attempt at refreshment, but Ana could not contain her nausea and, kneeling on the ground beside the graceless tree trunk, her forehead pressed against its cool bark, she vomited.

She slept until noon. Nando avoided asking any questions. Over a late lunch, Ana scrutinized him, wondering if he knew about her nocturnal escapade, then wondering about the events themselves, everything that had happened from the moment she had consulted the clock and seen the luminous hands indicating 2.35 a.m.

Transformed like an alchemist after a series of exquisite and dangerous experiments, Ana felt that she had, in her own way, made her peace with Pedro, but that she still needed to make peace with the monster. What strange revelation lay in wait for her that day with Guzmán?

While she prepared to go to the Science Museum, her mind retraced the steps that had taken her back to the house on Pedro Goyena Street, the taxi driver who had taken her, the woman who looked like Ilse, the half-open garden door, the kitchen with the dwarfs and their heated game of cards, the dead man in the chair with the broken finger, the vomiting, the fog under cover of which she returned to a new-minted city.

The last thing she remembered about that fantastical night was the slow, vaporous passing of the tram, how it seemed suspended in the air as though its long body were part of a merry-go-round. That and also the reflection of her face in a window – her blank eyes, her expression empty as a sleepwalker's.

7

Guzmán

You must retire, Professor. Take your collection of rats with you, take whatever you like, but then retire once and for all, for the love of God. There is nothing for you to do here any more, and there are people who need the space. Young people eager to work with new, fresh ideas. You, who no longer have any, should take retirement, Professor Guzmán, and be grateful for the time you have had at the institute. Retire gracefully, without complaint... Why would you have cause to complain anyway, if you have always done as you wished here?

They said it to his face now, though perhaps not exactly in those words: scientists tend to be polite, and bureaucrats like to avoid rudeness or anything approaching a scene. Anyway, Lucas Guzmán had no intention of giving either group what they wanted. He had worked at the museum for too long and had fully earned that little "space" which they now claimed, as if it had once belonged to them – those petty bureaucrats, those dimwits who reduced laboratories and workshops to mere "space". And he had earned it fair and square. He had published (admittedly some time ago, but should he feel obliged to match the output of a thirty-year-old at the age of sixty-seven?) as much as or more than the young people in whose name they wanted to take away his laboratory of evolutionary palaeontology, built up over forty years. Why, he had taught those young people himself, and also, paradoxically, the bureaucrats who were coming to him now with their demands. Young people – how ironic:

223

in his day it had been the old wrecks who wanted to snatch away your position, and now the tables seemed to have been turned. He, a monument to old wrecks, was the one doomed to be dispossessed.

Not only had he published more than them: he had single-handedly created the only rodentia collection in all of South America incorporating living and extinct species, all so that some of those new collectors of photos, those know-it-alls and conference-goers (as if you could sell a scientific education with a fancy whiteboard and a few catchy sub-headings) could come and tell him to trot off quietly home to Tigre with his "rat collection", so that they could "free up" the space for something else.

He had not created problems, just a collection of rodentia, but as far as they were concerned, rodents were no more than that: rodents, nasty little rats, varieties of kitchen mouse – and the museum was there for other things.

The museum was there to *show* things, and what was necessary for the noble purposes of an exhibition? Why, space! So, out with the laboratories, bin the collections, the skeletons, the casts and the old archives of stones that dated back to the Ameghino brothers. To hell with everything that could not be sold! Off it goes to the incinerator!

But he was not going to give them the satisfaction. Naturally, he no longer had any power, though once he had been able to exercise some scanty influence within the stratified organization of the museum. He no longer had responsibility for anyone (they had all left, though at least with a good education, thought Guzmán). He could not even use the stock of paraffin wax or the Sweiss microtomes, those marvels of Scandinavian technology which were now considered useless for everything except display – yet another "exhibit" – in serious oak cabinets. A microtome, for the love of God! A useful and perfectly functioning tool! But no: these days instruments were considered to be "artifacts", just as laboratories were "spaces", "research proposals" were "projects". Everything was piled up on shelves because it was fashionable to display things, but not fashionable to employ one's mind in anything more useful than how best to present a fossil. And if that fossil came from a prehistoric animal of great dimensions, better still.

Guzmán passed his hands over his bald head and heaved a sigh. In his time he had felt a devotion for, even an obsession with these animals, but he had also grown weary of them, to the point of abandoning them in favour of rodents, so much smaller and more humble. Why had he become disillusioned? Was it possible for anyone to tire of imagining a wild world populated by the most extraordinary and magnificent beasts that had ever existed?

Perhaps the right word was not exactly "weary", but he could not be bothered to dredge up a better one. At this stage in his life, Guzmán had ended up regarding such a passion (in fact any passion) as something dangerous – *too dangerous* – and, just like an opium addict ravaged by his need, he had sealed the doors of his house, obliterated the path to the smoking den, buried the pipe and the bottle of laudanum, then cut off his hands so as never to touch the stuff again.

Was that the right way to put it? Perhaps not exactly, but mental apathy obliged him to collapse some thoughts into metaphors that would be more worthy of a soap-opera writer than a scientist.

Unfortunately for those who wanted him long gone, old age had not taken too much of a toll on him: he still took the stairs to the fifth floor every day, and could recall the taxonomy of every one of the specimens he had managed to add to the collection without thinking twice. In spite of himself, he conserved a rigorous memory, although sometimes Guzmán thought that it must be the other way around, and that his memory was keeping him, because nowadays it contained more things he would have liked to forget. Some of them had to do with prehistoric animals, though Guzmán had also learnt to salt away those obsessive thoughts, those images of magnificent strange animals – monsters of land and water – that he could reconstruct simply by seeing the half-finished cast of a skeleton in the corridor of the museum's basement. In his imagination, they came vividly to life among the foul-smelling, poisonous plants and yellow swamps, curdled by sulphur and methane.

But Guzmán knew how to halt the process: he simply thought of any rodent, and concentrated on classifying it in reverse, that is, from the present to the past, following the evolutionary line of common ancestors to reptiles and even further back, as far as his fantasies permitted, allowing for a few long shots and slip-ups. After a few seconds of this, the monsters disappeared.

He had adapted that same evasive technique to dispel other annoyances in his life, such as those bureaucrats who came to his office whining about "space" and "retirement", or when Señora Hilda, his "housekeeper" (Céline had given her that ridiculous title and he had not only failed to oppose it at the time, but had let Hilda keep it after Céline did her moonlight flit) – Hilda the Executioner, he would have liked to call her – told him off because Guzmán insisted on cooking at night and leaving the apartment dirty. "This is a filthy pit!" she admonished, flushed and defiant, her head writhing with serpents, the *Hildagorgon*. Meanwhile he, perhaps a little cowardly, mentally rewound the universal history of the *mus musculus*, or common mouse, a modest specimen of which the outraged woman was dangling by the tail, compressed and dried thanks to the poison the Executioner herself sprinkled under tables and along skirting boards in sufficient quantities to extinguish the whole species.

That, of course, was the *mus musculus* species, from the old and much-loved Linnaeus, of the genus *mus*, also Linnaeus, subfamily Murinae – Illiger's classification, at the start of the 1800s – family Muridae, includes what those flunkies at the museum collectively call "rats", suborder Myomorpha, order Rodentia, Bowditch's classification, also nineteenth century, infraclass Eutheria, subclass disputed, class Mammalia, Linnaeus again, eighteenth century, subphylum Vertebrata, phylum Chordata and Kingdom: animalia.

And so the *Hildagryph*, the *Hildasalamander* could continue to give vent in the midst of a sepulchral silence, because Guzmán could not see her, she had disappeared and he was no longer listening to her; all that reached him was a distant murmur as he applied himself, once more, to that disputed subclass which had just come to mind and which might supply him with another fifteen minutes' mental occupation.

And there were the times that he received a note from Paris advising him that his son had suffered another relapse, but that the French state would take charge where the lad's mother could not – and much less so Guzmán with his slimmed-down salary from the museum of sciences, especially with the dollar costing three hundred pesos and with the coup that had been imminent ever since the General passed on to immortality.

All of these complications could be banished in seconds, that was why he liked rodents so much. They were easy, accessible. Like him, they kept a low profile and were mostly undemanding.

No doubt he would be calling on his special technique that afternoon, when the girl was coming to see him – but there was still a little time before that. Even if she was a punctual type, he still had at least an hour to make some coffee and go down to the café in the park to buy a sandwich. He had already given the lunch that Señora Hilda had made for him to José, who worked on the door to Administration, through which Guzmán made his triumphal entrance every morning. José was the only person he knew who appreciated the gastronomic puritanism of his housekeeper, especially since his debilitating second heart attack. Guzmán preferred not to consider the condition of his own heart and, as he was sure that he did not have many years left to live anyway, he was happy to make a gift of the lunches to prolong the life of poor José, who was much younger than him, and had various healthy children who needed him.

He, Guzmán, would probably die a spectacular and un-forgettable death, *hadn't he been thinking about that: what form to give the last ever act over which he would exercise control?* The opposite had been the case with Guzmán's father, who had succumbed to prostate cancer, a cancer he had hidden for years out of shame. Guzmán's father had been an extraordinary scientist to the end of his days. Few great men died of misfortunes that were commensurate with the lives they had lived. Kepler had died retching on a boat in the middle of a storm. Descartes had succumbed to a cold. Even Galileo had not died, as everyone supposed, under torture by the Inquisition, but as a result of a form of arthritis which plagued him for years. The pain in his bones finished him off, while he enjoyed visits from Milton in his little palace in Fiesole.

Bacon died of pneumonia, from trying to stuff a chicken with snow to see if the cold would conserve flesh (he proved the opposite with his own flesh). And if Sir Isaac Newton had not died of something foolish like mercury poisoning, then one of his many and well-deserved enemies would have killed him with an equation scrawled on a ball of paper and stuffed down his throat as far as the tonsils. No scientist had died like a Medici, stabbed twenty times in the heart or set about with an axe. Not even the emaciated Madame Curie, who was practically phosphorescent with gamma rays.

There were very few deaths like the ones Rilke demanded, made to the scale worthy of a great intellect, thought Guzmán, as he accepted once more – and with some puzzlement, in spite of all the years he had been taking him lunch – the profuse gratitude of José on receiving an insipid arrangement, a *panaché* of vegetables. Those great deaths, he told himself, are reserved for us pygmies.

One of these nights they might also take him away with his face covered, as they had a certain neighbour who lived in the building opposite, and whom he had seen, because he slept lightly and in his old age hunger or a full bladder sometimes woke him up, and, on that particular night, he had been standing at the window in the sitting room, drinking a diluted Martini – because vermouth helped him get to sleep – and then he had seen them, some in camouflage, some in mufti, dragging his neighbour into an ordinary car. He recognized his neighbour from the red pyjamas which he wore when he went out onto his balcony to water the plants. If it had not been for the red pyjamas, would he have imagined that they were taking away some delinquent? Or that those other men were policemen doing their job?

And on that night they would take him, as doubtless they had taken his neighbour, with his head wrapped in a sweater, off to some place that appeared to be remote – although in all probability it was just around the corner, the cellar of a launderette, or some harmless-looking shop – and the next day there would be a few lines in the newspaper, vague and opaque, like all the news that appeared in the papers in the last few months, to the effect that the army had carried out an operation in the capital to subdue various infractors of public order and security. But would that count as a spectacular death? Only if someone witnessed it, as he had witnessed the neighbour being taken away – otherwise he would simply have fulfilled a convenient dual purpose of disappearing for the bureaucrats and for his housekeeper. To disappear, not even to die a proper death: that was not spectacular, it certainly wasn't one hundred and twenty stab wounds or an axe blow to the temple – *because the truth was that he had no evidence that the neighbour had died, rather than ceased to exist in the configuration of everyday life* – it was a little like what had happened to the dinosaurs: suddenly they were no more, and in their place, more modest but much better equipped, the mammals which had spoilt that beautiful world of swamps and beasts.

Of course none of these musings on death and extinction could substitute for the name of that perfect rodent destined to save him from the bother of meeting that girl. For some reason he imagined her to be young, although the letter had not said much, only that she thought he might have known her father. In any case, she had not mentioned her surname and he had no interest in it; if he had any enthusiasm for remembering things, he would put it to better use – trying to reconstruct an image of his son, or of his wife, but no, he was not interested in memories. Nor did he have the slightest evidence, going on that brief letter that he had answered with a telegram, that the evening's vexation actually was a girl.

But it was nearly time, and he would have to hurry the sandwich.

Then again, perhaps not, thought Guzmán, and he smiled to himself, as he imagined the west wing of the museum, architecture's answer to the Bermuda Triangle. The corridors there were so similar to each other that one always had the sensation of going round in circles. That was also where they kept the oldest collections of skeleton casts, some examples of which had been formidably mounted. The corridors were dark and narrow and these beasts seemed to lunge from the tops of the cabinets, twisting their monstrous, misshapen bodies towards the floor. For anyone unaccustomed to such a sight – and even for those who were accustomed – those reptilian and nightmarish skeletons, with their empty eye sockets and talons, were like something you might see from a ghost train, where the smells of glue, formalin and dust, accumulated over years, help to make the experience gruesomely vivid.

Guzmán had suggested to José that he set the female visitor on a route leading through the heart of that labyrinth. As he had said this, he had handed over the implicit bribe: the *panaché* of vegetables. It *was* one of several possible routes, after all. Would José have done as he asked, or thought better of it? José was far too kind-hearted to be working at the institute: it was a wonder that they had not fired him, for all his good nature and heart attacks.

He was pondering all this, finishing off his sandwich and imagining the scene when they would find the girl's corpse, dried out like one of the mice *Hildacerberus* assassinated in her kitchen, when the door of his office opened and, with no ceremony, a woman appeared in the doorway. She was young, certainly, but not at all the "girl" Guzmán had imagined.

"Who would have thought that the way up to your office went via the basement," said Ana, with a smile.

Guzmán coughed, choking a bit, as though he had been caught in flagrante in a far-off corner of his mind. But he immediately recovered himself: in some ways, now that she was in front of him, this girl who was not a girl appealed to him even less.

"It is one of those mysteries of architecture – but there was no need to go down to the basement," he said, without blinking an eye. "There is a staircase to the left of the entrance which would bring you straight to this floor, and all – believe it or not – vertically."

"The doorman told me to come this way," said Ana, ignoring Guzmán's sarcasm. "By the way, that's an impressive collection you have down there. It's a shame that it's tucked away in a place that's so... so..."

"Dark?" suggested Guzmán.

His mean trick had backfired, but he had another up his sleeve – one that was elegant and infallible: 'the taxonomy of Houdini'. He tried to think of some outlandish rodent, one that could stand up to this woman, then he realized that they had not even introduced themselves. Here too, Ana seemed to take the initiative.

"Forgive me, Doctor Guzmán: my name is Ana."

"Lucas Guzmán. Let us not be formal: at my age very few things offend. And you may sit down too – you must be exhausted after that journey."

"Thank you."

She sat on the only chair, in front of Guzmán's desk. The remains of his sandwich, a pristine block of paper, a fountain pen and two old books bound in green and gold leather were the only things on the table.

"How can I help you?" said Guzmán. *She wasn't even pretty. Her features had a curiously Indian influence, high cheekbones, nose too wide, or too long – he couldn't decide – and the white skin and grey eyes of a Saxon. Her hair was tied in a ponytail, she wore jeans, a shirt that could have been a man's and trainers. No make-up. Why did women no longer pay attention to their looks? Céline would have hated her; she was – and no doubt continued to be – the exact opposite of this woman, but then Céline had liked to show herself off, and this one, or so it seemed, preferred inspecting skeletons in basements.*

"I'm not sure how to begin," said Ana.

"Begin with that letter of yours, then," said Guzmán, with no real intention of helping her, but rather of playing for some time in which to identify the ideal rodent for his purposes. Which would it be? It need not be a rodent… given the circumstances, perhaps this time it could be something from the order of Tubulidentata or the Chiroptera. No, his technique demanded rodents – and anyway, there were more than two thousand to choose among. What about an agouti, a capybara, a muskrat?

But Guzmán saw that the girl had begun to tell her story, and it would not do to miss the beginning, because the beginning of things contained a logical basis to which, even if everything else were lost, one could always return. The same was true, he told himself, with science.

"My father," Ana was saying, "came from Germany when he was very young, and spent the rest of his life in Patagonia, apart from some stints in hospital and getting treatment here, in Buenos Aires. He knew the mountains better than anyone, or better than most, and for a long time, in fact until he died, he dedicated his life to searching for…"

She stopped abruptly, and it was not as if she were trying to find the right word, but rather as if she were trying to decide whether to continue at all.

"Let me guess: the City of the Caesars," said Guzmán brightly. *But it was a farce: he did not feel bright at all, and this woman was annoying him as much as the story she had started to tell. No it wasn't the girl: it was the story, and the worst thing was that it gave him no time to…*

Ana, unsuspecting, smiled at him.

"Something like that," she said. "But not exactly. What he was looking for was a kind of chimera, an… obsession."

"Aha."…*now, to think of the rodent that was going to get him out of this. A crested porcupine. Something in this girl's manner recalled a crested porcupine; perhaps nothing so outlandish – better, a beaver. No, that wasn't it either. He was in trouble if he didn't have at least the name of a species by now…*

"I'm sorry, I'm not deliberately trying to make myself mysterious, believe me. I'm as rational a person as you are, and I would go so far as to say that we use the same methods

– so it's hard to say what I'm going to say to you. That letter I wrote to you was to verify that you were alive and still working here – you or your father, because it wasn't clear whether my father had written to you or your father, or even whether you or your father received that thing my father sent."

But "that thing" was so far down, so deeply buried! Geological layers had covered it, layers of madness, of frustration...

"Your father, my father – this is getting a bit confusing. Allow me to make something clear before we proceed: my father is not living, as you will appreciate, now that you have me in front of your own eyes and can see that I am old myself. And I suspect, from what you have said so far, that your father is also not living. Is that correct?"

"It is, but..."

"Permit me to ask another question: what was your father's name?"

"Víktor Mullin. I should really have started with that, shouldn't I?"

So it *was* that, then there could no longer be any room for doubt. But why had he not guessed as much, or at least intuited who this might be about? For Christ's sake... why had he not realized before?

"Víktor," repeated Guzmán, as though struggling to retrieve the name from deep within his memory. In fact, he was trying to deflect the girl's attention: that name had caught him off guard.

He remained for a few seconds with his fingers interlaced, and his gaze lost in a corner of the room that had for years been hidden by a spider's web.

"No, no I don't recall anyone by that name," he said finally, contriving an expression that fell somewhere between guilt and resignation. "It could be Alzheimer's, you know, at my age. But Víktor..." *And it was not altogether a lie because the name he actually remembered was simply "Mullin" or just "the German". It was an old name he confused with others, for example Céline's, and with the image of a world that he had done everything possible to forget – so he needed to return urgently to that beaver he had selected, or the crested porcupine or perhaps something even more ancient; he needed to set in motion the machinery of evasion before it was too late.*

"He must have sent it to your father, then," said Ana.

"Sent him what?"

"Because if it had been you, you would remember."

"But I still don't know what we are talking about. What is 'it'?"

"This," answered Ana, and she took from her bag the carbon copy of the letter.

Guzmán pretended to study the paper, while focusing his attention on the unusual topography of a fold running across the text.

"Really, what this note suggests is that my father sent something by post to Dr E. Guzmán. Would that be your father?"

"It's possible," said Guzmán. *Or would that perhaps be Lucas Ezequiel Guzmán, alias The Coward who had responded for him? And who had chosen the name "Ezequiel" for him? It must have been his mother. If he remembered anything about her, it was the rosary of violet beads that his father had brought from Toledo (as a consolation prize for never taking her there with him) and a leather-bound Bible, her bedside book. He was born of his mother's profound religious conviction and his father's supine indifference to domestic questions, Lucas Ezequiel, Apostle of Modern Palaeontology, the Prophet of South American Rodents. And the intended recipient of the original of that carbon copy, which Mullin had sent so long ago.*

But Guzmán was not prepared to go any further: he had managed to sidestep many other things, almost as important as this, in order to secure some tranquillity for the last years of his life. To go back over all that now...

His answer, however, had given Ana hope. *It's possible? Big mistake! He should have told her that his father was called Felipe and that he was Lucas and that the "E" of the letter belonged to one of those mad relatives of which no family can ever entirely rid itself!*

"Víktor sent your father a specimen – a tissue sample, perhaps, or some remains of an animal. Here he asked him please to fix the sample, in order to preserve it, and to wait for his arrival in Buenos Aires before divulging the result of his diagnosis. Do you have any idea what that may have been?"

Guzmán swung his chair round to face the only window in the office, which looked onto the park that surrounded the museum. Every day at lunchtime, some doves came to the window sill to share the leftovers of his lunch. None had come today.

"Perhaps your father mentioned something to you about it. Or the package never arrived," Ana pressed on, although her resolve was beginning to flag.

Finally, after a long and awkward silence, Guzmán spun round to face her again.

"May I ask what you think your father sent?"

Now it was Ana's turn to fall silent for a few seconds.

The cat's got her tongue, or perhaps it was the mice, thought Guzmán, and in a flash that word suggested to him the perfect candidate for a spectacular evasion: the last Cricetid fossil that he had planned to baptize with his own name: *aulisco-mys guzmánis. Now he could set in motion those automatic answers that were easy on the brain, because his mind's processes would be safely engaged in the systematics of that inhabitant of Monte Hermoso, Buenos Aires Province, during the Pleistocene epoch. How must Monte Hermoso have been in the Pleistocene? What wouldn't he give to contemplate, just for one minute, that landscape that he had so often imagined!*

"You see, it may simply have been an animal that seemed strange to him, because of some mutation or disease. You would not believe how often people find animals that are unusual, or have tumours, and they send them to the museum, as if someone here could do something for them…"

"My father wasn't that kind of person."

"I'm sorry – I wasn't referring to him, but perhaps he found an animal with a disease or a phenotypical anomaly and—"

Ana interrupted him:

"Do you know about the episode at Última Esperanza?"

"That story from the beginning of the century?" asked Guzmán, *although he was currently much, much further back in time, on a Pleistocene plain, with those* auliscomys guzmánis *that he was not yet sure would be accepted as a distinct species from the* auliscomys pictus *– the former having a procingulus that was more asymmetrical than the latter's, to start with – nor whether he could publish the work before they kicked him out for having concealed scientific evidence. No, not even "concealed": neglected to preserve it, which is very different. But what's done is done, as his father used to say, so* auliscomys guzmánis *it was, of the genus Auliscomys, Osgood taxa, also 1915. Which was when the Última Esperanza episode took place.*

"You do know it. Very well: I think that my father sent something similar to those gelatinous bones that were found in the cave at Última Esperanza."

The statement, finally wielded like a machete, was sufficient to drag Guzmán back from the Pleistocene.

"If that had been the case, surely the reaction would have been extraordinary! The ungulates became extinct thousands of years ago. If your father had found remains from these animals, he'd have his own bust in the museum now, beside Ameghino or even Darwin himself."

"You believe that it could have been an ungulate?"

"No: *you* believe it. I do not believe anything, I am speculating on what you say, nothing more." *Nothing more? Hypocrite! How often had he dreaded that someone, one of the German's associates, if not his very spectre, would come back to demand explanations of him? Because he had told Mullin that the box had never arrived, so Mullin had asked him, in that case, how did he know that it was a box? And he had laughed lightly, and convinced the German that it was he himself who had said that a few minutes earlier, and then he had made some sort of quip, like "we're none of us getting any younger", which had not amused Mullin in the slightest. And now, just his luck, it looked like the girl had inherited her father's poor sense of humour.*

"I don't believe that my father sent anything like that, because he was looking for something quite different."

Everyone is looking for something different, Guzmán would have liked to say, but he chose to say nothing. Silence protected him, giving him a space in which to return to the systematics of the *auliscomys guzmánis* and not think about that other time, that time when Céline had said, "Enough," because she was also looking for something different.

"Something else," Guzmán repeated in spite of himself, or perhaps it was his interior voice that had opened a fissure and found a way to be heard. "The truth is…" he began again, as though guided by that voice he had never heard before and which shocked him a little. But the girl got ahead of him.

"The plesiosaur in the lake," said Ana. "That's what it was."

Guzmán watched her, transfixed, aware that his expression was slightly idiotic. *He had never thought that this business would go so far. At that moment, more than anything else in the world, he despised his own indolence. Why had he not asked who the hell she was, before he had agreed to meet her? He would have saved himself all this bile, because now even the Auliscomys could not stop his memory, and much less the girl who was sitting in front of him, upright as a flagpole. Just like her father, like Mullin whom, thank God, he had only met once, and that was to tell him that his famous package had got lost in the Argentine post, as so many things used to get lost in all the state organizations – special deliveries above all. Mullin had the same grey eyes as the girl, less slanting perhaps, and set in a face that was hard-bitten, though it had that Germanic quality of strength that makes it difficult to calculate a person's age. He had died, anyway, he wasn't important any more. But his daughter was.*

"You know perfectly well that that's impossible," he answered. He was finding it very hard to quash the internal voice, which was refusing to return to the taxonomy of rodents, to the only method that could act as a buffer to the past or the present. Perhaps it only could work with one or the other, but not both.

"At least tell me why," asked Ana.

"Why is it impossible that there's a plesiosaur – or indeed any marine reptile that became extinct seventy million years ago – living in a lake of glacial origin in the Argentine Patagonia? You appear to be an educated person, not an ignoramus. Don't tell me that you came all this way to ask me that."

"I came to ask you what it was that my father sent from the cordillera, and, yes, I also came to ask you the same question you posed yourself, before calling me ignorant: why is a creature like that living in a place like that, when the last of them is supposed to have vanished seventy million years ago."

"I've already answered the first question: I have no idea what was sent by your father, Víktor" – *he had to be sure to use this other name, Víktor, one that was unfamiliar to the voice*

239

who knew him as Mullin, otherwise he would make the same
mistake he had made when he had let slip that he knew the
shape of that package before the German had said anything
about it – "although, unfortunately for you, I suspect that it
was a rare specimen, nothing more than that, and that it was
lost, or went to the wrong person, who processed it and then
forgot about it. Because, just imagine if someone had received
a box containing the fresh remains of a plesiosaur – neither
you nor I would be sitting here, and this museum would be
ten times as big and it would be on Fifth Avenue, or beside
Westminster Abbey, not in a suburb of Buenos Aires!"

He had been gradually raising his voice almost to the
point of shouting, but Guzmán realized that this was not the
product of annoyance, as it must appear to the girl, but of
fear, a sheer panic that the other voice was going to find a
way out and make itself heard, and that he would suddenly
confess to her that no, *it had not been the remains of a live*
animal, nor had it been a plesiosaur, but it was something
much more unnerving, something that perhaps she could not
understand: a true prodigy of evolution.

But Ana was not easily cowed. Just as she had negotiated
those corridors strewn with skeletons, now she watched him
from her chair with the half wary and half amused expression
of someone who is not satisfied merely with the evidence of
her eyes, but probes for something more, something which
Guzmán certainly had no intention of revealing.

"It would seem that some aspect of the subject bothers you,
deep down," she said, without altering her position.

Guzmán tried once more, with all the energy he could
muster, to reconstruct an attitude of indifference, to delve
a little further into the taxonomy of the Auliscomys: *tribe*
of Phyllotini – uncontested – class of Cricetidae, named by
Rochebrune round about the end of the 1800s... 1880, or
1881?

"It's impossible," murmured Guzmán. "Impossible."

"And if I told you that you are wrong?"

"On what evidence? Let's be serious for a moment, shall we? You came to ask me why, and I am telling you that it is impossible."

"You have misunderstood me: I didn't come to ask you if it was possible or not. Let's say that either I'm mad or that I know, beyond doubt, that it does exist, because I have also looked for it, as my father looked for it, and because I have seen it. I don't care whether or not you believe me, I can assure you that it doesn't matter to me any more, but listen: there is a cycle of appearances, a cycle of quiescence and of waking, like a hibernation that corresponds to some other factor – not temperature, not seasons, but something much more simple and logical: food. I can't be sure of everything, but there is definitely something that precedes it and obliges it to fluctuate in the same manner. If someone took the trouble to analyse the number of observations of the monster there have been in the last one hundred years during those cycles and, supposing the observations of the early travellers were treated as reliable, along with those of the Indians, I assure you too that they would find that the number of creatures has been falling and perhaps even that there is now only one specimen left in the whole lake. Let's leave my father out of it: what matters is that I believe everything I have just told you and I don't need to find out if it is possible or not, but *why* it exists, how it could have survived and, fundamentally, what it is. Will you help me now?"

Guzmán, at his sixty-seven years – nearly seventy, as he liked to boast – thought to himself then: why me? *He had never asked himself the question before, not even when they gave him the scholarship to specialize in evolutionary palaeontology at the school of the Technische Universität Clausthal in Germany where his father had also studied, thus setting in motion the events which would lead to the friendship, or at least the correspondence between his father – who was old and sick by then – and the father of the girl who was now fixing him with wide-open eyes, a frank, slightly troubled expression, waiting for his answer. He had not asked himself that question either, the day that he first met Céline, or the day that she agreed to marry him – even though his future did not lie in Europe – or the day that she agreed to move to Argentina to settle there for good (at least that had been Guzmán's intention); he had not asked himself "why me?" when Pablo was born, his son, their son, later rebaptized "Paul" by Céline, with a chromosomal abnormality that would turn their lives into a series of miserable events, because the most that could be expected for Pablo would be to survive, half-dead, with perpetual and expensive assistance, draining the life out of all those who surrounded him. He had not even dreamt of asking "why me?" when he felt, for the first time, that he had a kind of gift for studying certain monsters, when the expeditions, and nights spent on excavations, in the workshop and in libraries showed that he was very close to finding a solution to one of the greatest evolutionary problems in all of history – not merely the missing link, but perhaps the living link between what had been reptilian monsters and mammals. And of course he had not asked himself that question on the day that he received – like a sign from God – the mysterious package sent by Mullin from some unknown spot in the Andean foothills: three flat bones that fitted together perfectly, three bones from a cranium the hypothetical form of which he had spent exhausting hours shaping with his hands and his imagination, while his son's condition deteriorated each day along with his marriage, his reputation as a scrupulous scientist, his judgement, his health and life as he had hitherto known it. No, even as his life fell apart around him, he had preferred never to ask himself that question, sensing himself to be an indestructible star, an ego set alight by a wild theory. By the time he finally managed to dampen the flames, destroying the only thing that it was within his power and will to destroy – it was too late to ask himself anything.*

Now, finally, Guzmán answered Ana with the question that he had never posed before.

Ana observed him with a mixture of pity and helplessness: the stormy disquiet in her eyes was gone now. Perhaps Ana's presence signified something, Guzmán told himself – not a redemption, because that was no longer possible, nor yet a recognition of what he had done, or an acceptance, it was also too late for these things. But it was not too late to ask himself "why".

And suddenly it was as if the girl had discovered a method for reading his thoughts, all that he had not told her and would never tell her. It was as if she had decided that Guzmán's intransigence was not important, that his cowardly past mattered less than the discovery he had managed to make, albeit using despicable and underhand means, when he was young: a plausible explanation, a theory to make sense of the incomprehensible in a world that still required names for things.

"Because you…" Ana began thoughtfully. "I am going to be frank: this letter is the last and only link between Víktor, the monster and me. Or between my father's search and mine. The one thing I can be sure of is that it was sent to someone who would *know* what it was about. Even if your father were the recipient, or even if neither of you ever received anything, you would surely have discussed what Víktor had found. And if one of you did receive the package… at least you have had a long time to think about it since then."

Guzmán felt a new and sudden connection with this woman he had recently found so disagreeable, and whom he never would have agreed to see had he known her identity. He could not tell her that, but he smiled, for the first time without sarcasm.

"Let us suppose that I did think about it on occasion... and with some seriousness, if for no other reason than the story of Frey's expedition, and the findings at Última Esperanza. Let us suppose that there is an animal in the lake, an animal which common sense dictates should not be there because... well, why exactly?"

"Aren't you the one who said that it was impossible?"

"A plesiosaur, yes. A plesiosaur like the ones we know from the fossils collected by Mary Anning – of whom, by the way, you remind me of quite a bit – that would be impossible. But you are the one who spoke of a plesiosaur, not I."

"So?"

"Did you see it?"

Ana shook her head with a mute fury.

"I can't tell you that I actually saw it, because it was through a camera lens – I mean, the camera registered something that I was seeing, but couldn't distinguish. And, admittedly, the photos I managed to save are meaningful only to me, because I know every mark in that area and can immediately spot anything that is unusual, abnormal or out of place. But the camera is not the whole story. That night there was someone else on the shore. In fact, he was very close to the point where I should have been at that moment. Perhaps the light would have been enough... I don't know. I don't want to agonize over it now: it's over – I can't change things."

"I suppose there's no point in asking you for those photos... Were they taken at the time recorded in previous sightings?"

"Absolutely. When Lanz started shouting, I was directly in line with him, but on the other side of... of... whatever it was that came up in the middle of the lake. I shot off a load of film: most of the negatives came out over-exposed. All the time I could hear Lanz shouting like a madman, like when he disconnects from reality, but not the same, a different kind of shout – it was because of something he was seeing take place, and I knew that we were seeing the same thing from two opposing angles. I tried to get back as fast as the oars would allow me, but when I arrived all that I could manage to piece together came from Ilse, Lanz's wife, who had heard what he said."

"I don't understand," said Guzmán, perplexed. "Was your friend also unsure of what he had seen?"

"My friend, Dr Guzmán, is about your age and suffers from Korsakov Syndrome: his mind cannot retain anything that happened more than ten minutes ago – sometimes it's even less than that, but that wasn't the case this time."

"Unbelievable!" said Guzmán. "The only person who presumably got a good look is also the one who can't remember it. If you'll forgive me, this sounds like a bad joke."

"If this weren't about Lanz, I'd be the first to agree with you. But he has this quality: he's like a kind sonar for monsters. Perhaps that is precisely why they choose him..."

"Why?"

"Because they know that he is as watchful as the lenga trees in the forest, the myrtle bushes, the fish in the lake. None of them can report on what they see, and so monsters are safe around them."

"It strikes me as too lyrical an interpretation of this business, Ana, but anyway, this Lanz is not a kind of sonar for monsters, but a sonar for species – see how I can be creative too?"

"I hope that you are now going to tell me what you have been thinking all this time."

"I would ask you not to get your hopes up: I have no evidence and I'm afraid that, unlike you, I believe this to be very far-fetched." *Far-fetched? A sonar for monsters... that is also what he had been, and it was even possible that he still was one, an outdated sonar. He was out of commission, like those Russian satellites that orbited the Earth, completely forgotten now, so much fancy junk that the astronauts of the future were destined to contemplate with pity, if they ever caught sight of it on their way to Mars. Such a sentimental analogy did not pain him however, but, like one of Hilda's broadsides or a visiting bureaucrat, it made him feel gratifyingly stoical.*

"There's another thing," said Guzmán. "Classification, as you will know, is a fallible art, because it relies on the knowledge that is available at a given moment, in the same way that a crime can only be analysed on the basis of existing evidence – but that evidence does not identify the criminal, only the circumstances of the crime. It can fail, without a doubt, but, more seriously, it can also be useless. To classify a chimera is to give it a name, an entity, and that also means to lose it. I warn you, Ana, that when you bestow a reason on something, you lose it for good."

Ana said that she agreed, and only then, as if he had been waiting for her to accept a sacrament that united them, paradoxically, in a scientific sacrilege, Guzmán returned to the theory that he had once promised himself never to think of again.

"As a hypothesis, I am inclined to think that this could be a divergent line of the pelycosaur. Do you know what they are, or what they were?"

Ana nodded, but Guzmán continued as though the reply had been negative.

"I suppose that they are less attention-grabbing than the great carnivores and, for that reason, very few people can identify them. The original Pangaea was a land of amphibians and primitive reptiles: everything was perfect, the plants had oxygenated the atmosphere and the world was shining, until the planet began to explode inside. At the end of the

Permian period the world's greatest ever mass extinction took place. Lava contaminated the oceans and almost all aquatic and terrestrial life disappeared. Even the trilobites. All that was not killed by volcanic sulphur was liquefied by the ice that covered everything like a shroud for thousands of millions of years. But during the Permian heyday, long before the dinosaurs evolved, the real rulers of this planet were the synapsids, or "mammal-like reptiles". They covered the world. There were herbivores, carnivores and omnivores around the equator and in the tropics. Then came the extinction, but here evolution took a risky turn, favouring one line which later led to the mammals we know today. The first synapsids were the pelycosaurs which had a... (how could he describe the evidence that he had destroyed, how could he present his argument without being able to use it?) a cranial architecture that was... unusual, very unusual, which allowed for the attachment of a new set of muscles extending to the jaw. These muscles were fundamental for feeding and for communication, two far from lowly factors... Palaeontologists believe that the only line of the pelycosaurs to have prospered were these original mammals, the ones with this new kind of cranium. Well: I beg to differ."

"But that theory is much more chancy than if this were a plesiosaur: not only would you be talking about an animal that became extinct sixty million years ago, but also about a species in transition that does not even appear in the fossil record."

"Don't be so sure. There are fossils of the edaphosaurus and the dimetrodon, the two pelycosaur species from the Permian that have dorsal crests. Evolution is a random process and it is not the strongest that survive, but the best-adapted. Adaptation," repeated Guzmán, "not strength. If we consider for a moment the possibility – a remote one, agreed, but that's what we're looking for – that one line of the pelycosaurs evolved towards the mammals, that is, that it acquired characteristics commonly found in some present-day mammals as a result of undergoing similar selective pressures, then we could postulate the existence – a remote one – of a 'living fossil', a specimen clinging to the shirt tails of some 'primitive' species. That does not mean that it hasn't undergone the same evolutionary process, simply that it retains the old form, because it has turned out to be advantageous."

"Do you mean that natural selection sustained a 'form' that was adequate to the circumstances of the earth during the extinctions: mammals did not change, but this creature did because, in common with the mammals, it was adapting to the same habitat?"

"Something like that. If you accept the notion that an unknown line of pelycosaurs has survived until the present day, then we would have to go back 225 million years to follow the trajectory of your creature. Some quirk of evolution could have caused that unknown line to establish itself as a phylogenetic tree without branches, that is a thread pursued only by the pelycosaurs which gradually acquired the characteristics of mammals by convergent evolution. During the Cenozoic period, Patagonia was formed. A million years ago saw the start of a great glacial age, and throughout that time the majority of Patagonia was covered by extraordinary ice masses with such powers of erosion that they managed to wear away the rock bed and scoop out very deep valleys. The last glacial period ended some fourteen thousand years ago. The ice subsided, then the course of rivers was modified, and the valleys created by the glaciers filled with water, creating most of the lakes we know today. They are very deep lakes, in a V-shape, and not very productive. The water in them is practically distilled, because it comes from melted ice. All that – the low temperatures, scant nutrients, the sharply angled lake beds and the effect of wind blowing off the mountains

– makes it difficult for aquatic vegetation to take root and hinders establishment of complex trophic networks... Could there still be, therefore, a line of these animals lost in space and time? Was there an evolutionary path, over two hundred million years, culminating in a monster unknown to science? It is possible, especially if one listens to those specialists in planetary biodiversity who claim that there could be more than ten million living organisms on this planet, and that we only know about one and a half million of them. A tenth – imagine it – and that's erring on the generous side."

Ana shook her head doubtfully.

"But then, why does it not appear more regularly? Why are the descriptions so different from one another? The '*cuero*' the Indians talk about is not the same as the creature my father looked for, or the one Frey was after. And that animal is not like the one Onelli was looking for, or like the one at Última Esperanza..."

"Wait a moment. Let's suppose that there were various Patagonian populations of these animals that were halfway between reptiles and mammals: they lived in subterranean valleys as old as the mother rock of the Andes; as the great rock masses rose out of the earth, creating valleys between which there was no communication, these populations gradually became isolated. The isolation could have produced a new species – perhaps that occurred, but there is no record of it. The Patagonian cordillera has some important characteristics: lower peaks, transversal valleys, numerous lake systems, U-shaped valleys, moraines and passes that allow humid air to flow from the Pacific Ocean, favouring dense forestation. In this setting, and with constant volcanic activity, nearly all the isolated populations became extinct... but if the valley they inhabited had been sufficiently hospitable, in terms of food and protection, it is possible that one group, or a remnant of it, quietly survived to the present day... it would be a rarity, without doubt: these would have to be creatures with a very low reproductive rate and tremendous longevity, averaging 150 to 180 years, with long periods of hibernation, corresponding to a five or ten-year climactic cycle, as you suggested a minute ago."

"The cycles could be connected to solar storms, which somehow stimulate the growth of the algae; their proliferation in turn sustains some other species, which these animals feed on when they come out of hibernation..."

"Or it could be something more complex... and the algae neutralize the species that usually eat whatever it is these creatures eat when they become active. Or perhaps the algae are simply a sign, like an alarm clock, because they change some crucial characteristic of the lake."

"The alkalinity!"

"For example, or the level of dissolved oxygen, or some mineral compound that becomes apparent through oxidization. That is a common process in the trophic cycles of African lakes: an entire chain can be maintained thanks to the presence, in a specific moment of the year, of a metal which then forms a salt which forms part of a layer of micro-organisms which – well, I'm sure I don't need to tell you how a trophic chain is made."

"The feeding and the hibernation could be linked through the cycles of any one of these variables. But the temperature? Bear in mind that the temperature of the water below twenty metres is constant and freezing."

Guzmán dismissed the objection with an impatient wave of his hand. "Once they had acquired the characteristics of mammals, they could be partially endothermic. Perhaps these creatures were capable of maintaining their body temperature at about twenty-eight or thirty degrees, like a platypus today... Anyway, I'm sure you must agree that your monster remains problematic – even if we've found some theoretical solutions – and that these speculations do not explain why the creatures are never seen, nor how they have managed to survive. Your monster is an imperfect entity, Ana, who lives in spite of natural selection, not thanks to it. An amputed being that has learnt how to makes the most of its stumps..."

Guzmán felt himself becoming tetchy again. A long time ago, when the subject was still important enough to absorb all his time, he had realized that the theory of the pelycosaurs became less convincing the more you explained it. It suddenly revealed itself as a great theatrical piece, in which every element of the ensemble must have a purpose. The theories served a preconceived idea, just as characters are necessary for dialogue, and dialogue for scenes. And it was that rationality that made him feel most uncomfortable. It made him think of that episode with Mullin, and he asked himself what it was that he had held in his hands and destroyed, if not the illusory product of two obsessives, one of whom thought he had found what the other was looking for, and the other who thought that a lifetime's search was over.

He said nothing now, sunk in a petulant silence.

"Please carry on," said Ana. "Even if you do think the idea's preposterous."

"That's exactly the problem."

"That it strikes you as preposterous?"

No: that it does not strike me that way, but this is something that you would never understand. Or perhaps you would, but I don't want to find out.

"Preposterous ideas are not unusual in science, and scientific method is the mesh that sifts them. That's not the case here. Please consider that only one of every ten thousand species leaves a fossil record that serves to identify it. That means that the majority of species, in all times, have ended without leaving any trace of their presence on earth more lasting than that of a crab on sand."

"That's not important to me."

Why was he really talking about the monster? Or was he talking about all of them, himself, his father, Ana's father, of those imperfect beings who live in spite of Darwin, hidden, hunkered down, searching for a way to survive? Was it not that communal madness that kept them all alive?

"You're right. None of this is important."

"So?"

Guzmán heaved a sigh.

"We must assume that the creatures live in very small groups of individuals, that the lack of genetic variation has brought them to the brink of extinction. The creatures' habitat could be in subterranean amphibious caverns, and eventually they would make their way into the lakes via tunnels. However, since there is no light in these caverns, the whole ecosystem would have to depend on trophic networks based on chemosynthesizing organisms. Their skin would have to be very special, with no kind of pigmentation; their reptomammalian legacy might have left them covered with large scales, like the Asiatic pangolins, that would give them a mimetic superficial structure, making them undetectable, almost invisible. This kind of covering could diffract light so, at a distance, they might look like rocky islets, light glinting on the lake or the shadows of clouds. Being aquatic, too, their extremities would be webbed, with interdigital folds or membranes. Their shape would be hydrodynamic, minimizing friction in the water and improving their speed. They would also have a layer of subcutaneous fat, as well as some physiological mechanism to maintain body heat when they were awake."

"The waking periods would be during the summer," Anna added, "when heat in the atmosphere would be enough to warm the body."

"Hunting activity would be at twilight, though, during the time of maximum activity and greatest capacity of mimesis, thanks to the ambiguity of the light. That, as you say, fits with the sightings, but it also means that the time they come out to hunt is also the time when they cannot be detected. The sightings would have been lucky exceptions, or made possible by some prevailing condition that interfered with the mimesis."

Ana spoke, then, with a sad wonderment.

"I don't know how to explain it, but that night the darkness shone, and the camera caught that too: a darkness that was more opaque than all the other darkness."

Guzmán stared at her, engrossed, as though this were a scene that they were remembering together; then he swivelled his chair towards the window. A dove with dappled markings pecked at crumbs on the other side of the glass.

"There's nothing much else to say," he murmured, without looking at her.

Silence overtook them then. The quality of the evening light outside suggested that several hours had elapsed since Ana arrived. Neither of them had noticed the passing time and now it seemed that neither noticed the silence, each one deep in thought. On his side of the desk, Guzmán studied the faded sky through the window; on hers, Ana inspected her hands.

Finally Guzmán stood up and went to pick up the coffee pot.

"Would you like a coffee?" he asked.

"Thank you, but there's someone waiting for me downstairs. I can't believe how late it is – look at the time."

"Is your friend a fellow monster-hunter?"

"He's a patient unbeliever," said Ana. "Luckily more patient than unbelieving."

It was almost dark now. At this time in the evening, a stony quiet habitually rose from the depths of the museum and covered everything, as though transforming the whole building into a fossil from the inside outwards in successive and enveloping layers, until the great, imposing mass of cement seemed to cast its cold silence even on the air in the gardens outside, as the sky overhead darkened.

Guzmán never wanted to miss this spectacle, which meant leaving the office at exactly the right time in order to sit on the bench that was in the little square opposite the museum. Today, however, it was more likely that he would go straight home, with a possible diversion to the supermarket to buy something stronger than vermouth. He would need to take a few secret gulps before confronting Hilda, because he suspected that his usual evasive technique would not work – not today.

Ana put the letter back into her enormous raffia bag, and took out a brown paper envelope which she placed on the desk.

Guzmán guessed that it contained the photographs.

"May I ask," he said, "if you mean to keep looking for it?"

Ana stood up, smoothed down her shirt, put the bag on her shoulder and stretched out her hand to shake his: it occurred to Guzmán that she was about to leave his office, and his life, as simply and suddenly as she had entered it, and that that was probably the best outcome.

"I suppose that I'll try one last time – and then another, and another, until the same thing happens to me as happened to you and I stop thinking about it."

Guzmán drained his tiny coffee cup, and took her hand with relief.

"I wish you luck," he said amiably.

"Thank you, and I hope you'll forgive this sudden intrusion," said Ana, from the door.

"Not at all. And remember that there is a stairway that leads directly to the main entrance."

"All the same I might prefer to take the other route…"

"Of course: take whichever one you prefer."

As Ana was about to close the door, Guzmán motioned her to wait.

"May I ask you something else? If your father believed that the thing he had found was so important, why would he send it by post?"

Ana looked at him, surprised.

"Víktor was German, Doctor Guzmán. The Germans have blind faith in the postal service. Víktor found whatever he found, he sent it to someone he knew could help and then he went on his way. Wasn't your father also like that?"

"I don't think so."

"When did your father die?"

Guzmán senior had died of cancer in Santa Rosa de la Pampa, in a mobile home that was stationed halfway between San Rafael and Buenos Aires, two years before Mullin's discovery. When he had sent the package, the German must have believed that Guzmán father and son were the same person – either that or he did not care which of them received it, so long as they both shared his fascination with creatures from the past.

In fact that had not been the case: the father's fascination had never come close to the blind passion of the son.

He was about to tell her a lie – as if the girl could not easily have checked up later – but Ana shook her head and said that it was not important anyway. Víktor had obviously respected him enough to send that package, without allowing for the failings of the Argentine postal service.

She said goodbye again and closed the door quickly and decisively. He heard her footsteps for a few seconds afterwards: she had obviously not taken the staircase that went directly to the door, but gone via the labyrinth in the basement.

She must be a difficult woman to get on with, thought Guzmán, and he remembered some words of Goethe, whom his father had read as a writer, and he, almost exclusively, as Romanticism's impenetrable scientist: "The thinking man's greatest comfort is to have explored what can be known, and to have quietly revered that which cannot be explored."

Quietly? How could he have got it so wrong! One could never be at peace with the inexplorable; there would never be anything akin to reverence: just frustration and thirst. The thinking man does not resign himself, and for that reason Ana would one day find the monster, or the monster would find her.

Guzmán put his notebook, fountain pen and the two green books away in his briefcase, and made his way downstairs in the half-light. In the little square, he sat down for a moment on the bench, summoning up the energy necessary to go back home.

The last rays of the sun had disappeared in the west some time ago, leaving merely a trace of faded yellow, like oxidated picric acid. He tried to imagine that same park at the time of the Pleistocene, darkened by voracious ferns. And he imagined that the silence, imposed now by the museum, would have been the same millions of years ago, when all the creatures destined to die that night held their breath as one.

8

Klára

According to Mutti, she – Klára – had been born under the sign of Gemini, some time in May or June 1944, a year before the end of the war. This nugget of information was as reliable as that other, about her parents dying in the hold of the boat that was taking them to America. She had been born with an uncertain name, on an uncertain day, into a family about whose identity she knew absolutely nothing, in a place somewhere in Europe. Mutti used to say that her mother was from the Balkans, and that her father had the dark, fragile looks of certain people from Serbia.

And that was it. No one in the world knew anything else about her or her background. Had her parents taken part in the war? Were they involved in the resistance? Would they have tried to oppose the regime that ended up destroying them? Could they have committed a crime in the name of some cause? Had they ever been taken prisoner, denounced, tortured? In which jails? Would they have been in concentration camps? And in what guise: as prisoners or warders?

How many possible versions of their story were there?

"Blood will out": that was one of the first expressions that had made an impression on her, when she was already grown up. She could not understand it, and had asked Lanz to explain this concept that seemed to describe some sort of haemorrhage. And Lanz, who had always been truthful with her, explained that there were no blood ties in her case and that that was a good thing, because everyone has to learn to be alone in the world and the lesson would come naturally to her. It was like a gift.

From then onwards, Klára had regarded her own essential loneliness as a gift, even if she did not always experience it that way. She saw her life as an amalgam of two lives: one as daughter of Mutti and Lanz, sister of Ana, and then the other. A few people referred to that other her as "the Hungarian". It was almost a *nom de guerre*.

They've given her the window seat, on the right side of the aeroplane. Judging from the colour of the sky, she knows that at the moment they are flying vaguely north and east. Over on the other side, through the left-hand windows, the sun is setting and those passengers have started to pull down their blinds. Her window displays the sky like an amphitheatre seen through dirty acrylic. They are flying above a layer of clouds lit from underneath; the original white has been tinged yellow, and now magenta, and very soon it will be blue. She wonders if Ana is at this moment down by the lake on the Melancolía Sound, taking her twilight photos with Víktor's old camera. What would Ana say if she were here now, watching the sun set from this same seat, ten thousand metres high? What would the lake look like, the stone house, Lanz's boat, the cabin, the wood? They would probably be no more than specks on the grey expanse of the cordillera. And people would not be visible at all; wars, clashes, bombs – all of it would be reduced, perhaps, to a delicate swirl of dust.

She is leaving everything behind, in that peachy luminosity to the west: Mutti, Lanz, Nando, Ana, La Pedrera, a dead boy, the co-operative, the Pascual group. The Hungarian.

The air hostess interrupts the hum of the engine to ask Klára and the white-haired man sitting next to her if they would like something to drink. The man asks for a lemonade and she for a glass of water. In the airport, before boarding,

Nando gave her some tranquillizers. Then he had held her, and she had let herself be held. That too is behind her now.

"Are you nervous?" her companion asks, smiling, when he sees her take from her bag the silvery strip of pills. The question startles her. She must not get into a conversation with anyone. She does not want to. Once again she is leaving her life behind.

Pascual is not here. Neither is the co-operative. She and Pascual were the ones who organized all the work, and when they took Pascual away, the whole Mapuche group seemed to dissolve for a few days, swallowed up in the wilderness, as if it had never existed. But they were indigenous people, used to suffering and resisting, so they had suggested to her that the group continue, with Antonio – Pascual's brother – and two other activists, one inside and one outside the group. That had ended in less than three weeks, with the news that the co-operative was going to close down. They had tried to continue running an underground operation, while she and Antonio secretly searched for Pascual.

Everything had fallen apart so quickly that she found it hard to remember the details. Without the co-operative, there could be no school, no clinic and no community. But without Pascual there was also no group, and she could not replace him – even if she had wanted to – because he was Mapuche and she was... who knew what she was? If something had united them, it was the permanent, tireless battle for an identity. She had never allowed herself to be seduced by eloquent promises, nor let down her guard after some small achievement: Pascual took no prisoners and barely stopped to draw breath; she had learnt her style of activism from him. And one day she had realized how much he meant to her and told him so, but Pascual had said nothing.

The last they had heard was that he had been moved to the penal institution at Neuquén. The trail went cold after that, and there were no official records of other transfers. Nor had there been any "official" reasons given for his detention, other than the obvious ones: that he was an activist of Mapuche descent, with no political affiliations to speak of, who ran a co-operative that aimed to bring cohesion to a scattered community living on land supposedly surrendered to the treasury – some thirty hectares in the foothills of the Andes around Barda Roja.

And it was at that time, during their covert and dismal search for Pascual, that a body had been thrown into the ravine of the Melancolía Sound, very close to La Pedrera.

"Would you like another drink?" asks the hostess, whose little trolley, replenished with bottles, has come clinking back down the aisle.

"I think she's gone to sleep," says the man with the white hair, and Klára, with her face turned to the window and her eyes firmly shut, imagines him mimicking the action of someone taking a pill, and the hostess, with all her experience of air travel, casting her a tender glance. But when the trolley has passed by, the man murmurs:

"I can save dinner for you as well, if you like."

"Thank you," she says, without looking at him.

"Not at all."

The night continues on its asymmetric course through the sky, smattering ink to the east, threatening the faltering reds to the west. Klára hardly notices the space surrendered to the night.

She had not found out about the ravine incident until a week after it happened, when she went to meet Nando in a pâtisserie in the town centre. That particular memory makes her smart with guilt and shame. What significance did Nando have in her life anyway? She cannot work it out. Nando is the very opposite of Pascual – Ana's lover, a dear friend she had known for years, and the only one who really protected, in his way, those two old people who constituted her entire family. Had she also sought protection from him? At some point she had needed a safe haven, a break from fighting that was never possible where Pascual was concerned.

It doesn't matter any more. It is because of Nando that she is on the plane. A year ago, Nando knew nothing about Pascual, or the co-operative. He, like everyone else, thought that Klára was a social worker on a project connected with the Indians, and that she taught in a rural school near Barda Roja. She had never had any intention of hiding the truth from him, until the day when Pascual taught her to use a gun, the first time that she was going to stay in the clinic all night. This is how you take off the safety catch, he had said, sliding back the top part of the revolver, his finger well away from the trigger. And this is how you load it.

That night, alone in the middle of the mountains, she had not slept a wink, not so much because of the gun – although she was certainly aware of it beside her campbed – but because of Pascual. Not long after that, they came for him at dawn. Nobody heard shots, then again no one had been close enough to the post. Pascual had been alone, and the only trace of what had happened were the signs of violence and devastation that had been visited on the room. Pascual himself had warned that this might happen.

Was it her tension, her uncertainty or the absence of Pascual that had brought Nando closer – or simple loneliness?

She had reeled at the news of the episode in the ravine: that body in the dispensary represented her last chance to find Pascual alive, albeit barely alive. Nando had never seen Pascual, although he had heard about him by then; she had told him everything a few days before Christmas, and from then on she had had his reproaches and jealousy to contend with, as well as her own guilt and confusion. Instantly she

261

regretted telling him, but by then it was too late, and she could only ask him not to tell anyone, even Ana. Nando had asked her why, and she had said that she neither wanted nor had the right to involve other people in her problems. But in fact Nando had meant something else: why Pascual? Why the co-operative? Why could she not forget all that once and for all? Because of Pascual, she had answered, that Christmas night at La Pedrera.

And that had been the end of whatever was starting between them – until the incident in the ravine.

The illusion that the body might be Pascual's had not lasted long. Beneath his swollen skin, Pedro, as Ana called him, was another stranger, another person like her: nameless, or with a name bestowed on him by fate, like hers.

Perhaps she should not have listened to Nando. Perhaps she should have stayed, and kept searching. Wait until the worst was over, then start again, with Pascual or without him. But for once, Antonio had agreed with this man he did not know, and for whom he would surely have felt contempt. As things were, there was nothing they could do, either for the Mapuche community – which had already disbanded now that there was no school or working clinic – or for Pascual himself. She could not help thinking of him each time she saw Pedro – three times in all, including the last time. Nor could she keep away from Barda Roja and the places that linked her to Pascual, as Antonio had suggested. She had thought that La Pedrera would be a good refuge, until Lanz started talking about the men in black who were spying on them from the edge of the forest.

Klára had not wanted to move there when Ana and Nando went away, but she could not refuse either, given that the old people were going to be alone with Pedro. According to Ana, Pedro was caught in "suspended animation". She said this with a smile, as though the technical phrase were part of a private joke, or a combination of words that described the situation with great exactitude. Precision was always a source of pleasure to Ana, who seemed to have started living in a rather hazy reality since the changes at the lake. Klára did not understand why they had not sought help in studying the phenomenon. At the same time she was relieved that there were not teams of people nosing around the area, reporting on the microclimate that had transformed the Melancolía Sound. At any rate, Ana was alone in that fantasy world, in which there was a young moribund man and a prehistoric creature, each of them elusive in his own way. In the end Klára had to agree to spend three days in charge of the house.

So Ana and Nando had taken the bus to Buenos Aires, on the trail of the only clue they had about Pedro: a scrunched-up scrap of paper bearing a handwritten address. Luckily, that paper seemed to have survived Pedro's ordeal rather better than he had – assuming it really did belong to him, and this was not a macabre coincidence. They had gone to follow other trails too, pertaining to a scientist who might be dead and to an unlikely monster. Ana accepted anything that looked plausible on the surface.

Klára had sensed that these would be her last days at La Pedrera.

She had never liked the house, but Lanz had insisted on staying there after Víktor died, and Mutti did not oppose him, although she would have liked to go. They had stayed on in that monument to loneliness, as isolated as a pair of hermits. When Ana came back, she did not want to leave them. Klára had supposed that Ana would go and live with Nando in the city, but Ana had surprised her, and Nando too: both of them seemed to prefer playing an eternal waiting game.

But she did not want to live between the walls that had once housed Víktor. It was not the loneliness of the place that daunted her – what was that loneliness next to her own? – but the obsessive spirit that had impregnated every stone. She had never wanted to live there, and had left as soon as possible, first with the excuse of her studies, and then jobs she didn't have. Thanks to that early elusiveness, Mutti, Lanz and Ana had never known what she did, not exactly.

A life with no roots need not bear foliage, flowers or fruit. In that, she agreed with Ana: they both had floating roots, like water hyacinths, those large aquatic plants.

They had come for her. While Nando and Ana were away they appeared, as if they had been spying on the house, waiting for the perfect moment. Unlike that time with Pascual, this time they came in the afternoon, in broad daylight. It was the first time they had shown themselves.

And it was as if they had always known, right from the start. Ana said that Lanz had been raving about black men who were spying on him from the cover of the woods, or the shadows down by the lake. He turned out to be right, but as Ana said, it was very hard to disentangle past events in Vatti's life from his current fears. He had always seemed gifted with a kind of clairvoyance, even during the fog of illness. And as he had been their victim once, long before, he could recognize them now.

There they were, ready to spring from the shadows. And they did not knock on the door: they came right in. First they went to the cabin, to the room in which Lanz was sleeping. Mutti couldn't stop them. Lanz woke up and found them in the middle of the room, with their drab clothes and their guns pointing at his head. Lanz probably had no idea where he was, whether in La Pedrera or Crvenka, but he kept still, paralysed with fear, until everything blew up inside his head. The violence of his convulsions was enough to stop the men. They left him and proceeded to examine every centimetre of that room, then the darkened living room, the larder, the bathroom. Everything was knocked over, manhandled. Mutti quickly acted to stop Lanz swallowing his tongue. He was foaming at the mouth and his eyes had swivelled backwards, leaving two blind and bloodied orbs. His hands and feet were tightly clenched. They didn't care about any of that. Mutti threw herself over Lanz's body, as if to protect him from a bomb, and there she stayed until the last of them had left the room. Then she picked up the iron washbasin that was filled with water every morning and, with all her strength, hurled it against the window pane. With one blow it shattered into pieces. The sound reverberated across the ravine, as though amplified by thousands of hollow trees. In the garden that separated the cottage from the house, the men paused, startled, then walked on, dark and undeterred, like giant flies.

The noise of the broken glass had alerted her, before the men were able to enter the house itself. She caught sight of them through the window: they looked jittery, like carnivorous animals for whom any sudden noise grates on the ear's extreme sensibility. Unabashed, one of them approached the window, bending slightly towards the glass, and tried to make out the interior of the living room. She thought that the brightness of the day outside would frustrate him, but she was wrong. On the other side of the glass the man's narrowed eyes suddenly opened wide, and he shouted her name to the others without looking away. She read on his lips the name which Pascual and the others in the group had called her. She even managed to see his face, coarse and pockmarked with scars; one eye was sunken and a lifeless black, like glass. A flaccid eyelid flopped over the eye, completely covering it, and giving his features a repugnant, demented cast.

When the man left the window to get the others, she moved as quickly as she could. She knew that Ana still had Víktor's Winchester, a lever-action large-calibre rifle. Both Lanz and

Víktor had cared for it as one would a child. After Víktor's death, Lanz had been careful to clean and grease it at every change of season. He would never have used it for hunting, or to shoot at tin cans, as Nando did on the occasions Lanz took the rifle off its throne for its quarterly clean. That rifle had travelled with Víktor through Patagonia, slung over his shoulder on a leather bandolier that Ana had also conserved, carefully wrapped around the weapon.

Now Klára found it there, exactly where it was meant to be, in the clutches of the inseparable bandolier, beside a box of cartridges.

Pedro was sleeping on his side on the bed beneath the window. Light flooded over him, as though mercilessly pointing out his defencelessness. His back had been covered in sores for weeks, and now the only way he could breathe without help from the machine was like this, on his side. His lungs had filled with phlegm, and the functioning area was of such scant volume that the air barely had time to enter before it was expelled, without any effort on his part. The rest was a dim rumbling of liquid in cavities.

His breaths were quick and fluttering, like a bird's. When she lifted him, she had the impression of lifting a skeletal frame deprived of its feathers. With her hands under his arms, she could carry him easily, partly because he was so light, and partly because fear strengthened her. This way she dragged him to the only place in the house they might not be able to enter: the cellar.

Ana and she had played there as little girls, hiding from Mutti, who hated the dank smell and the confinement of that room, which measured barely six metres square and was as deep as a dungeon. The stone steps seemed to descend for ever, and the floor was often flooded. Mutti questioned how anyone could sleep knowing that a space resembling a crypt lay beneath the house. Ana and Klára, on the other hand, were happy to venture down into the bowels of La Pedrera, like explorers, decked out in Mutti's shawls and green bead necklaces with candles and a bundle containing food and more candles, "in case we get stuck down there for ever". Thanks to these childhood games, Klára knew every inch of the cellar and, most importantly, how to disguise the secret entrance that led to the stairway.

Lanz had designed that trapdoor so that the oblique cuts coincided with the grain in the pine and the fortuitous arrangement of the planks. For someone unfamiliar with the house, it would be almost impossible to distinguish the faint lines that marked a square in the floor planks, perfectly merging as they did with joins between the wood and cement.

It was invisible to anyone but them. Víktor had forgotten about it, Lanz never went down there and Mutti struggled to find it. Ana and Klára were the sole mistresses of a deep pit that had never served any purpose, other than to infuriate Mutti on the occasions when she finally discovered them down there. Even now, in the dark, Klára would have known from memory how to find that cover, simply by counting paces from the wall.

So it was to that secret door that she dragged Pedro's limp body, together with the rifle and a lamp. There was no time for anything else because, even as she was prising open the wooden cover, sinking her nails into dirt-clogged cracks, she could hear them beating on the front door, and then the squeaking of hinges as it gave way. Hidden from view in the stairway, she took Pedro down into the cellar first, then the rifle, then – holding the lamp between her teeth – she closed the trapdoor behind them. There was a lock on the inside, a sort of bolt she and Ana had put there as a last-ditch defence against some disastrous scenario they had once invented. The bolt was still there, but it was too rusty to be drawn. She managed only to slip the end of the bolt across the edge of the cover: they would still be able to open it, but with a much greater effort than she had needed.

Just then, the rifle slipped out of her hands and fell, glancing off the steps, to the ground, where the water muffled its impact with a small splash. She knew that she could take Pedro no further than the lower steps, that she would have to sit him there, wrapped in the blanket that she had accidentally dragged with him to the cellar. For a few long minutes she manoeuvred his body into the right position. She could hear, overhead, the sound of boots on the living room's tremulous wooden floor, footsteps in the kitchen, a crashing of metal, then silence. They had gone up to the first floor. She prayed then – crouching on the stairs, holding Pedro so that he would not slip, trying to warm him, to imbue his lassitude with energy – that Mutti would stay in the cottage. She knew that the noise of the breaking window had been intended as a signal for her to act quickly; Mutti had such good instincts that it was surprising she had never discovered the secret Klára had been hiding for the last few years.

She propped Pedro up against the wall and went down to look for the rifle. Her whole hand immersed in the freezing water, she scrabbled at the ground in the place she thought the rifle must be. She wanted to avoid getting completely soaked in that murky cesspool. However, the lugubrious atmosphere of the cellar did not frighten her as much as the silence that had been thickening on the floor above them these last few minutes. She was sure that they had not gone, but she had no way of knowing what had happened to Mutti, or Lanz. If the old man had suffered another serious attack, surely this time it was going to be his last.

From the ground, now with the rifle to hand, watching the trapdoor, she saw Pedro's face fully illuminated by the lamplight. He was dying. A bluish tinge spread over the skin that was not covered by the blanket. He looked like a drowned man underwater. She climbed up the steps between them, and held for a long time his frail swallow's body.

Some time later, she was not sure how much later, she heard the front door opening and a lighter footfall approaching the entrance to the cellar. Fingernails scraped, like a rat, at different sections of the floor. Then she heard her name, Klára, and a muffled sob.

Climbing out of the pit, the first thing she saw was Mutti's face, and a wild expression of frustration, hatred and pain, such as she had never seen in her before.

After taking Pedro back to the living room, they went together to the cabin, where Lanz was lying, pale and defenceless, on the bed. He seemed to have aged several years. His forehead shone with sweat, his hair was dishevelled and one of his eyes stared strangely.

Mutti, disconsolate, watched him. "There's nothing to be done," she whispered.

"I know," said Klára.

"What now? They will come back, Klára."

"Vatti needs a doctor, and Pedro too."

"I don't want to be on my own."

"Pedro is going to die. He can't take any more."

"That's probably for the best."

Mutti's voice floated in the air for a few seconds. "Don't look at me like that," she said, without changing her tone. "It's the best thing that could happen to him."

"You don't understand…"

"There's no hope for him, Klára! They tried to kill him once, and now they'll come back to finish him off!"

"Mutti… it's not like that…"

"What would happen if they find him? What if they managed to wake him up?"

"Ilse!"

Klára had never shouted at her before and it was years since she last used her name. Usually it was Mutti, Mamita, Mamá. How could she explain that they had not come for Pedro? How could she begin to explain who the woman was that they certainly *were* going to come for?

"I'll be back in two hours," she said, and hugged her. Then she embraced Lanz, who lay shaking on the bed.

On the way to the city, as she steered Ana's truck along the road at the top of the ravine, she decided that she would return to La Pedrera only to get the old people and Pedro, and take them to Marvin's clinic, where they could wait until Nando and Ana arrived.

Pedro died in the ambulance as they were passing the cypresses, almost at the spot where his body had been thrown out of the car months before. Marvin said later that his lungs were so full of liquid that he had literally drowned.

The man sitting next to her has turned his head towards the aisle, and with this tiny gesture, he makes her a gift of privacy, expanded by the square of the window and its rotund landscape of air.

They are still flying eastwards, but she does not want to think about the end point of the journey. At this moment, Klára would give anything not to think, to forget all that has happened, and to travel back in time to a place beyond the reach of Ilse and Lanz's memory, when she was perhaps just a few months old. An olive-skinned man with dark hair would be holding her, while her mother, a woman of vigorous appearance, uncovered her breast, preparing to feed her. Her mother would be smiling at her between two red ringlets, perfect as copper spirals. Perhaps this man and woman would have nowhere to go and fate would already have decreed their destiny, because, as Lanz says, if there is anything predictable in war, it is death. But at that moment, in which she would remain frozen in time, the hold of the boat would still be only one of a thousand possible lives waiting for her, in a future as empty as the sky outside.

Now, beyond her window, the sky drinks in the night and slowly turns a cobalt blue, silent and vast as the bottom of a lake.

9

Epilogue

Dearest Skinny-ribs,
I'm writing you this second letter because the last one, a rather laconic missive I sent in August, has not been returned — maybe that means nothing, all the same it makes me hopeful that you may have received it and that this silence is a good sign. If you got my previous letters, you're probably thinking that I'm mad to have forged a letter, in your name, to Ilse. I think Mutti probably knows everything anyway, but doesn't want to admit it. Nando let me use your Remington, and for once that odious machine came up trumps, because when I gave Mutti your letter (or rather mine) she immediately recognized the decapitated "g"s and the lack of accents, two irritations that always bugged me and made you laugh.

At any rate, those weak or broken keys gave the letter a credibility that came in very useful, given the circumstances...

You might ask — as I ask myself — if there's any point continuing with this pathetic lie — does it actually benefit Ilse to receive more letters, to keep turning a blind eye to what she must know in her heart of hearts? I don't know, Skinny-ribs. I'm not sure of anything much any more! I watch the men working out in the lake, Mutti's impassive expression beneath her wrinkles... the day that woman dies, the whole world will mourn without knowing why. It will be like the loss of a great secret.

So there it is, Klára. I've been rereading the book that you left on my bedside table, before we set off for Buenos Aires, as

273

though it were a sacred text, and I can't draw any conclusions about it. It doesn't give any clue as to where you are, or if we'll ever see you again.

I sense that Nando knows something, but I don't dare ask him. The few times I have broached the subject, he has been politely evasive. Like that fight the two of you had on Christmas Eve – he told me it was to do with politics. I think that was only a half-truth. I didn't want to ask you about it at the time, and then it was too late. Anyway, I've reached the point of accepting that there are some questions that cannot be answered: it's just the way things are.

But I'm not writing in order to waste your time with half-baked theories about the past. I want to tell you how we are now. Spring is already in the air, and once again, I feel amazed at the powerful beauty of this inhospitable place. I can't believe that we spent a whole summer and much of the autumn literally in that swamp of red algae. Now it's as if all that had never happened: the algae have gone, together with those suffocating airless days, so still it made you think that the whole continent had moved to the other side of the Pacific. It's strange, how quickly and easily one can forget terrible things. I always thought that process applied mostly to good things, that happy memories came to mind less readily than unhappy ones, but no – everything can be forgotten.

The stagnation in the lake went on for two more months after you left – that is, assuming you have left. I have to imagine that is what happened, Skinny, because there is no alternative, except to tear up this letter and sit down to cry on the banks of the lake, like when we were children. I'll tell you something: for the first time in my life I think I would rather not know why you weren't here when Nando and I returned from Buenos Aires (or perhaps you were here, but not for me). Was Nando the last person to see you, to be with you? I don't know. I don't really trust him, or the things he tells me, and especially not the things he doesn't tell me. Was he really with you in the city – was that when you told him about the things that had happened while we were away?

The second time they came was not very nice either, but at least we were prepared, and the third... let's say that they still have not gone, and that it looks as though they will not leave until they find what they are searching for, even if it's no use to them. All I know about the first time is what Mutti told Nando and me... I'll never understand why you spoke to him about it and not to me, your own sister.

Klára, I don't feel I can go on without getting some answers – it's so hard to live with this uncertainty!

The algae have gone, that's for sure, and the lake has recovered its old crystalline and chilly blue. There's no more monster – not on the surface, anyway – and those fish that lay dead or dying on the shore have gone. I'm done with the photos and the water samples. Even Lanz's deterioration seems to have stabilized into a state of permanent but relatively benign confusion. For two months he's been calling Mutti "Sashenka", and Mutti answers him as if this were normal, but with a very sad face.

He started using that name around Christmas, do you remember? Ilse didn't say anything at the time, as if she didn't know what was going on. Now I am quite sure that she knows, and that Lanz's regression wounds her in a way that none of us can salve, because we'll never experience anything similar. You know her, and perhaps you also know what this is about. But don't worry, I'm not going to ask you to tell me. If these lines reach you, and you write back, that would be enough, or if you came home...

All the same, I know that I cannot blame the old people for having secrets. Each one of us has hidden something. The same is true of monsters. Because, as Doctor Guzmán, the palaeontologist at the science museum, says, when something becomes permeable to reality, it is lost to speculation. So giving names to monsters forces them into an open existence that they have not previously had, and obliges one to confront them, which is never very comfortable.

It is curious to think that, while those people appeared here, Nando and I were in Buenos Aires, on the trail of monsters...

That journey helped me to make peace with the city, which I had hated as much as I once hated Víktor. Don't get me wrong: I'm not thinking of going back there, but at least it's no longer a bad memory. I'm choosing this place, as Víktor did once, and the old folk and Nando. This is my home, I could not live without these grey walls and my well-travelled desk, or the view of the lake from the window.

I am not at peace, exactly, but better than before.

We put the divan bed back upstairs some time ago. The living room is now back to the way it was that Christmas Eve, when everything started. I can remember your eyes, when Mutti was telling some Hungarian folk tale or a children's story – how they shone, as if you would have liked to lose yourself in that invented landscape. Then I think of Lanz's attack, his inflamed eyes, Mutti holding him to stop him falling to the floor, and after that, I have a hazy memory of you and Nando in the kitchen.

How I wish I had asked you what was going on!

Trying to get information out of Nando is like talking to a brick wall. I'm the same in some respects, and perhaps that is why we have struck a bargain of silence that lets us both off the hook. We haven't slept together for months. You don't need to know – I realize that – but I want to tell you anyway. Perhaps he found out about my pregnancy at the same time as I did, on the journey from Buenos Aires. Three times they had to stop the bus in the middle of nowhere, so that I could get out to throw up. From that day on, without either of us saying anything, everything changed.

The nausea was over very quickly, and the changes keep coming with a spontaneity that neither surprises nor frightens me. The baby is there, within my swelling belly. It will grow all that it needs to. One day it will come out into the world and nothing else will seem important, I'm sure. I also know that Nando will be nearby, and that's all that matters.

When we were children, I used to think that I could convince you with reasoning, that I could fill up our empty memories just as one stuffs a rag doll with straw, using more or less plausible explanations, more or less plausible details. I was drawn to nature, because its questions are harder to deny, not because they are easier to answer. You always did your best to believe in me. But I'm flawed, you know; there are pieces missing. It is the indetermination principle: as soon as one manages to grasp one concept, another one escapes us. It's impossible to play a game with missing pieces all the time; a bit like that cricket game in Alice in Wonderland, when the mallets were flamingos and the balls armadillos. I suppose that these are the rules of physics and thus of the universe, and one should accept them without protest. Play the game, guess at forms we cannot know, or forget about them and get on with life. Live in harmony with the yawning holes. I think I might be rambling...

Ilse's been on at me again: has Klára written? Who's going to change the gas cylinder? A few minutes ago, before I started writing to you, she was commenting that the men from the prefecture would die of cold if they went into the lake – but she was really thinking about the monster, and so was I.

I saw it again on the last day of summer. It was like a kind of private leave-taking, quite appropriate to our on-off romance over the years. When would the next time be? Would there be a next time? In which year? On which hidden cycle would that depend? Those were the questions that interested me more than identifying its true form. In other words: it was no longer the monster, but Guzmán's creature. Once and for all it had a name – perhaps not one that befitted it – but a name, and an identity that Guzmán had come up with: a history, a colour, a possible appearance, an evolutionary history.

It was 21st March, the last day of the world – if you believe the millenarian prophecies – and the autumn equinox. That day and that night should be of equal length everywhere on the planet. It was no small sign.

Shortly beforehand, we had buried Pedro in the depths of the lake near to the left bank of the ravine. In that same area, I was rowing quietly across the calm surface of the water. Leaning over the edge, I peered into the water's reddish viscera, thinking I might see Pedro's body still floating down there, face-up to the sky, levitating, suspended in a mesh of algae, as though trapped in a spider's web. The equinox sun began to descend in the purple sky, and the algae slowly transformed the lake into a black hollow.

And then I knew that it had happened again. It had happened behind my back, not far from the boat, and when I heard that sound of a plunging submarine, of water displaced beneath the surface, it was already too late, and the last trace of the eddy generated by its movement was already disappearing in a smattering of bubbles.

This time I looked around me to see if any witnesses were to hand. The trees along the shore watched the spot where the apparition had been, all dazzlingly green except for reddish marks of sap, which made them look like blushing children caught peeping through the crack in a door. The ghostly trunks of the lenga *trees formed an outlandish vanguard; behind them, some diseased myrtles, some* ñire *trees – chastened by their crippled limbs – red mitraria bushes, amancay, cypresses fighting vainly to throw off the fungus and creepers that covered their boughs... it was a whole army of nature, dressed in the colours of revelation.*

Then, as if Pedro had been calling me from the depths of the lake, my instincts told me to look down again, where the reflection of the sky's clear colours were lost in a phosphoresence of algae. And I saw a dark silhouette against the light emanating through the water, a black, tapering shadow, that passed under the boat with the speed of a killer whale.

I could not swear that I saw it. I can't be sure that it was not a floating branch, a trick of the light or a more normal animal enlarged by my own mind – and perhaps I will never know. I know for sure that the extraordinary light emitted by the phosphorescence was eclipsed for an instant by something that disappeared then into the depths, in the direction of the bank.

I can't help wondering if it could have been heading for the shelter of one of those iridescent caves about which Guzmán spoke. Since our conversations, I keep imagining the base of the mountains as a great sponge, made of stone, covered by a tarry layer of fauna that died millions of years ago. A prehistoric bed, home, too, to the silent "cuero" of Indian legend, and Pedro's resting place.

I know that you did everything you could and that he would have died sooner or later. I only wish that his death had been in my hands. It's a terrible thing to say, and I'm afraid that it's to do with the love I felt.

At least I was able to choose the place of his burial. It was a strange night, very hot, with a jet-black sky against which the moon was spectacularly radiant. We buried him like a Viking, head first into the black water, strapped to a raft that was weighted down with four large rocks in a cross formation. They say that people who die after a happy life should enter the water feet first, the opposite of birth, to close the cycle of life correctly. I suppose we could have set the raft alight to make it more of a ritual, but that would have been too

PAOLA KAUFMANN

dangerous. Nor would it have been possible to bury him in the woods, where animals immediately uncover any buried secrets.

Earth casts out, water covers: that old Indian saying is one of several that are written in the caves, beside the cave paintings.

So there it is, Skinny-ribs: our graveyard is rather a special one. Did anyone ever tell you the theory about the lake's bottom? It's interesting: they say that there is no real floor, that geological layers of forest, one on top of the other, disguise the true bed. They say that there are areas where sonar signals are lost, as though the lake actually extended right through the earth. Lanz used to laugh his head off at such ideas... But I assure you that the abrupt change in level on the left side of the ravine inclines one to believe in that theory of an infinite depth.

I have a feeling that nothing that falls into the lake on that side will ever be found. Nothing that lives in those depths will ever be discovered. I'm not a fan of crank theories, but I am beginning to believe that that part of the lake could be connected with the Antipodes, as Lanz said.

Sometimes I wonder if Víktor is in one of our morgue's concealed depths, still intact, preserved by the cold. If one could unfold that geological concertina, might one find a watery graveyard of cadavers, bodies that have no relation one to another except for a common thread of misfortune, obsessions, persecutions? How many, like Pedro, are down there in the inky depths, intertwined, embracing, as in the mass graves Lanz has been talking about these last few months? How many unhappy monsters are there? Will they ever be discovered?

Acknowledgements

I would like to thank Luis Cappozzo and Fernando Novas of the Museo Argentina de Ciencias Naturales "B. Rivadavia" for helping me to construct a theory based on evidence invented by me, purely for the purposes of this fiction.

The Museo de la Patagonia, in Bariloche, kindly opened their doors to me to recreate the monumental expedition of 1922.

Walter Rodríguez, a journalist on the *Diario Río Negro*, and staff in the archive, helped me to find cuttings relating to the monster.

Special thanks to all those who contributed to the writing of this novel, enriching it with their comments, suggestions and corrections. They are many, and much loved.